For Lee—
Thanks for making
Best fishes,

TWICE BITTEN
A Matt Davis Mystery

By

Joe Perrone Jr.

Twice Bitten
A Matt Davis Mystery
by
Joe Perrone Jr.

Copyright © January 15, 2012
Joseph Perrone Jr.

ISBN-13: 978-1468199581
ISBN-10: 1468199587

DEDICATION

This book is dedicated with love to the memory of my late uncle, Joseph Ricca, who passed away on the date of my 66th birthday, March 31, 2011, at the age of 91. He was a terrific husband to my Aunt Tess, and wonderful uncle to all his nieces and nephews. He was an entrepreneur, a skilled wine maker, and an innovative cook. His warm personality, brilliant intelligence, and enormous sense of humor were gifts I always treasured, and he is missed greatly.

"And these signs shall follow them that believe; In my name shall they cast out devils; they shall speak with new tongues; They shall take up serpents; and if they drink any deadly thing, it shall not hurt them; they shall lay hands on the sick, and they shall recover."
—King James Version of the Bible, Mark 16: Verse 18

Joe Perrone Jr.

Prologue

Alabama—spring 1984

The meeting place was situated on a gentle hilltop, up a series of dirt roads off the main highway, in the rural enclave of Overton, about twenty miles outside Birmingham. Two metal gates, fastened in the middle by a short length of chain and an oversized padlock, were the only security measures needed to keep curious passersby from investigating the battered metal trailer located a quarter mile farther up the road in a narrow clearing. A wooden platform stood in front of the trailer; it was covered by a makeshift arbor made of branches. The heavy woods surrounding the venue guaranteed privacy, and ensured that the sound of the singing and shouting that generally accompanied the service would not escape beyond the confines of the clearing.

This evening, there were more than seventy-five people in attendance. The crowd was comprised of youngsters in their late teens, a scattering of folks in their thirties, forties, and fifties, and even a handful of octogenarians. All were about equally divided by gender. The young people all wore jeans and tee shirts; their necks adorned with decorative strings or chains with crosses suspended from them. Mostly, they were students at nearby colleges, and all were natives of Southern Appalachia, drawn together by a common interest—religion. Several dozen cars and trucks were parked on either side of the road leading up to the clearing, and the people milled around in small groups by the locked gate, awaiting the arrival of their spiritual leader, known simply as Brother Richard.

Brother Richard, in his late forties with a graying blond ponytail, promised "salvation for all those who come with an open heart." He attracted participants by posting notices on bulletin boards in dormitory lobbies and at other churches, and by slipping flyers under the windshield wipers of cars parked in the lots of various retail strip malls. Tonight's service would be "special"— he had assured them of that fact at the end of the previous week's gathering—and would provide the promise of salvation for all those in attendance. As a result, there was a feeling of great anticipation, and a nervous murmuring that filled the air—much like the sound of an active beehive.

Several of the boys carried guitars, and at least half the girls had tambourines or finger cymbals. One elderly man had a banjo strung over his shoulder. Periodically, brief smatterings of improvised music burst forth, and singing and laughter could be heard. At exactly eight o'clock, a weathered black Chevy pickup slowly approached the gate, the sound of its tires crunching on the small stones in the roadway announcing Brother Richard's arrival. Immediately, all activity ceased, and everyone huddled together and grew silent.

As Brother Richard exited the pickup, he was accompanied by his wife and two small children who followed him at a distance. All the girls present immediately gathered around him, their eyes focused upon a large wooden box he was carrying aloft in front of him with both hands. Its top was made of metal mesh, and there appeared to be something alive within the confines of the container. As the preacher made his way through the hushed crowd, a palpable tension spread among the followers who moved back to permit him to pass. He stopped at the gate, placed the box carefully on the ground, unlocked the padlock, and removed the chain. Several boys immediately opened the two gates, and everyone filed through the opening behind Brother Richard, who marched directly to the trailer, entered it, and closed the door behind him.

In a little while the religious leader emerged from the trailer, dressed in a pale green, medical-scrubs type shirt, worn outside his jeans, a gold cross dangling from a chain around his neck. He was carrying the wooden box and a leather-bound copy of the Bible. Taking great care not to disturb its contents, he placed the box down gently behind him on one of the steps leading into the trailer and flipped a switch mounted on its side. Instantly, the wooden platform was immersed in bright light emitted by numerous floodlights strung across the top of the arbor. Holding the bible aloft for all the young people to see, Brother Richard closed his eyes and muttered a brief incantation that sounded as if it were in a foreign language—perhaps Latin, perhaps something else entirely. One thing was for certain; no one other than he could understand its meaning. When he finished, he opened his eyes and rolled them upward, permitting the whites to be seen, before he closed them

again.   More incantations followed.   Then, just as
suddenly as it had begun, it all ended.   The sounds of
night birds and frogs could be heard distinctly above the
hushed human murmurs blanketing the gathering.

"Brothers and sisters," said Brother Richard.   "We
are gathered here for a purpose."
Amen! shouted the crowd.
"*What* purpose?" he shouted, his voice growing in
intensity.
To worship the Lord! came the reply.
"What sayeth the Lord?"
Love is the truth, and the truth shall set you free!
"And the truth is the Lord.   What is the truth?"
The truth is the Lord!

Brother Richard closed his eyes again, and began
to sway side to side, apparently speaking in tongues.
The young people also began to sway, and several of
them shouted unrecognizable words.   Whether they were
answering the preacher or repeating his words was not
clear.   This behavior went on for another ten minutes or
so, until he raised both arms in the air and shouted
"Hallelujah!   Amen!" into the night sky.   Everyone
answered with Hallelujahs and amens of their own, and
he smiled with pleasure.
"Brothers and Sisters, I promised you tonight would be a
special night, and I intend to keep my word.   But, first,
we need to get right with God.   Let us sing our blessed
hymns, in His name, amen."   As if on cue, several of the
boys began strumming their guitars, while the girls with

tambourines and hand cymbals joined in with a rhythmic beat of their own. The older members of the crowd just observed in silence. Brother Richard, who was now swaying side to side and clapping his hands, began by singing, "*A-a-a-a-a-men, a-a-a-a-men. A-a-a-a-a-men, amen, amen!*" as the young people joined in, answering his verses in counterpoint, with choruses of Amens:

> "*...Sing it over!*"
> *A-a-a-a-a-men, a-a-a-a-men. A-a-a-a-a-men, amen, amen!*
> "*See the baby. Wrapped in the manger*"
> *A-a-a-a-a-men, a-a-a-a-men. A-a-a-a-a-men, amen, amen!*
> "*On Christmas mornin'*"
> *A-a-a-a-a-men, a-a-a-a-men. A-a-a-a-a-men, amen, amen!*
> "*See him in the Temple,*"
> *A-a-a-a-a-men, a-a-a-a-men. A-a-a-a-a-men, amen, amen!*
> "*Talkin' with the elders...*"

The hymns continued unabated for at least half an hour, accompanied by frenzied shouting and hand waving, and culminating in the singing of *Amazing Grace*. When the music ended, everyone grew silent once more. The preacher gave the Bible to one of the young women, and reached behind him for the box. This was what they had come for. A murmur spread through the group. Total silence. Brother Richard slowly raised the box above his head for all to see. At first, nothing happened. Then, a very soft buzzing sound began to emanate from the box. Initially, no one recognized it for what it was. Then, as the noise grew louder, and its source became more apparent, there was anxious murmuring, interrupted periodically by shouts and screams. Brother Richard slowly lowered the box to a folding table that had been erected in front of him, and reached for the lid. By now, the buzzing had become a loud chorus of rattles. With great care, he opened the box—and a hush came over the crowd.

At the rear of the assembly, standing in the shadows, stood his wife, Raynette, and the couple's two small children. This was the progeny's first visit to watch their father preach, and the experience that night would have such a profound effect upon one of them that it would change the course of that life forever; whether it was for better or for worse was a question for another day.

1

Roscoe, NY—May 10, 2011

It was just past ten on a Tuesday night, and Stewart Street was deserted and dark. A light drizzle filled the air. It had been raining continually for the last three weeks, and Wayne Sabolewski cursed the dampness that seemed to envelop him like a shroud. Dressed in tattered jeans, a long-sleeved insulated undershirt, and a suede vest stained with beer, food, and God knew what else, the nineteen-year old moved silently in the shadows toward his target, the Grime Be Gone Laundromat. He was tall for his age, but rather skinny in contrast; his blue eyes that once sparkled with youthful energy were now dull from his constant drug usage. He had long, unkempt blond hair. In his rear pocket, he carried a small pry bar, just perfect for jimmying open back doors and coin boxes; it certainly had seen its share of both.

Wayne's hands, encased in a cheap pair of leather work gloves, had started to shake, and his mouth grew dryer by the minute; a sure sign that he couldn't wait much longer to fix. Wayne was a Meth addict. He hurried toward the laundromat, situated just south of the newly renovated credit union building—the only three-story structure in Roscoe. The financial institution certainly held more money than the laundromat, but with the remote camera guarding its ATM window and its steel doors, breaking into it wasn't something Wayne was prepared to tackle. By contrast, the laundromat occupied one of the oldest buildings in town, and featured a simple hasp and padlock on its dilapidated, wooden back door. Thirty seconds of work with the pry bar, thought Wayne, and he'd be in "Fat City."

Over the last five years, Methamphetamine use has hit epidemic proportions throughout the country, and Roscoe has not been spared, despite its idyllic setting in the mountains. When the average person thinks about drug use, it is usually associated with big cities, tenement buildings, and minorities. But, the statistics belie the common misconceptions. The use of crystal Meth or "Ice" (as it is often called by those in its grasp) is most prevalent among poverty-stricken, white teenagers in rural areas, where its relatively low cost makes it hard to resist. Once hooked, addicts will do almost anything to secure a fix. Since the drug is cheap, more often than not "anything" turns out to be petty larceny or, especially in the case of female Meth addicts, casual prostitution.

Everyone in town knew Wayne as an abuser of the drug, as evidenced by his rotten teeth, sallow complexion, and pencil thin body. Wayne could just feel the euphoria that would sweep over him in less than half an hour when he scored. As with most drugs, the effects of the Meth were short-lived, but for the six to twelve hours that the dopamine "rush" lasted, it always seemed worth it. Once the drug wore off, however, there was always the inevitable profound depression that all "Meth" addicts dreaded, followed by the unrelenting pressure to, once again, get high.

Wayne crept down the alleyway between the two buildings, rounded the corner, and quickly made his way to the battered back door of the laundromat. Without hesitating, he pulled the pry bar from his pocket and went to work. Twice, the uncontrollable shaking of his hands caused him to drop the tool, and each time he cursed to himself as he retrieved it from the ground. Finally, with a loud grunt, he managed to pry the hasp and its half-inch brass screws loose from the wood frame surrounding the entrance. Using his shoulder, he forced the door open, and silently moved inside. He moved quickly, prying open the covers of one coin box after another, and dumped the collection of quarters into a cotton sack he had brought with him. It took less than ten minutes for Wayne to fill it. He estimated the "take" at close to fifty dollars, more than enough to keep him in "Ice" for the remainder of the week. With a triumphant, "Yes!" he exited the door, and made his way outside. Billy Stillwater, the drug dealer who kept Wayne and most of the other "users" supplied with Meth, hated taking the coins, and charged extra for the inconvenience; nevertheless, he always accepted them. "What the hell," he'd say, "money's money; ain't it?"

Clinging close to the numerous storefronts for protective cover, Wayne hurried down the several blocks toward the spot where his supplier's pickup truck was usually parked. He prayed that Billy would be there, and prayed, too, that the fucking rain would stop. As he rounded the corner, he looked up the road and much to his relief saw that, indeed, at least one of his prayers had been answered. The truck was there. At the same instant, he noticed that it had stopped raining. Silently, and with a feeling of shame, he thanked God for the two small favors, and hurried to the truck.

Stillwater sat alone in his battered, brown Chevy pickup. He was carefully positioned about a half-mile from the center of town, just outside the city limits. It was there that the name of the street and its twenty-five miles-per-hour speed limit (conceived by an earlier city council as a means of increasing the town's meager flow of revenue) changed from the Rockland Road to Route 206 (the Walton Road as it was known to the locals) and a more appropriate limit of fifty-five.

Stillwater was an ex-serviceman who, lacking any real talent for making money legitimately, just naturally fell into the drug "profession." His Special Forces training—along with an ego that matched his six-foot-three-inch frame—gave him all the "equipment" he felt was necessary to conduct business effectively. The reality, however, was that he had forgotten most of what the service had taught him, and his physique, once rock solid, had turned to mostly fat. His brown eyes, once clear and engaging, were often heavy lidded and unfocused.

Anyone looking to score Meth knew right where to find Billy, and so did the police. But of course he never carried the drugs on his person—he was way too smart for that—so, it was unlikely that local law enforcement would ever catch him red-handed, especially with its lack of personnel. Billy kept his stash stored in a collection of Mason jars, the locations of which changed several times a week. His "lab," where he brewed his deadly

Twice Bitten: A Matt Davis Mystery

concoction, was buried deep in the woods somewhere between Roscoe and Walton, and its location was a well-guarded secret.

"What ya got for me, Wayne?" said Stillwater. He had a cheap cigar clenched between his rotten, yellow-stained teeth (what few he still possessed) that gave off a rancid odor that nearly caused the youth to retch. Bits of a beef burrito that he consumed earlier in the evening clung to the ragged surface of his unkempt beard. The front of his pale blue, denim shirt was stained with coffee and whatever he'd spilled on it since it was last laundered. Ever vigilant, he moved his dark brown eyes nervously from side to side, scanning the landscape for any evidence of law enforcement.

"Here," said Wayne, shoving the bag through the open window of the vehicle. "Gotta be fifty bucks—at least!"

"Lemme see," said Stillwater. "I'll be the judge of that." The drug dealer ran his fingers through the bag's contents, estimating its worth. "More like forty, I'd say."

Wayne shuffled his feet and licked his parched lips. "Yeah. Whatever. Just let me have the stuff, okay?" He was in no condition to bargain.

"Relax," cautioned Billy, with a menacing tone to his voice. "Get in. I ain't doin' no business here on the street. You oughta know better than that."

Wayne scurried around to the passenger side of the Chevy, opened the door, and got in. Stillwater put the vehicle in gear and accelerated down the road, heading toward a well-hidden parking area used by fishermen to access the nearby Upper Beaverkill River.

He admonished Wayne to "stay put, or I'll kick the livin' shit out of you," turned on a small flashlight, and started down the narrow dirt path that led to the river. Several times, he thought he heard someone behind him, and each time he stopped and glanced over his shoulder to be certain his client wasn't following. At last, convinced it was just his imagination playing tricks on him, he continued down the path until he came to the river. He marched downstream a ways until he located the distinctive pyramid shaped rock jutting out from the middle of the water that he used as a marker for his stash. Opposite the rock, located on the near shoreline, was a solitary rhododendron bush. Billy knelt down and retrieved a Mason jar, filled with small packets of crystal Meth, from its hiding place at the base of the shrub where it was concealed beneath a cairn of small rocks. For an instant, he thought of carrying the jar back with him and finding another hiding spot for it, but since it had only been there for a short time, he decided he could wait a few more days. He extracted the requisite number of packets, and then placed the jar back beneath the rhododendron, carefully covering it with the stones.

When he returned to the vehicle, he and Wayne conducted their business, and then Stillwater got back in his truck, quickly made a three-point turn, and left the boy standing alone in the parking area, minus his bag of quarters, but possessing, instead, a three-day supply of Meth. By the time the Chevy exited the dirt road onto the asphalt of the highway, Wayne Sabolewski was already high as a kite, and it was beginning to rain—

again.   Stillwater flipped on the truck's wipers and headed out into the night.

With a couple of hours to kill before he was to meet someone else at half-past midnight, Billy decided to drive over to the town of East Branch and grab a cup of coffee at a fast food restaurant.   He could have gone to the Roscoe Diner, but since that was where all the state troopers hung out, he opted for the Quickway instead. Besides, if things went right at the meeting, he'd soon be on easy street.   He whistled the melody from "Daydream Believer," as the rain began to intensify—along with his expectations.   He had no idea what the night held in store for him.

2

Roscoe, NY—the following day

My name is Matt Davis, and I'm the Chief of Police in Roscoe, New York, a quaint Upstate fishing village with just over six hundred residents. Long touted as "Trout Town USA" by its Chamber of Commerce, most recently Roscoe was officially voted the World Fishing Network's "Ultimate Fishing Town USA," garnering more than a quarter-of-a-million votes—a glowing testimony to its overwhelming popularity with fly-fishermen.

The position of Chief was supposed to be a "tit job," compared to my former occupation as a homicide detective in New York City. A friend secured the job for me as a sort of favor after an on-the-job brush with death forced me into early retirement. I figured that the bucolic setting in the Catskill Mountains would not only soothe my soul, but also allow me to pursue my favorite pastime, fly fishing for trout. I was wrong on both counts.

I'd just spent the better part of a week preparing the annual budget for my four-man department—including a request for a patrol car—and I'd had all the paperwork I could handle. If the town council didn't like my asking for the car, well, that was too damned bad. It wasn't like I was asking for a new one, mind you; I just wanted a "real" patrol car. I couldn't have cared less whether it was the latest model or a used one—even something donated would have been fine with me—as long as it was owned by the *town* and *not* by yours truly. I'd been using my own '91 Jeep Wagoneer as my official vehicle ever since becoming Chief, but "enough is enough" was how I put it to Mayor Harold Swenson at the last council meeting. To his credit, Harold asked me to "put it in the budget, and we'll see what we can do." So, I did.

It was drizzling as I pulled the Jeep onto the thinning gravel surface of the parking lot and slid to a stop alongside a car parked in the spot designated for my own vehicle. I laughed aloud at the car's distinctive license plate; it belonged to the mayor, and it read: His Honor. It was affixed to the bumper of a somewhat garish red Cadillac CTS whose spotless finish gleamed brightly, the rain beading as it hit the car's surface. Interestingly enough, the town's only new Cadillac belonged to its singular chief executive. The irony wasn't lost on me. Power had its perquisites; that's how it was back in the city, and it was no different here.

"Morning, Nancy" I said, as I waited patiently for my secretary to buzz me through the security door separating headquarters from the entry vestibule. Nancy glanced behind her at the clock on the wall. "More like afternoon, don't you think, Matt?" *Thrust.*

"Whatever," I muttered. *Parry.* "Where is he; in my office?"

"Yep."

Nancy and I liked each other from the moment we first met, and we loved to engage in the verbal fencing that kept our working relationship from growing stale; to casual observers we might even have appeared at odds.

Nothing was farther from the truth. Glancing at my wristwatch as I passed through the doorway, I realized Nancy was right. Hell, it was nearly nine. *Shouldn't have made that trip to the landfill this morning,* I thought. *Oh, well. What's the point of being on salary if I can't go the landfill when I want to?*

I hurried down the hallway until I reached my office. The door was ajar, and I could see the mayor through the opening. Although not a large man, he had a firm, upright carriage that commanded instant respect, and a distinctive mane of silver hair that caused him to appear taller than he was. He always dressed immaculately, and today was no exception; a regimental, red and white tie over a pale blue, button down shirt, complimented a dark blue, two-button suit perfectly. He was the quintessential big fish in our small, country pond. He appeared agitated; walking back and forth with his hands clasped tightly behind his back. *Probably came to tell me I'm not getting the car.*

"What's up, Harold? Been waiting long?"

"Not too long, Matt. Just got here a few minutes ago."

"I didn't realize we had an appointment today."

"We didn't."

"Oh."

It wasn't that I didn't *like* Harold; I did. It was just that I would have appreciated a bit more respect from my "boss." So, it was only natural that the mayor's first words caught me completely by surprise.

"I got you the car!" he exclaimed. "It wasn't easy, mind you, but I persuaded the boys to go along. You owe me, Matt—big time!"

I was speechless.

"Well, don't you want to know what we got you?" The mayor was ebullient. He bounced up and down on his toes, waiting for me to respond.

"Well...you kind of caught me off balance there, Harold. Okay, what is it?"

"It's a Jeep!" exclaimed the mayor. "Lot newer than yours, of course, but almost the same color. It's only got thirty thousand miles on it, too; in fact, it's still under warranty—well, at least for another six months or so."

I was a bit disappointed. First, off my '91 was the last production year for the authentic Wagoneer, so everything since then was ersatz in my opinion. Undoubtedly, whatever Harold had secured for me was probably actually a Chrysler product, and therefore not *really* a Jeep at all. Secondly, I'd hoped for a real police *cruiser*, maybe even a new Ford Crown Victoria Interceptor. The seminal American automaker had virtually cornered the market on police cars ever since Chevrolet discontinued the old rear-drive Caprice. *Who am I kidding? This is Roscoe; remember?*

"Uh...that's great, Harold. At least I can stop using mine."

The mayor looked genuinely upset. I could tell I'd hurt his feelings.

"I'm sorry, Harold," I offered. "It's just that I was hoping for something...well, something more...*traditional*. But, it'll be fine, I'm sure."

Harold's face brightened. "It's got a light bar, Matt—newest one—halogen! Car's got all kinds of stuff— digital siren, all-wheel drive, new radio, the works—it's really neat."

I started to smile at the outdated adjective, and then stifled it.

"Oh, I almost forgot," said Harold. "Gotcha a raise, too. What do you say to that?"

"A raise—"

"Okay, it's not much, but it's *something*. Twenty- five bucks a week—and I had to beg 'em for that."

I scratched my head, and then it hit me. The election! That's what this was all about. The mayor needed my support, and this was his way of enlisting my assistance in securing his re-election.

"Well, Harold, I certainly appreciate it."

Actually, Harold did a damn good job balancing the needs and wants of our little community—on a budget that was perilously deficient. And, to make matters worse, it was a thankless job. I didn't understand why he even wanted it. *Better him than me.*

The two of us stood there without uttering a word for a full minute. It was a Mexican standoff. Finally, I broke the silence. "So...uh...when do I get the *new* vehicle—euphemistically speaking, of course—next week?"

"*Today*—if you still want it. You *do* want it, don't you?" Harold appeared desperate.

"Of course I do. Where is it?"

"It's over at Joe Chesler's garage in Livingston Manor. I thought I'd have him spiff it up for you. He's already had it for a couple of days. It should be ready."

"Good. Good. I'll have Val drop me off later to pick it up."

Harold stood in place like a bellhop waiting for a tip.

"Oh, yeah," I added, "and thanks, Harold. Thanks a lot...*really.*"

"No need to thank me, Matt. But there is one thing you could do that would make me *and* the council very happy."

"What's that?" I asked, a note of caution tempering my enthusiasm.

"Find that fucking Meth lab!"

"Oh, that."

"Yes, *that!*

Rumors of a Methamphetamine laboratory located somewhere on the outskirts of the city limits had been circulating for several months, but with the limited resources I had at my disposal, I was having a difficult time developing any leads. I knew *who* the local dealer was, but we certainly didn't have the manpower at our disposal to put a twenty-four-hour tail on him. Just the same, I made a mental note to have my new patrolman, Pete Richards, make it a priority. He was a savvy guy with lots of big city experience, and I figured he was the best man for the job.

"We're doing the best we can to find it, Harold. But, we're a little bit limited in the manpower department."

Harold winced. "Then use it *better*, Matt. The council doesn't like seeing little boys and girls all strung out on that crap. And neither do I."

I took a deep breath, trying to maintain my composure. "I don't know what else to tell you, Harold. We'll *find* the lab. It's just a matter of time. I've got Pete working overtime on it—"

"No overtime!"

"Not literally," I sighed. I was acutely aware of just how much that word irritated His Honor, who hated the thought of paying *anyone* one more dime than was absolutely necessary.

Apparently satisfied that no additional reimbursement was called for, Harold beamed and headed briskly out of the office.

Ah, what the hell, I thought. *He's doing the best he can. At least I don't have to run for re-election.*

As soon as Harold was gone, the phone rang. Nancy answered the call on the second ring. "Roscoe police" she said softly. "How may I help you?" The voice on the other end of the line was so loud that she had to pull the phone away from her ear. "Where's Matt?!"

"Excuse me. Who's calling, please?"

"Goddammit! They've done it again!" said the voice on the other end of the line.

"Who's done *what* again?" asked Nancy, her patience growing thin. "And don't yell, or I'll just hang up this phone right now!"

I could hear the man's voice from where I stood. "I'm sorry," he said. "I didn't mean to yell. This is Don

Brann, over at the Grime Be Gone Laundromat, and they just broke into my place again last night. Emptied out all my machines—the coin boxes, that is." Nancy held the phone away from her ear so the two of us could receive the news together.

The caller continued, "I need Matt to get over here right away. This is the second time this year, and I've just about had it."

"Okay, okay," said Nancy. "Just a minute, let me write down the information. What's your phone number, Don? In case Matt needs to call you back. I don't know for sure when he'll be able to get over there and..."

Twenty minutes later, I pulled my Jeep to a stop in front of the laundromat. The exterior of the building was badly in need of repair, and I found myself wondering how such a place could provide a decent living for its owner, if, indeed, it did. It was no wonder that Don was so exercised over the break in; he probably needed every dime just to survive. I walked inside and found him sitting on one of the cheap, plastic chairs located in the rear of the establishment. He was reading the local paper.

"Anybody we know get married?" I cracked. That's mostly all the publication contained: marriage announcements, obituaries, and advertisements—but, the people still bought it. Old habits die hard.

Don stood up and, ignoring my initial inquiry, announced, "They did it again, Matt. They got every last quarter."

He could ill afford the loss. Every business in Roscoe operated on precarious footing ever since the economic downturn that seemingly occurred simultaneously with the Obama administration's ascent to power. Whether the two events were related was a subject of much discussion in the local drinking establishments; but regardless of the truth, the fact remained that things were tough all over. And even though I'd suggested on several occasions that he empty his coin boxes every evening, Don had apparently ignored my advice. However, I didn't chalk it up to stubbornness, but instead allowed that it was more an adherence to a set of "country values," which presumed an innate goodness in the individual. Either way, it was costing Don money.

Don's spirits appeared to be in a sorry state, and when I accompanied him to the rear of the building, he showed me the damaged door as though he were revealing the body of a deceased relative. Whoever had broken in hadn't majored in finesse. The door was a mess.

"Sure sorry about that, Don," I said, examining the broken hasp and cracked doorjamb. "Have you considered upgrading your security? Obviously, what you've got here doesn't offer much in the way of resistance. Hell, a boy scout could probably get in here with not much more than a pair of pliers."

Don winced.

"Sorry, Don. But, am I wrong?"

"Nah. You're right, Matt. But, couldn't you just *catch* the guy? It shouldn't be *too* hard to find a guy with a shitload of quarters. Am I wrong?"

The sarcasm registered hard.

"Probably not, Don. But, things aren't like they used to be in the old West, you know. We can't just 'round up the usual suspects' on a whim. I'll send Bobcat over to dust your place for prints, but chances are we won't find much."

"*Great,*" said Don. He was obviously disappointed. "Guess I shouldn't open up until he gets here, huh?"

"Probably not. But, I'll get him over here as quick as I can, okay?"

"Sure."

I knew it was probably a waste of time, but I had to offer the merchant some glimmer of hope. Chances were that it was a local teen with no record, but one never knew; maybe we'd get lucky.

"If it was me, I'd check into getting some metal doors installed—with *real* locks on 'em." I knew Don probably couldn't afford them, and he wouldn't listen, but he ought to. "Or maybe try installing one of those dummy surveillance cameras—up high where nobody can reach it. At least that might stop the locals. Of course it'd be a lot better if you had a *real* camera. But, in the meantime I'll see if we can't make an extra pass or two by your place over the next couple of weeks. Sometimes, if they think a place is easy, they'll come back again fairly soon. How's that sound, Don? Okay?"

"Sure, Matt. Whatever."

Walking out the front door, I wondered how in the world I'd ever keep my promise.

Inside my car, I keyed the microphone and called "Bobcat" Walker, my recently reinstated patrolman.

"What's up, Matt?" responded Bobcat over the airwaves.

"I need you to get over to Don Brann's place."

"What happened, another break in?"

"Yep."

"It's probably drugs," offered Bob. "Don't ya think?"

"That'd be my guess. Oh, and make sure you've got your fingerprint kit."

"Not a problem," replied Bobcat. "I've got my kit—and crime scene tape, too. Four rolls."

"Well you won't need it—the tape I mean. I told Don not to open up until we've dusted the place. Being closed for an hour or so isn't going to hurt his business—especially with all this rain, but hurry up anyway."

"Okay, Matt. I'll get right over there."

Bobcat had only been back on the job for a few months, following an unpaid suspension for "failing to follow proper procedure" during the arrest of a murder suspect. The incident was an ugly one. The suspect had just confessed to accidentally killing a young girl he had been abusing, and Bobcat had absentmindedly manacled the man with his hands in front of his body instead of behind his back as mandated by proper police procedure. In the blink of an eye, the suspect grabbed

Bob's service revolver, and before anyone could stop him, placed the gun in his mouth, and fired, ending his life.

At the time, Bobcat's suspension seemed harsh to some, but it wasn't nearly as bad as being fired, which is what several members of the council had called for. Walker knew he had handled things badly, and it was only because of my lobbying that he still had a job.

"Bob?" I called back into the microphone. "Are you there yet?"

"Not quite, Matt. But I'm on my way."

"Well make it fast. I don't want Don to feel like we don't care."

That was the problem, I thought. We *did* care. But, with only a four-man police force there was very little we could do unless we caught someone red-handed committing a crime. It wasn't much different than it was back in the city—only on a smaller scale. The truth was, many crimes went unsolved.

A few hours later, Bobcat walked into my office, his face flushed. He'd just returned from the burgled laundromat. "Well, Matt," he said, "I dusted all the washing machines and dryers, the coin boxes, the front door, back door, the door frames, even the handle on the john."

"And?"

"Whatta ya think?" Bobcat stood in the office doorway, hands on hips.

"Let me guess." I paused for effect. "Nothing?"

"Bingo," said Bobcat. "Nothing, nada, zilch, not a damn thing. Well, not quite nothing." Bobcat held up a see-through plastic evidence bag containing a piece of cellophane tape with a piece of acetate affixed to it. "I *did* get a pretty good thumb print off one of the coin boxes, but I doubt that it'll amount to anything."

"Well, check it against our 'in house' records first, just in case it's a—"

"I know, juvenile. Already did it."

Then, run it through AFIS." (AFIS stands for Automated Fingerprint Identification System, which is used by all fifty states, Canada, and Mexico.)

"Done."

"Jesus. If I didn't know better, I'd think you were a real cop."

Bobcat frowned. He was still sensitive about his tenuous situation, following his suspension.

"Sorry, man. That was a cheap shot."

"It's okay," replied Bob, with a theatrical sigh. "I'm tough. I can take it." Only, now he was smiling.

"Good man. Oh, by the way, don't forget to get a set of elimination prints from Don. We don't want to—"

"Already did it," replied Bob. "Got 'em right here." Bobcat waved the evidence bag at Matt. "First thing I did. Like you always say, 'always eliminate the victim's prints first,' right?"

"Right," I said with a smile. "I knew there was a reason I keep you around."

"I'll get started on this right away."

Ever since Bobcat was reinstated, he'd really tried hard to do whatever he could to restore his reputation and good standing with the department. As far as I was concerned, the suspension hadn't been necessary. The mayor and council had dictated it—not me. Had it been my decision, Bobcat probably would have gotten off with a reprimand. It was bad enough he had to carry the burden of the suicide, suspending him just added insult to injury.

An hour later, I decided to stretch my legs and took a stroll back to the office immediately behind my own, the one shared by my three patrolmen. Approaching Bob from behind, I couldn't help but notice that my "second-in-command," had put on a little extra padding during his forced absence. His dark blue tunic bulged over the edges of his leather belt like an incriminating fleshy donut. Now wasn't a good time to say something, but at some point I'd have to address the issue.

"So," I inquired. *"Anything?"*

"Well," said Bobcat, "after I ruled out Don, I ran the print through AFIS, but I couldn't find a match. So, I checked our 'juvie' files—"

"And?" I was cautiously optimistic.

Bobcat shrugged his shoulders.

"Nothing there, either," he sighed. "No match."

"Shit."

"Sorry, Matt. If you ask me, my money's still on a druggie."

"Yeah, mine too."

"You want me to tell Don?"

"Nah. I'll tell him."

"Sure thing," said Bobcat.

"I'll be back in a half hour," I told Nancy, as I started out the front door of headquarters. "I'm going over to tell Don the good news—*not.*" Nancy laughed in reply.

I walked outside, and started toward the laundromat. A slight drizzle was falling, and I pulled the collar of my windbreaker up to prevent the rain from getting inside. But, my actions had the opposite effect, and water that had already accumulated on the fabric ran down my neck, causing me to shiver involuntarily. It seemed as if it'd been raining for weeks. Hell, it was nearly June, and I still hadn't wet a line. It wasn't that I expected to fish a lot, but this was getting ridiculous.

As I passed the IGA food market (actually, it was called by some concocted, chichi name now, but everyone still referred to it as the IGA), I looked across the street and noticed Wayne Sabolewski leaning against the old, abandoned movie theatre. I made a mental note to have a little chat with the latest of the town's Meth addicts. Apparently homeless, but always visible on the street, the youth was as good a one to start with as any. He generally hung around the collection of retail stores in the center of town, so finding him wouldn't be a problem. Although it would probably be a waste of time, because no doubt one or more of his fellow druggies would vouch for some cockamamie alibi they'd concoct. There wasn't much of a rush, though, because he and his half-dozen-or-so buddies were married to the town like rust to a railroad spike. I shook my head in disgust at the thought of the loss of their collective youth.

After I broke the news to Don, I called my wife, Val, and arranged to pick her up so we could go over to Livingston Manor and retrieve the newly acquired police vehicle. While, the "new" used Jeep might not have been exactly what I was hoping for, at least it would pick up my spirits. Hell, I thought, the week could only get better. But I was wrong, for a storm was heading my way, and its name was Evil.

3

Roscoe, NY—earlier the same day, just past midnight
Wayne had been at the Roscoe Diner for several hours, nursing several cups of coffee, and waiting for his head to clear, before he was asked to leave. Now, as he slipped and slid his way along the muddy road that led to the parking lot where he and Billy Stillwater had conducted their business earlier in the evening, he was confident that he'd seen the last of Billy for that night. His head still buzzed a bit from the Meth he'd consumed, but his mind was focused nevertheless on one thing— getting more.

He knew that Billy's hiding place was somewhere along the river's edge, but exactly where he couldn't be sure. The rain was coming down in sheets, but Wayne was undeterred. He could hear the sound of rushing water as he moved closer to the river; its contents swollen no doubt to near overflowing by the relentless deluge. His clothing was drenched, but his thirst for more of the horrid drug could not be quenched.

Suddenly, a flicker of light pierced the darkness. He stopped dead in his tracks, straining his ear for any trace of accompanying sound. Nothing. Wait. There. A car was coming. No, it was a truck. It was Billy. *Shit.* He turned his head toward the main road, and sure enough, much to his dismay, he saw the steady stream of illumination cast by the pair of headlights belonging to Billy Stillwater's Chevy.

Shit, he thought. *What's he doing back here?*

The truck pulled to a stop in the parking area; its motor was cut, and its headlights extinguished. Wayne crouched behind a Rhododendron bush, and held his breath, praying that he wouldn't be seen.

"Fucking rain," cursed Billy Stillwater, through teeth clenched tightly against the butt of a cold cigar. It was nearing twelve, twenty-five, and if he didn't step on it he was going to be late. This could be the biggest payday of his life, and he wasn't about to screw it up—especially not because of some goddamn rain. The Chevy's windshield wipers squeaked in mechanical protest against the liquid assault of its invisible enemy; they were just barely holding their own as they swept back and forth across the scarred surface of the glass. The rain was falling so hard that Billy could hardly make out the roadway, which was dimly illuminated in the narrow beams of light cast by his truck's outdated headlights. At least he didn't have to worry about hitting a deer, he thought as he sped toward his date with destiny. *Odocoileus virginianus,* or white tailed deer, the species sought after by local hunters, virtually never move about during a rainstorm, preferring instead to bed down until a storm passes.

Pulling off the Quickway at the Stewart Street exit, Billy made the left at the end of the off ramp, crossed under the highway, and sped through town to the blinker light at the intersection of Old Route 17. He slowed the

Chevy almost to a stop, looked left, then quickly to his right toward the Roscoe Diner, before pulling out and heading left toward the access road where he was to keep his appointment.

He pushed the light switch on the dashboard halfway in as he entered the access road, leaving just the parking lights to illuminate his way down the narrow, muddy roadway that led to the seldom used parking area near the river. When he got there, he found it deserted. What if they didn't come, he thought. He need not have worried.

In less than a minute, another set of headlights glowed in the distance. These belonged to a second pickup, a red Ford, which was slowly snaking its way along the narrow roadway, headed straight for the parking area.

Oh fuck, thought Wayne. *Just what I need.* He continued to crouch behind the bush as the other vehicle pulled along Billy's and stopped. It sat with its engine idling quietly, its exhaust pipe emitting a steady breath of steam that was quickly swallowed up by the rain. In a minute, its occupant killed the Ford's headlights, then the engine, and for a moment there was only darkness and silence. Billy exited the Chevy and approached the Ford. Apparently, the passenger door was locked. He banged loudly on the door, until finally it was opened, and he climbed inside. Immediately, the cab's interior glowed brightly, as the light from the ceiling fixture illuminated the pair within before it was extinguished, plunging the area into inky darkness. It took a few minutes for Wayne's eyes to adjust to the darkness, but soon he was able to see again. He figured now was as good a time as any to make his escape. He crept past the two vehicles as stealthily as he could, praying that the noise of the rain would obliterate any trace of sound he might make.

"Did you bring the money?" Billy asked, not bothering with a greeting.

The driver reached across to the glove box, opened it, and extracted a white envelope, handing it to Billy. "It's all there, just like we agreed—ten thousand—and you don't say a word to anybody—*ever.*"

Billy grabbed the envelope with a tobacco-stained hand and quickly rifled through its contents with the other. Satisfied that the amount was accurate, he smiled broadly and reached out a hand. "No hard feelings, right? I mean you'd do the same thing. I know you would."

The driver returned the smile. "Of course I would. Hey, how about a little drink to seal the deal? For old times sake?"

Billy shivered against the cold dampness of the night. The sooner he could get out of there the better he'd like it, but what the hell—he could use a drink. "Sure," he answered. "Why not. For old times' sake."

The driver reached across the seat and re-opened the glove box, this time extracting a small, dark bottle bearing the familiar label of a popular bourbon whiskey. Billy didn't need a written invitation. He grabbed the bottle, unscrewed the cap, and brought the open end of the container to his lips. "Here's to swimmin' with bowlegged women," he laughed, quoting a line from his favorite movie, *Jaws*. Then, he took a long, deep draught of the liquid, which burned a bit as it slid down his throat and headed toward his unsuspecting stomach. Billy waited for the familiar glow that usually followed, but it never came. Instead, violent cramps assaulted his insides, causing him to double over in pain. Something was terribly wrong. This wasn't bourbon; this was something entirely different. Suddenly, he was having trouble breathing. He turned to the driver, who held a heavy, commercial grade flashlight in the air, poised to swing. "What the fuck—,"cried Billy, lifting a hand meekly in self-defense. But he was too late. The flashlight struck him hard on the side of his head with a heavy thud, as blood splattered everywhere.

Billy struggled to remain conscious, opened the car door, and slid off the seat and onto the muddy ground, the envelope full of money falling in a puddle beside him. The combination of the rain and the fall revived him slightly, and somehow he got to his feet, and staggered blindly to his truck. He needed help, and he needed it fast. "Can't...breathe," he whispered, as he climbed inside the cab. "Gotta...get...help." He fumbled in his pants pocket and found the ignition key. His vision was growing dimmer, and his efforts to breathe resembled a dog panting in the hot sun. In the meantime, the driver calmly exited the car, walked down the path to the river, and heaved the flashlight as far as possible into the water.

Then, the driver returned to the truck, walked to the passenger side, scooped up the envelope containing the money, wiped it dry, and hissed, "That'll teach you to blackmail me, you useless piece of shit." Those words were the last words Billy Stillwater ever heard. The last *sound* he made was a long, siren-like wail that was swallowed up by the sound of the rain beating on the metal roof of the truck as he literally vomited his life onto the floor of the Chevy and died.

"Good riddance to bad rubbish," said the killer before starting the engine, carefully turning the car around, and driving slowly down the muddy path, toward the main road. The rain continued to fall, washing away any trace of evidence.

Wayne had almost reached the main road when he heard the sound of an engine being started behind him in the parking area. Soon, he sensed the approach of one of the trucks coming fast in his direction. He turned and looked back—straight into the headlights of the oncoming vehicle. It was the Ford. Before he could react, it had pulled alongside him, and its driver was yelling something at him through a partially opened window.

"You didn't see me," shouted the driver. "You didn't see a damn thing. Understand?"

Wayne could barely make out the words through the noise of the rain, but nodded anyway, water running off his head and down inside his shirt, his heart pounding inside his chest.

"If you so much as say one word about me to anyone, I'll find you and I'll kill you. *Do* you understand?"

"I w...w...won't say a word. I s...s...swear it."

"Good. Now get lost!"

In an instant, the truck had turned left, accelerated onto the main road, and was heading toward Walton—and away from a much-relieved Wayne, who even now was walking into town, zombie-like, his mind filled with questions that would probably never be answered.

As he walked, the rain continued to pour down on him, and no sound came from the parking area.

4

Roscoe, NY—two days later

My phone rang at seven in the evening. I had just finished dinner (my favorite: meatloaf) and was watching the local news, when Val brought the phone to me in the den. It was one of my two patrolmen, Rick Dawley, and he had some bad news. It appeared that after less than two years of my being on the job, the homicide rate during my brief tenure in Roscoe might have just doubled.

Rick was with a fisherman who had just discovered a dead body lying in a pickup truck. Apparently, he was on his way into town to report what he'd found when he intercepted Rick, who was patrolling that part of Roscoe, and flagged him down.

As I headed to the crime scene, just for the hell of it I switched on the new light bar, and then just as quickly switched it off again. Who was I kidding; there was nobody on the road to see it. I pulled the Jeep off Route 206 and onto the dirt road leading toward the parking area. With all the rain we'd had over the last couple of weeks, the unpaved road was mostly mud with a little grass along the midline. Rick's blue and white, vintage '92 Ford Bronco, with an after-market light bar of its own, was pulled alongside a rusted out, brown '89 Chevy pickup. There was one other vehicle in the parking area, a late model, silver Honda SUV with New

York tags that read: LUV2FSH. Rick, dressed in gray trousers, brown garrison belt, and a requisite dark, navy blue tunic with gray tie, stood alongside the fisherman's vehicle, about twenty feet away from the deceased's truck, engaged in animated conversation with its owner.

"Officer Dawley," I said, nodding in Rick's direction. Both he and the fisherman nodded back automatically, and I added a quick, "Sir," in response to the latter.

"The deceased is in the pickup," said Rick, pointing at the Chevy. "It's Billy Stillwater."

"*Really?*" I said, the word more of an exclamation than a question. It may have been my imagination, but I could have sworn that I detected a subtle smile on Rick's face.

"Yep. It's him."

This time there was no doubt as to the smile.

I shouldn't have been surprised. Billy Stillwater was a suspected Meth dealer whom we'd been trying to catch ever since I took office. It was his lab that we'd been trying unsuccessfully to locate for the last several months. The fact that someone might have wanted him dead was no shock at all. In fact, the only thing surprising was that it had taken this long for him to meet his demise.

I donned a pair of latex gloves and started for the truck. As I neared it, my nostrils were immediately assaulted by the distinct odor of ripe, decaying flesh. A squadron of flies buzzed continuously within the interior of the vehicle; individual bodies bombarded the windows like miniature baseballs in a batting cage. Although the smell emanating from the truck was offensive, I'd smelled worse. Putrefaction generally commences between twenty-four and forty-eight hours after death. A combination of decaying red blood cells and sulfur gas contained in the intestines accounts for "that death smell," as some refer to the odor. I covered my nose with a handkerchief just the same.

This was the second unnatural death that had occurred within my jurisdiction since I took office just two years ago. The other *corpus delecti* was discovered a year earlier by none other than yours truly while attempting to enjoy a day on the river. *That* corpse was six-months old, seriously deteriorated, and barely recognizable as human. *This* one probably "assumed room temperature" only a couple of days before its discovery, and was easily discernible as that of a male Caucasian in his late thirties. Although we knew the victim's identity, we would still run his prints through AFIS to determine his "real" name, since Stillwater was most likely an alias. An additional check with NCIC would determine whether anyone was looking for him, but there wasn't any hurry to get that done. He wasn't going anywhere.

Apparently, something he ate or drank gave him a bit of an upset stomach, because the front of his blue, denim shirt was stained with what appeared to be bloody vomit. The right side of his head was badly lacerated, most likely from a blow with a blunt object, which was probably the cause of death. There didn't appear to be any other signs of injury; there weren't any bullet holes visible, or knife wounds, either. But, we'd need to wait for the autopsy to determine the exact cause of death.

I've always been fascinated by what motivates one human being to take the life of another. In many cases, it's hatred or jealousy, with the violence often committed in the heat of the moment—an act of passion if you will. We've all read the sensational headlines in tabloids detailing the sordid descriptions of wives beheaded by jealous husbands, or husbands poisoned by likeminded spouses; in fact, the number one motive for murder (according to some sources) *is* domestic violence. Therefore, when a fisherman discovers the body of a local Meth dealer, with no "significant other" in his life (as far as we knew), it would appear that the motive for his murder most certainly did *not* fall into that preeminent category.

Oh, did I mention what Number Two is on the "Motives for Murder Hit Parade?" Give up? It's "no apparent motive." Surprised? You shouldn't be. Translated, it means that probably those particular crimes were never solved. Unless I missed my guess, the motive here would turn out to be either robbery or competitive greed—or both. It was my fervent hope that it wouldn't end up being "Number Two."

I closed the door to the pickup and turned to face the witness. "So, you're the one who found him, huh?" I asked of the fisherman.

"Yes, sir."

I watched his body language carefully to see if he appeared nervous or guilty. But all I saw was a man who was wet, tired, and a little shaken. He was about six-feet tall, wore those new lightweight, breathable waders that we ordinary working stiffs can't afford (but all wish we had), a chest-mounted fly box worn over a tan Orvis fishing shirt, and a matching water-repellent baseball hat with the obligatory embroidered patch. His rod and reel were up to the same standards. I was tempted to dislike him out of hand, but resisted the temptation until he gave me better cause.

"You come here often?"

"At least once or twice a week. I live over in Liberty."

"So you—"

"I'm retired," he said, answering an unasked question.

Why do they always feel they need to explain everything about themselves?

He wasn't done.

"I was here a couple of days ago, and I noticed the truck then," he told us. "I didn't pay too much attention to it, because I figured whoever owned it was probably fishing too—maybe further up or down stream. To tell you the truth, I was just as happy I didn't run into him. Had the river all to myself for a change—even with the rain, it was still good to be alone."

He definitely didn't appear nervous or guilty, and I doubted that he was connected with the murder, but you never knew.

"So, when you came back today and saw it still in the same spot, you became curious and thought you'd take a look. Is that right?"

"Right."

"And that's when you came looking for us."

"Right."

"Okay. Well, I appreciate you letting us know. Officer Dawley will take down your information. Just make sure you give us a number where we can get in touch with you, okay?"

"Sure." The man turned and started toward his vehicle.

"Oh, Mister," I called out to him.

He stopped and turned around. "Yes," he said. "Is there something wrong?" He had a confused look on his face, and I felt kind of guilty for what I was about to say. But, I said it just the same.

"Have you got your fishing license, Sir?" I was barely able to hide the smile that threatened to spread across my face.

Relieved, he slipped his hand inside his waders and unzipped the waterproof pouch in the front. He pulled out a neatly folded piece of paper and offered it in my direction. He was the one who was smiling now.

I waved the document away, without examining it. "That's okay," I said. "I just needed to check. Have a good evening, Mister...uh. Actually, I don't believe I caught your name."

"Oh, I'm sorry. It's Carl Johnson."

He extended his hand and we shook. "I'm Matt Davis," I said. "I'm the Chief of Police. I'll call you if we have any other questions."

While Rick was busy stringing yellow crime scene tape around the perimeter of the parking area, I got to work examining the crime scene in detail for anything obvious. No point in taking impressions of any tire tracks; they would surely be useless. The rain had turned the mud to soup, and because of that, any definition that might have been helpful was washed away almost as soon as the tracks were made. I took a few photographs anyway, mostly to note the position of the deceased. Knowing what little I did about the victim, my best guess was that this was probably a drug deal gone sour and that somebody would be bragging about it in a bar before the week was out. Little thieves have big mouths.

A "biker's wallet" hung from Billy's leather belt by a length of chrome chain. I examined its meager contents, finding a New York State driver's license—expired, of course—showing his age as thirty-five, a pre-paid credit card (probably depleted), a convenience store discount card, and a red business card for a "titty bar" over in Downsville, called Twin Islands, which opened about a year ago. Scribbled on the back of the card were the name Donna and a local phone number. Oh, and surprise, surprise, there was no cash—not a nickel—which seemed to lend some credibility to my initial assessment.

I took a half dozen more pictures of the interior, returned to my car to retrieve my fingerprint kit, and began the tedious task of dusting the vehicle, inside and out, for prints. My best hopes were the Mason jar, the wallet, and the door handles of the truck. It was doubtful that I'd get anything usable, but procedure was procedure.

When I'd finished dusting, I bagged the hands with plastic bags, and put the wallet into an evidence bag. There were another dozen or so bags, each one containing a "sandwich" of fingerprint lifting tape pressed against a special acetate sheet. Each bag was numbered to correspond to a list I'd made, detailing exactly where the print was found. One of the bags contained prints taken from the victim himself. Chances were, all the other prints would match his. If we were lucky, maybe they wouldn't.

"You might as well go on home, Rick. I'll wait here for the EMTs and the tow truck."

"You sure?" he asked.

I knew Rick would stay as long as I needed him, but his time would be better served writing up his report of the incident while his memory was still fresh. "No problem," I said. "There's no point in both of us losing sleep. I'll see you in the morning."

As the taillights of Rick's Bronco disappeared, I called emergency services to come collect the body. I was sure the local auto body shop in Livingston Manor that I usually used for towing was already closed, so I phoned an outfit that prowled Route 17, between Monticello and Binghamton. They'd tow the truck over to the little impoundment lot alongside the Quickway, where it passes over Stewart Street. Eventually, the vehicle would be auctioned off, but for the time being it was still evidence, and would be safe behind the padlocked doors of the chain link fence surrounding the lot.

The EMT unit arrived within ten minutes, and the body was bagged and loaded in no time at all. It would be taken to the county coroner's office down in Monticello, where it would be autopsied and formally identified. The tow truck was another story, and by the time it arrived, hooked up the pickup, and towed it to the lot, I wasn't surprised to find the hour was past midnight.

It was nearly one by the time I pulled onto the parking pad outside my garage, and made my way inside to join my sleeping wife. I was bone weary, and in no mood for chitchat, so I undressed in the bathroom, then returned to the bedroom and carefully slid in next to Val, being extra careful not to wake her. Tomorrow promised to be a long day.

Some tit job, I thought, as I drifted off to sleep.

5

Suburb of Birmingham, Alabama—spring of 1992

Miss Hattie Godsey was eighty-nine-years-old and an avid gardener. Her large, well-constructed ante-bellum home on the outskirts of Birmingham, Alabama, had been in the family for five generations. The seven bedroom house stood on a three-acre parcel in upscale Vestavia Hills, along I-65, just southwest of Birmingham. As the matriarch of the Godsey family (and present guardian of the estate) she prided herself in the decorative gardens she had planted over the last half-century. Crape Myrtles, Rhododendrons, Camellias, and diverse species of roses, all planted with care in eye-pleasing designs, adorned the grounds. Different ferns, interspersed among the flowers, gave a soft, feathered look that added to the natural feel of the garden. A walkway featuring a herringbone design of pinkish paver stones set in special, dark green sand, led from the house to the formal gardens. On either side of the path were several rows of various-colored Hostas. A white-painted, wooden wishing-well stood sentinel midway along the walk, with matching wrought-iron benches on either side that visitors could sit on as they contemplated the imaginary requests they might make. Not to be outdone by its surroundings, the structure itself wore a blanket of dark green ivy that gave off a warm, comforting aroma that welcomed relatives and friends.

The snake glided effortlessly through the grass. It was a copperhead, about average in size for its species—just less than three feet long. Its "intelligently designed" pattern of tan and brown markings allowed it to blend in almost seamlessly with its surroundings. Although its species accounted for nearly thirty-seven percent of all human bites in North America, its venom is rarely fatal, mostly causing great swelling and discomfort. Rattlesnakes were far more deadly, possessing a potent strain of neurotoxin delivered through an efficient pair of hypodermic-like fangs. But rattlesnakes had a built-in warning system that alerted most people who encountered them in their natural habitat. One *almost* had to go looking for trouble to be bitten by a rattlesnake. Not so with the copperhead.

Today, before the June sun warmed the air to an uncomfortable level, Miss Hattie planned to plant some Jemison Lilies in a special location near a limestone birdbath situated in the far corner of the garden. She wore powder blue coveralls over a pink, paisley blouse, and a matching blue sun hat given to her the previous Mother's Day by her only daughter, Julia, who always seemed to know just what her momma wanted. *Bless that child*, thought Miss Hattie, who still thought of her offspring as a young girl, despite her actual age of nearly sixty. In one hand she carried a trowel, and in the other a basket containing the delicate bulbs of the lilies. *Mustn't waste these precious days*, she thought. Like most folks her age, not a day went by without her being aware of the strident ticking of her biological clock. And while she welcomed that inevitable meeting with Jesus, she surely wasn't in any particular rush—especially on a day like today.

Miss Hattie wiped away a bead of perspiration from her age-spotted forehead, and reminded herself to "not overdo it," as her daughter so often admonished her over their weekly lunches together. Holding the basket of bulbs off to the side, she gently knelt down on a bare patch of topsoil that she recently prepared for planting, digging the trowel into the soft, loamy ground to maintain her balance. She never wore gloves, preferring instead to feel the rich, dark soil between her slender fingers. It made her feel one with the earth; a relationship that was not too far in the future—inevitable even—but, as far as she was concerned, was not necessarily welcomed. One by one, she carefully inserted the bulbs into the soil in neatly arranged circles, each one larger than the succeeding one. It would be a pretty arrangement, she thought.

She never saw the snake—until it was too late. The initial strike wasn't even very painful; it felt more like the sting of a large hornet or wasp on the back of her hand—almost as if someone had slapped her. The copperhead, or *Agkistron contortrix,* as it is know by herpetologists, has solenoglyphous fangs (long, hollow, articulated fangs which fold against the roof of its mouth when the jaws are closed) that transmit venom to its prey. They are proportional to the snake's body size (in this case they were probably less than a third of an inch in length). Copperheads tend not to be aggressive, but will often make a half-hearted strike containing a low level of venom as a warning when cornered or threatened. Unfortunately, Miss Hattie had probably startled the snake in reaching for the final bulb in the basket, and it reacted thusly.

In most cases, the copperhead's bite is not serious and requires only minor medical treatment; that is because its venom is not nearly as toxic as that of other poisonous snakes and because copperheads generally do not inject very much. An individual might experience pain and swelling, perhaps accompanied by minimal bleeding and a change in pulse rate. If untreated, the bite can cause nausea, vomiting, and intestinal discomfort—perhaps even loss of consciousness—but, rarely death, much less permanent injury. Rapid treatment with antivenin usually stems the effects of the neurotoxin, and recovery is generally full, with little or no permanent damage other than some scarring.

Initially, Miss Hattie felt a bit light-headed, almost giddy (fairly typical in the case of a venomous bite). Her first thoughts were of Julia, and she wished her daughter were there. Next came the pain—not from the snakebite itself, but rather from the massive heart attack she was suffering as a result of the shock to an organ that was already weakened by congestive heart disease—and then finally, there was the merciful loss of consciousness and subsequent cessation of breathing that ended her worldly existence. In all, the entire episode took less than three minutes, bringing to an end a life filled with dreams and aspirations (both realized and unfulfilled), and leaving behind a void in the wellspring of humanity. The snake slid silently away unaware of the consequences of its actions.

Miss Hattie's body was found the following day after she failed to answer the door when her daughter came to pick her up for their weekly lunch date. Fortunately, owing to Miss Hattie's relatively sudden demise, the snake's neurotoxin hadn't done much damage, and therefore Julia was spared the site of the bloated, blackened flesh that might have otherwise been visible had her mother died from the snakebite alone. What she found instead was what appeared (at first glance) to be an old woman who apparently fell asleep on the ground amidst the gardens that she loved so very much. Only a small, half-dollar sized circle of bruised skin on the back of her right hand, surrounding two small puncture wounds, gave evidence of the secondary cause of her demise. The coroner, recognizing the wound for what it was, still listed heart attack as the primary cause of death, but also documented the snakebite as a contributing factor.

As executrix of Miss Hattie's estate, Julia was charged with submitting copies of the death certificate to the appropriate agencies, including several to the various life insurance companies that indemnified her mother's life. Owing to her mother's characteristic generosity, Julia was not surprised to find that the beneficiary of one of the policies was a church that Miss Hattie frequented over the past two years called The First Pentecostal Church of Signs Following; ironically, its members routinely handled poisonous snakes as part of the service. The practice was dictated by an obscure passage in the King James Version of the Bible to which the worshippers subscribed, and one that Julia frowned upon, having made her feelings know to her mother on more than one occasion. However, true to her somewhat stubborn nature, Miss Hattie dismissed her daughter's concerns, and resolutely embraced the church further by naming it beneficiary of the relatively small policy. The remainder of the estate went to charity, except for the house, which as expected was bequeathed to Julia.

The following week, a thoughtful and well-written obituary appeared in the local newspaper, summarizing Miss Hattie's life accomplishments and listing heart attack as the cause of death; there was no mention of the snake.

Evil smiled at the omission.

Roscoe, NY

"Pete," I said, "it's like closing the barn door after the horse is out." I had called him in for a little chat about finding the Meth lab that the mayor had "discussed" with me, and now Pete Richards stood quietly waiting for my next pearls of wisdom. "Since Billy Stillwater is officially dead, we can probably assume that the location of his Meth lab has become a moot point. *But,* just on the odd chance that someone else has assumed the controls, I want you to be especially mindful of being on the lookout for where it might be."

"Sure thing, Matt," said Pete. "But you and I both know that we'll probably never find the damned thing until some hunter stumbles across it while chasin' down a deer he nicked with an arrow."

"You're probably right, Pete. But, it doesn't matter *how* we find it, or even *who* finds it. What's important is that I keep my word to Harold."

"Gotcha." If nothing else, Pete was succinct. "Anything else?"

"Nah. Keep me posted, okay?"

"Will do."

As Pete left the office, I thought how different things were here, as opposed to the city, with paid informants just waiting to tell you anything you wanted to know—*if* the price was right.

I received the coroner's report a few days later, and while it noted the blow to the head, it listed the official cause of Billy Stillwater's death as "asphyxiation, caused by the effects of a poisonous substance." To my surprise, the toxin cited was *not* Methamphetamine; it was Strychnine. *Strychnine?* I was totally perplexed. I figured for sure that our boy had overdosed. But Strychnine, well, that just came completely out of left field—and it elevated matters to a new level. After all, this was Roscoe, not the set of some daytime soap opera. We weren't used to this type of activity. This wasn't a case of suicide or stupidity; this was cold-blooded murder—but why? If this wasn't a drug deal gone south, then why had someone wanted a piece of crap like Billy Stillwater dead? Maybe it was another dealer wanting to cut in on Billy's action. Or a parent, whose teenaged son or daughter was hooked on "product?" Billy surely wouldn't be missed, that much was certain.

Initially, something else bothered me; I had wondered about the vomit all over the front of Billy's shirt. But now, as I continued reading the findings of the report, it all became perfectly clear.

> ...the likely cause of death was from *lactic acidosis,* brought on by the ingestion of strychnine. This would account for the vomiting, preceded no doubt by nearly continuous convulsions. Death most likely resulted from suffocation caused by paralysis of the neural pathways that control breathing, or perhaps even from sheer exhaustion from the convulsions themselves.

Not a pleasant way to leave the planet, I thought. Stillwater was—excuse me, *formerly was*—a drug dealer. He had also been a user, a fact known to everyone in the area; dead at thirty-five, he had the appearance of someone twice his age.

Whoever had "shared" the toxic highball with Billy hadn't counted on the fact that unless one died in a hospital, there would almost certainly be an autopsy, in which case the actual cause of death would point to the Strychnine. Perhaps the killer hoped that whoever found the body would assume that Billy hit his head on a rock, staggered back to his truck and died—end of story. Case closed. Or maybe, quite simply, they just didn't care, as evidenced by their ultimate choice of the *true* "weapon."

I picked up the evidence bag containing the victim's wallet. Thumbing through its contents, I extracted the frayed Twin Islands business card with the name Donna and the phone number scrawled across the back. I ought to have a chat with Donna—*if* I could find her. However, like most male hangouts, places like Twin Islands didn't open until at least lunchtime—especially on a weekday—so I decided to first seek out Wayne Sabolewski, the most visible of the town's drug addicts. I seriously doubted that he was my number one suspect in the murder case, but the details of his well-known symbiotic relationship with the deceased might at least yield a starting point in the investigation. Besides, I was way past overdue in my obligation to grill him about the laundromat burglary. I *definitely* liked him for that one.

Because of the rain, I figured I'd most likely to find the teenager skulking around the protected doorways of the small knot of retail shops concentrated in the three or four block area that made up the heart of Roscoe. I was right. The Jeep's windshield wipers glided across the glass in a slow, hypnotic, one-two beat, fending off the steady drizzle as I crept up Main Street, made a left onto Old Route 17, and started toward Maynard Street, just past Maple. It was just after I slapped the signal lever to indicate a left turn that I spotted him. The kid was squeezed inside the doorway of an abandoned Chinese restaurant. He was barely protected from the rain by a tattered awning hanging at an awkward slant below a faded neon sign that read: Mai Moon Take Out. You knew things were bad when a town couldn't support an oriental take-out joint—although, in fairness to Roscoe, the food hadn't been that great to begin with. So, when the downturn in the economy hit, it just made the inevitable closing a *fait accompli*.

I made a quick U-turn and pulled the Jeep to a stop in front of the vacant building. Almost immediately, the Sabolewski kid started moving.

"Hey, Wayne," I called. "Hold on. I just want to talk to you for a minute."

"I didn't *do* anything," he whined. Dressed in tattered jeans and a hooded sweatshirt, he was hopping around like a Mexican jumping bean, shuffling from one sneakered foot to the other.

"I'm sure you didn't. But, I still want to talk to you." I turned off the engine, and got out. Wayne continued walking slowly back toward Stewart Street. "Look, don't make me have to catch you. Just stop right there and relax. I just want to ask you a couple of questions."

Whether it was the tone of my voice or that he didn't want to get any wetter than he already was, it didn't matter; he stopped walking. He ducked inside the doorway of a second hand, clothing shop with no name to its credit, and I quickly closed the space between us and joined him there. He was shivering, partially because he was damp, but more likely because he needed a fix. He was also scared. I figured I'd go for broke. But I had to be careful; as with any suspect, I couldn't afford to ask him any questions that might tend to incriminate him. For that I'd have to read him his Miranda rights, and then he'd probably dummy up until the state had provided him with a lawyer.

"So, Wayne," I began. "How're things between you and Billy Stillwater?"

"Whattaya mean?"

"Just what I said. When's the last time you saw him?"

"Why?"

"I just wondered; that's all." I was looking for any sign that he might know something—*anything*.

Wayne shrugged his shoulders. He might have appeared lost, but he certainly didn't appear guilty. I tried another tack.

"How about the laundromat?" I asked. "Been by there lately?"

Immediately, the youth's face darkened, and a deep furrow creased his forehead. "I didn't do it!"

The kid probably wasn't a murderer, but he *was* an idiot.

"Do *what?*" I asked. "Did something happen at the laundromat? What *didn't* you do, Wayne?"

"Oh, come on, you can't prove I robbed that place."

Bingo, one for two!

"How'd you know it had been robbed? I didn't say anything about a robbery. What did you do with the money? Did you score off Billy?"

Silence.

"Look, I'm pretty sure you broke into the laundry. But, if you own up to it, my best guess is you'll probably only get six months probation. But, if you know anything at all about what happened to Billy and you don't tell me, well, I don't think I can help you. So, you'd better go ahead and tell me now, before it's too late."

"What happened to Billy?" Wayne's eyes were open wide, and he appeared genuinely dumfounded. His response certainly wasn't the one I had anticipated.

"Why don't *you* tell *me?* When did you see him last?"

Wayne scratched his head, making an obvious effort to remember. He didn't appear to be having any luck.

"A week ago?" I asked. "*Two* weeks ago? How about *Tuesday?*" I threw the last one out there just to see if I'd get a response. It worked.

"Okay, okay, I saw him on Tuesday," sighed Wayne. "But, what happened to him?" he asked. "Is he okay?"

I figured there was no point in playing games. "He's dead," I replied. "Someone found him in his truck." His reaction was one of genuine shock.

"But that's impossible. I saw him Tuesday, after I—"

"After you robbed the Grime Be Gone?"

"N...n...no. No," he stammered. "I swear. He was alive when I left him."

"And what time was that?"

"Around ten, maybe ten-thirty."

"Okay, so where were you between, say, eleven that night and three in the morning?"

"I was at the Roscoe Diner," sighed Wayne. "Ask the Greek. He'll tell you. I had a cheeseburger and a Coke. It's the truth; I swear it."

The "Greek," was George Popadopolous, the owner of the storied eatery. If George said Wayne was there, you could take it to the bank. I'd check to be certain, but I tended to believe the kid. Wayne started to say something, then thought better of it. He was stupid, but not *that* stupid.

"Okay, I'll tell you what, Wayne. Why don't we take a ride? We'll just go on over to headquarters and talk about this a little more."

I opened the rear door to the Jeep, and motioned him to get in. The mayor had done the right thing and had a wire grille installed between the driver's compartment and the rear passenger compartment, along with automatic door locks that could only be opened by the driver. Wayne started to get in, but then hesitated.

"Look, kid, I just want to make one thing clear: you're not under arrest or anything like that. I only want to ask you a few more questions. See if we can't get to the bottom of this, okay?" A look of panic spread across his face. "Relax, Wayne. You can leave anytime you want. I promise."

The teenager got into the back seat, and I closed the door. As I pulled the Jeep away from the curb, the boy started to cry. He was no hardened criminal, just a lost and confused youth, strung out on Meth. I really hoped he'd be sent someplace where he could get help. I promised myself to do whatever I could to make that a reality.

When we got to headquarters, Nancy buzzed us in; and I took Wayne back to the holding cell. I deliberately left the door wide open, so he'd know that I meant what I had said about his being free to leave. He sat down on the cot, with his back against the wall, and closed his eyes. He appeared on the edge of exhaustion.

"Would you like a soda?" I asked.

Wayne shrugged his shoulders and nodded.

"Okay. I'll be right back."

When I returned, Wayne was sitting quietly in the holding cell, his head in his hands. I couldn't help but feel sorry for him. He never knew his father; his mother left him with his grandmother when he was only six-years old, and the two never saw nor heard from her again. By the time he was sixteen, he had dropped out of school, and spent his days wandering back and forth between Roscoe and Walton, getting himself hooked on

Meth somewhere along the line. His grandmother passed away when Wayne was eighteen, and the state had auctioned off the house for taxes, changing his status from occasionally homeless to officially so.

I sat down next to Wayne on the metal cot that occupied the majority of space in the small containment unit, and handed the kid the can of soda. He gulped it down without hesitation.

"Look. Wayne. I'd like to help you. Maybe get you off the Meth. Would you like that?" He looked up at me like a lost puppy, his soul showing through his eyes. He nodded his head. "Good. But, I'll need you to admit to breaking into the Grime Be Gone, okay? And, I'll have to arrest you—just so we can get you into rehab."

He nodded again.

"That way I can get the judge to release you on what's called a personal recognizance bond. We'll get you transferred over to the rehab center in Monticello, and after you get yourself clean we'll see about maybe finding you a job and a place to live. Okay?"

He nodded in agreement.

"*And,* of course, you'll have to pay Don back for the money you stole and the damage you did breaking into his place. If you can do all that, the judge will dismiss the charges, and it'll be like it never happened. What do you say, deal?"

He nodded his head again, but a bit more enthusiastically this time. What other choice did he have, I thought. If he *didn't* plead guilty, I really couldn't charge him (but, *he* didn't know that). If I let him go, he might get by for a while, but it was only a matter of time before *his* body would turn up somewhere, just like Billy's—and I think he knew that.

"I'll be back in a minute with some paper and a pen. You can write down how it all happened. Then, we'll get things moving with the judge and social services."

It might have been my overactive imagination, but I could swear I saw a sigh of relief exit the poor kid's body. At least *something* good had come out of the day. I walked up front to Nancy's office, being careful to cough as I entered. "I need some paper and a pen, please, Nancy."

"Beat a confession out of him, did you?" asked Nancy with a wry smile on her face. She knew better, but still enjoyed busting my chops.

"Yeah," I replied with a smile. "I beat him to a pulp. You better get back there, later on, with a washcloth—clean up the bloody mess."

Nancy handed me a pad of yellow, legal paper and a ballpoint pen. "Here you go, *Adolph*," she said with a laugh.

"Thanks, *Frau* Cooper," I replied in my best imitation of a German Gestapo officer's accent.

Wayne seemed to be in a better mood when I returned to the holding cell to give him the pen and paper. He sat quietly, as he worked on his statement. I watched him for a few minutes, and then left him alone with his thoughts. I truly hoped this would be the beginning of a new life for him.

"Listen, Wayne, I'm going to have to lock this cell while I take care of some business." An anxious look spread across the youth's face. "Don't worry. I should be back in about two hours, and you can either take off then (I knew I was going out on a limb, but, what the hell) or you can stay the night—in the cell, of course. You can think about it while I'm gone. I'll tell Miss Cooper to check on you every once in a while."

I stopped by Nancy's office on the way out, and apprised her of the situation with Wayne. "Would you mind calling Frank Merritt over at social services? Tell him I've got a kid who needs to get into rehab, and he should be coming over there in a day or two, just as soon as I can get him before the magistrate."

"Are you going to arrest him?"

"I'm afraid I have to. But, I'm going to try to get Judge Holscher to release him on a personal recognizance bond *with* the stipulation that he makes restitution *and* completes rehab. He's writing his statement now. Just tell Frank that I need him to coordinate things with the rehab center, and if he has any questions he can call me."

"Sure thing, Matt." She picked up the phone, and then set it back into its cradle. "Oh, by the way, I was watching the weather channel this morning—"

"And?"

"And it looks like we *could* get a break in the weather tomorrow. I thought you might want to know—seeing as how you've been cooped up so long with all this rain."

Nancy knew me like a book. She was well aware that I hadn't wet a line since last fall, and would dearly love to spend a little time on the water fishing.

"We'll see what it looks like in the morning. Maybe I can sneak out for an hour or so before office hours. If I'm not there when you get here," I laughed, "Start without me."

"Sounds like a plan."

"In the meantime, I should be back in a couple of hours. I'm headed to Downsville to interview that gal over at Twin Islands."

Nancy grimaced in mock disgust at the mention of the risqué bar. "Well, be careful what you touch there—and for God's sake, be sure to wash your hands."

"Yes, ma'am. I promise."

I took my time driving to Downsville. The rain became fog at the higher elevations along the section of Route 206 known as Cat Hollow Road, and then changed back into a steady drizzle when the road emptied into the town of Downsville at its lower end, where it met up with Route 30.

While "on the job" in New York City, I'd had my fill of sleazy bars that served watered down drinks, and offered diseased hookers masquerading as exotic dancers, so I wasn't in a hurry to be in another one; not that the place I was headed to was even close to being on a par with those in the city. But sleaze was sleaze, no matter where you found it.

It was just past one in the afternoon when I slipped the Jeep into the potholed parking lot at the rear of the two-story, yellow stucco building that housed the bar. I deliberately chose not to park in front, because I didn't want to spook any would-be informants, especially Donna, whose name had been hastily scrawled on the back of the business card I carried in my pocket.

The steady beat of the bass track from a song playing on the juke box inside reverberated through the cheap front door, which was nothing more than two sheets of plywood nailed to either side of a frame made of two-by-fours, with a hole drilled into it to support a five-dollar lockset. There was no need for anything more substantial since the bar's owner, who lived upstairs, emptied the cash drawer of the register on an hourly basis. I imagined that the security arrangements for the apartment above were far more substantial, and no doubt included a firearm or two. However, that information was not what I was seeking.

I had opted not to wear my uniform, and, dressed the way I was in jeans, button-down cotton shirt, and a windbreaker, my appearance was that of any tourist looking, perhaps, to use the bathroom—which was exactly where I headed. The old prostate had reached a point in its never-ending quest to overpower my bladder as to be a constant source of annoyance. Its size not only necessitated more frequent visits to the John, but also at the same time prevented me from emptying the dysfunctional vessel of its contents. It was a veritable "Catch-22."

The music from the jukebox was so loud that I could feel my diaphragm resonating to the sound waves of the bass track; and it actually hurt. No wonder people drank so much in these places. The bar was a horseshoe affair that wrapped around an island supporting rows of liquor bottles and a rusty, old NCR cash register. Atop the island was a pole attached to the ceiling, and temporarily attached to the pole was a youngish girl, probably no older than twenty, who gyrated mindlessly to the beat of the music. Her outfit (if you could call it that) consisted of a red, string bikini bottom, and two red pasties attached to her ample breasts. She was about five-feet, three-inches tall, with dark hair worn loose to her shoulders, and she had a rhinestone stud punched through the left nostril of her pert nose; not my taste, to be sure, but apparently just what the customers desired. Even money said her name was Donna.

It turned out I was right.

7

Alabama—2005

Ronald David Trentweiler was a survivor. A three-year stint in FCI Talladega (Federal Correctional Institution) for armed robbery would certainly test his mettle. The medium-security level facility housed a full range of prisoners, among whom Ronald had ranked just above a DWI offender in the meticulously maintained pecking order (owing to the relatively benign nature of his offense). After all, there weren't many "props" for someone who held up an ice cream parlor in Moulton, Alabama—with a BB gun, no less—especially when the "take" had amounted to under two hundred dollars. It hadn't been much of a crime, but it *had* been just enough to net Ronald his "three spot," and to secure him his place in the Class of '08 at Talladega.

In the beginning, things were tough for the lanky twenty-four-year old serving time in a prison populated with mostly hardened, career criminals. Being so young and good looking—with his sandy hair and sparkling blue eyes—he was gang raped by a group of Mexicans in the first week of his incarceration. Then, several weeks later, he nearly had one of his ears cut off by a sharpened spoon wielded by a black "queen" jealous of attention paid to him by the man's "butch" counterpart. Within a month, however, Ronald had fallen in with the "right" group (they were Aryan Brotherhood sympathizers), adopted a physical fitness regimen that saw him add thirty pounds of muscle to his slender frame, and begun to develop a skill set that every inmate needed to live out his sentence in relative security.

But, time was time, and regardless of how it was earned, its passage was the same—slower than shit. However, the Lawrence County High School dropout had put his three years "time spent" to good use, and by the end of his stretch, he had acquired a myriad of skills. Among them were forgery, brewing (turning cider into "moonshine" with the help of raisins smuggled from the prison kitchen), and knife making (a "required" course). Additionally, during his final year, he had developed a brisk "retail" business trading in "uppers," "downers," and "poppers" supplied to him by an outside acquaintance that passed them to him during weekly visits (in exchange for a fifty-fifty share of the profits—naturally). In the end, the most useful skill of any he learned turned out to be that of double-talking—or, more precisely, the ability to bullshit *anyone* about *anything.*

But, even those blessed with God-given talent need inspiration; someone to recognize their abilities for what they are, a mentor to help cultivate them. For Ron, his authority figure was the Sunday morning preacher who visited the prison each week.

The man's name was Brother Daniel, and he was always dressed impeccably, usually in a three-piece suit of expensive origin, with his long, pomaded, wavy hair glistening beneath the harsh lights of the prison dining hall where the services were held. A silk handkerchief that matched his tie was always present in his breast pocket, accompanied by a fresh carnation in his lapel. His name was Brother Daniel, but to Ron, he might as well have been The Savior Himself.

8

Downsville, NY

The Twin Islands bar was a dump. Its ancient tin ceiling had been painted a flat black to hide its defects, and the walls were papered a hideous red, with bogus fenestrations stenciled on them. The place smelled of mildew, beer, and stale urine. The bartender was a fat slob named Johnny Warinski who I'd busted less than a year ago for beating on his wife. He managed to avoid jail time when his "honey" declined to press charges. I never understood women like her; the more their men mistreated them, the better they liked it. I guessed it was a self-worth issue—not my problem. I sat on a stool near the end of the bar and ordered a Coke. Johnny filled my glass to overflowing and waved his hand to signify "no charge." *What a sport.*

When the music finally stopped, Donna grabbed a seat on the stool next to me at the end of the bar, lit up a cigarette, and sat quietly, puffing away disinterestedly. I removed the card I had found in Billy's wallet, and slid it across the worn surface of the bar top in her direction. At the same time, I flashed my badge. "We found that card in Billy Stillwater's wallet a few days ago."

Donna picked up the card, turned it over, and muttered, "So. Big deal. You found a card with my name on it in a Meth dealer's wallet. That doesn't mean I killed the son of a bitch."

"Who said anything about Billy being killed?"

Donna sat next to me, half naked, uninhibited, breasts heaving from the exertion of her last dance, and smiled. My eyes focused on a bead of perspiration that was making its way slowly between them toward her navel. "News travels a lot faster around here than you might think it does," she said, her voice breaking my concentration. She took a long drag on the cigarette, and stabbed it hard into a waiting ashtray.

This wasn't going to be easy. She might have only been twenty-or-so, but this was a hardened woman, accustomed to scratching out a living—and her claws were fully extended. "I didn't *say* you killed him. I doubt that you did. I'm just trying to get a sense of what might have led up to his death. When's the last time you saw him?"

"Maybe a week or so."

"Did you see him often?"

"Maybe twice a week. Whenever—you know how it goes."

I knew, all right. She probably traded sex for drugs. It was a common practice back in the day, and probably no less so here in the sticks. If she hadn't seen him in a week, she was probably hurting—unless she'd already found a replacement supplier.

"Did he ever mention anyone having a beef with him? Another dealer, maybe?"

"Nope."

A real wordsmith, this one, I thought.

"Did he owe anybody money?"

The girl laughed aloud.

"Okay," I laughed. "Never mind; forget I even asked."

She smiled.

"Anybody owe *him*?"

The girl scratched her head. Obviously, something I said had rung a bell. "Ya know, he *did* say something about his 'ship finally coming in,' or some shit like that."

"Like maybe he had made a big score?"

"I'm not really sure. But I know he was planning on getting out of this dump. He kept talking about going to Florida."

"Did he mention anyone by name?"

"No. Billy wasn't like that. He was always kind of vague, you know. He talked *around* things, dropping hints, teasing; he had a way about him. No big surprise, though—him being dead and all."

Her voice trailed off, and I could almost read her mind. Another week or two and Billy would just be a distant memory, especially if someone else had already taken his place.

"Do you have any idea why anyone would want him dead? Anyone have a beef with him—anything like that?"

Donna shook her head and lit up another cigarette. She had nothing more to say, and I was done here. "Nice dance," I said. I handed Donna a five-dollar bill, and headed for the exit.

As I walked out through the front door, I could almost feel someone's eyes watching me. Something told me I'd be back. But, for now, I needed to get back to headquarters—and Wayne Sabolewski.

9

Talladega Prison

In the beginning, Ron would just sit quietly and watch, marveling how the silver-haired preacher would use a perfect turn of phrase or Biblical passage to illuminate his message. As time progressed, he took even more and more notice of how Brother Daniel handled himself; watching intently, as the preacher plied his "trade." Just like a doctor or an engineer, he was a true professional. And, judging by his clothes and the gaudy, gold jewelry he wore, he was making it pay—somehow. But, he certainly wasn't getting rich preaching to a bunch of convicts. So where did he get his cash? Ron wanted— no, *needed*—to know. He decided to ask. Why not, he thought. He had nothing to lose.

One Sunday, after the service had ended, Ron approached one of the guards and asked if he might speak with the preacher for a minute. The guard was understandably apprehensive and nudged Ron away, telling him to move on. But, Ron persisted, until, at last, the sentry relented. "Okay," he replied. "But, don't try anything smart. And, only for a minute." He tapped his nightstick on the hard, concrete floor to emphasize his authority, and then idly brushed the front of his starched tunic.

Cautiously, Ron moved toward the preacher. *Jesus! He's taller than I thought he was.* "Excuse me, Brother Daniel," he said. "Can I speak with you for a minute?"

"Why certainly," replied the preacher. Ron caught a whiff of the heavily scented cologne the man wore, and couldn't help noticing the extensive dental work adorning the inside of his thin-lipped mouth. What was it his mother had always said about not trusting anyone with thin lips? Well, never mind.

"I was wondering," he began. "What do you—"

"Did you have a question about today's message?" The preacher's suit today was navy blue; it's cloth iridescent and without a wrinkle in evidence. A white, baby rose popped against its deep, dark surface.

"Well, not exactly," began Ron. He looked around to be sure no one else was listening. "It's more about you, actually."

"Me?"

In the next ten minutes, Ron poked and prodded the preacher about his profession—and his private life. He wanted to know everything: from how much the man made, to how many hours a week he worked. For his part, Brother Daniel was even more forthcoming than Ron had hoped he would be. It was obvious that the visiting preacher was proud of his accomplishments, and Ron used that pride to his own advantage. He flattered and cajoled him, until finally Brother Daniel offered to take him under his wing.

Each succeeding month saw the preacher revealing more and more of his "trade"; and before long the two appeared to have forged a true friendship—at least that's what Brother Daniel thought. In actuality, Ron was merely cultivating a resource, extracting from the preacher every bit of his knowledge and technique. By the end of his prison sentence, Ron had gleaned all he needed to prepare himself for life on the outside—and, more importantly, for his chosen vocation: "Man of God." He'd even usurped the preacher's name—not Brother Daniel, of course—but Brother—as in Brother Ron. However, once he was released, unlike his namesake, he hoped never to see the inside of a prison again.

10

Roscoe, NY

I had plenty of time to reflect upon things on the ride back to headquarters. Assuming the judge and the district attorney agreed to my idea of a plea bargain for Wayne, the big "laundromat caper" was effectively solved, and maybe, just maybe, Sabolewski would get a second chance at the life that most kids took for granted.

I thought, too, about Donna's reaction to Billy's death, and how cheaply some people valued life—even their own. One minute she's having sex with an overweight drug dealer that she probably despises in exchange for a drug that will most likely kill her; and the next day she's searching for another equally repulsive stranger to take his place—so she could keep on killing herself. It all made no sense.

The rain that had been falling on the way to Downsville seemed to have abated, and I speculated upon the accuracy of Nancy's reported weather forecast. Just an hour or so on the river with a fly rod in my hand would be a welcome relief from the events of the last week.

I sure hoped she was right.

When I got back to headquarters, Nancy greeted me with a smile on her face.

"Let me guess," I quipped, "You've decided to adopt the kid."

Nancy shook her head. "No, but *somebody* should. He's not all that bad, really—except for the drugs, of course. My guess is he just needs somebody to take him fishing."

"I wish it were that simple."

"Anyway, I spoke with Frank like you asked me to, and he said he'd make sure they had a place ready for Wayne."

"Thanks, Nancy. I appreciate your taking care of that."

"Serve and protect," laughed Nancy. "That's what we're here for."

"Yeah, yeah, I know. I guess I better get back there and see what kind of writer he is." I started down the hall toward the holding cell. Assuming Wayne was still agreeable, I had an arrest to make.

He was, and I did.

I left headquarters with Wayne safely under lock and key, and my mind focused on fishing the next morning. I was out of 5X tippet material, and I knew just who to see about it.

I pulled into the gravel driveway of Frank Kuttner's fly shop about fifteen minutes later. The first thing I noticed was that the old picnic table, which had been located on the grassy region adjacent to the driveway, was gone. I made my way past the painted, white house that sported a dark green, tin roof and oversized porch, and then stopped short of entering the shop, located to the rear. I swiveled my head to the left and, looking back over my shoulder, again surveyed the empty spot where the picnic table used to rest. It was still gone.

The little bell attached to the glass-windowed door tinkled as I pushed my way inside the shop. As usual, Frank was seated at his fly tying bench, with what appeared to be an Atlantic salmon, wet-fly hook held in the jaws of his ancient Thompson Model A vise. A few wraps of 3/0 black UNI-Thread, tied in just behind the eye of the bronze hook marked the point of Frank's progress. Several completed flies sat attached to a magnetized bar, mounted on his fly tying bench. I knew Frank didn't trout fish anymore, and there were no Atlantic salmon within five hundred miles, so I deduced that he was tying a custom order for some sport.

"Who are those for?" I asked. "Dewey?"

"Nope. Haven't seen John for a couple of years."

"Brian?"

"Nope."

"Well, who—"

"None of your beeswax."

"So what happened to the picnic table?" I asked.

"Firewood."

"You *burned* it?"

"Yep."

"So where will your—"

"Got a new one comin' tomorrow," said Frank, looking over the top of his half-lensed tying glasses. "Okay with you?"

"Sure...I guess."

"Tea?" He knew my drink of choice was hot chocolate, but always offered *his* favorite, just in case I'd decided to come over from the "dark side," as he referred to my preference.

"Hmmm," I said. "Sounds tempting, but I think I'll have some hot chocolate instead, okay?"

"Gimme a minute. Got a new copy of *Fly Fisherman* here someplace." Frank brushed aside some packets of feathers, and rummaged through a stack of manila envelopes until he found the magazine. "Here," he said, "Read this while I put the water on."

Ten minutes later I was sipping Nestlé's finest from a mug, as Frank sat opposite me, drinking Earl Grey tea from a delicate porcelain cup. As if on cue, Frank's wife, Mary Ellen, came through the door, carrying a large plate with two generous portions of fresh crumb cake on it. "Here," she said, "I thought you boys might like some cake." She set the plate containing the cake down on the wooden coffee table that separated the two of us, along with a couple of cloth napkins that she arranged neatly across from one another. "I'll leave you two alone," she offered in my direction. She smiled quickly, and before I could so much as say "thank you," Mary Ellen had disappeared out the door.

"Think she's a keeper?" Frank asked, with a wink.

"Could be," I replied.

"I'm thinking about it," he smiled.

"Could do worse."

"Never you mind."

"Billy Stillwater's dead," I said.

"Good. Somebody *shoot* the son of a bitch?" Frank had no love for anyone who made a living by selling drugs to young people.

"He was poisoned—with *Strychnine,* no less."

"Strychnine, huh. You don't say?" A puzzled expression spread across his face. "Got any idea who done it?"

"Not a clue."

We both sat quietly for a minute or two, each sipping his beverage of choice and nibbling on the succulent coffee cake that Mary Ellen had graced us with. The only sound was the steady "tick tock, tick tock" of the old German cuckoo clock on the wall behind Frank's tying desk.

"Got any ideas?" asked Frank, breaking the silence.

"Not a one. But I'll call you as soon as I do."

"Oh, *please* do. You know I won't be able to sleep a wink until I know."

I looked at Frank and smiled. "You're really cold, you know."

"Nahhh. I'm a regular pussycat."

"More like a pussy."

"Meowwww."

I started to get up. "Thank Mary Ellen for the cake, will you? It was fabulous."

Frank rolled his eyes and patted his stomach. "But not as good as Val's carrot cake."

"Just tell Mary Ellen I said it was great, okay?"

"I *might.* Might *not.* Don't want her to get a swelled head."

"You'll tell her?"

Frank stood up, walked over to the door, and held it open for me. "Good luck fishin'," he said with a smile.

I was halfway home before I realized I'd forgotten the 5X tippet.

11

Scottsboro, WV—Christmas Eve, 2008

Ron Trentweiler served twenty-eight months of his three-year sentence at Talladega, earning early release for good behavior. It had been six months since his subsequent relocation to the little town of Scottsboro, population 3,000—give or take a few military enlistees. He had chosen the place for two reasons: because it was as far from his hometown of Moulton, Alabama, as he could afford to go; and specifically because of its proximity to the small, relatively affluent city of Martinsburg. He set up "shop" in nearby Scottsboro, calling his congregation the Devoted Church of Jesus with Signs Following. Ron felt that Scottsboro's less educated residents, who provided Martinsburg with its unskilled workforce, would be the type of folks that would be most receptive to his type of ministry. What he hadn't counted on was just how poor his "congregation" would be. So, over the last few months, Brother Ron (as the "Talladega graduate" called himself) had barely scratched out a living, and was becoming less and less satisfied with the way things were going. He needed to do better.

Tonight, as he eyed the small congregation of worshippers that had crowded into the narrow, makeshift church his ministry called home, he tried to estimate what the meager "take" might be. Just as Moulton had been situated not very far from a prison,

Scottsboro, too, was similarly located; in this case near Martinsburg Correctional Facility. Like Ron, some of those in attendance had also served time. And, while among them they might not be carrying more than a few hundred dollars, Brother Ron was certain of one thing: No matter how much or how *little it was,* he fully intended to possess it *all*—every last dime. The meager savings that he had accrued in prison were almost gone, and he desperately needed to supplement his welfare payments to pay the rent on the mobile home he now occupied. He was now twenty-seven, with very little to show for his time on the planet. He was desperate.

It was cold and damp, and yet despite having only a plug-in electric radiator for heat, the atmosphere in the rundown storefront building was euphoric, thanks in part to the misplaced optimism of those inside—but mostly owing to the collective body heat they generated. Trentweiler had secured the space without a deposit, in exchange for the promise of two month's rent for the first month's use, payable at the end of December. It had seemed like a paltry sum at the time, merely three hundred dollars in total, but donations to the new "preacher" and his church had been sparse, and now with barely enough put aside to fulfill the bargain, Brother Ron fidgeted nervously, wondering whether he had made a deal with the devil—so to speak.

He need not have worried, however, for that evening an angel of sorts was destined to change his life.

12

Roscoe, NY

It was just after seven in the morning, when I lined up my little seven-foot, nine-inch, four-weight Powell fly rod. As it turned out, I wouldn't need the 5X tippet after all; from the look of things, it was going to be all small stuff. A fairly decent spinner fall of "Tricos" (short for *Trichorythodes*, a genus of minute Mayflies) was on the water, so I carefully attached a delicate 7X tippet to the end of a ten-foot spring creek leader, tied on a parachute imitation, and waited. Almost immediately, I spotted a sizable riser (probably a resident brown trout) gently sipping bunches of the barely-alive Mayflies from its lie, tight against a rock ledge on the far side of the creek. Unfortunately, there were several large boulders between me and my target, and they provided enough resistance against the moderate current to produce considerable drag on the floating fly line. I just could *not* seem to make that perfect, drag-free presentation that the situation called for, no matter how hard I tried. Finally, on my fifth attempt, I managed to throw enough slack line into the cast to permit my imitation to begin its journey toward its target in perfect attitude—without a bit of drag. I held my breath, and then exhaled slowly through clenched teeth and tight lips, as the tiny fly neared the trout. Just as it reached that magic zone where a strike could be expected, the fly stopped dead.

"What the hell?"

Holding the rod tip high, I rummaged with my free hand through the pockets of my vest until I found my mini binoculars. One look confirmed my worst suspicions; the fly was hung up on a tiny twig of a Rhododendron bush that spilled over the edge of the rock ledge.

"Shit." Now I had to wade across and get my damn fly back.

Moving slowly to maintain my balance, I placed one booted foot in front of the other, and carefully made my way across the swollen stream, reeling in slack line as I went. When I arrived at a point where I thought I could reach the snagged fly, I raised the rod tip high in the air and began to slide my free hand slowly down the length of the leader toward the fly. A slight movement on the ledge caught my eye and I stopped dead in the water. A four-foot long rattlesnake lay sunning itself just within easy striking distance of my exposed hand; had I moved another foot or two, I surely would have been bitten. The motion my eye had detected was the flicking of the reptile's forked tongue—undoubtedly surveying the air and sensing my presence. Instantly, a shiver went up my spine, and I was transported back to a time nearly a year-and-a-half ago, when I discovered a body while fishing my favorite "secret spot." I'd had the same reaction then. Images of bleached bone and bits of flesh flashed in front of my eyes. Composing myself, I backed away ever so slowly, keeping my eyes riveted on the snake, while pulling steadily on the taut leader, until at last the nylon snapped cleanly, leaving the fly where it lay. "Damn thing could have at least rattled," I cursed, as I carefully backed my way out of the water on unsteady legs.

Suddenly, fishing didn't seem nearly as attractive as it did when the day began—and, to make matters worse, it had started to rain and a storm seemed imminent.

Unfortunately, there was another storm coming my way, and as I would soon learn, it bore no relationship to the weather.

13

Scottsboro, WV—Christmas Eve, 2008
Standing in the shadows of the shoddily constructed "stage" at the rear of the space he had rented to serve as his "church," Brother Ron watched with curiosity as a good-looking, young woman entered through the glass door at the front of the building. It was unusual for females to attend his services, especially any as attractive as this one. She was of average height, and appeared to be in her mid-to-late twenties, with long, dark auburn hair worn straight. She had on tan, corduroy slacks, a light blue, man-tailored shirt tucked in at the waist, and a loose fitting brown, suede blazer. On her feet were immaculate penny loafers. Among the other shoddily dressed attendees, she stuck out like a spider in an ant farm. But what really caught his attention were her eyes; they were dark brown—and *enormous*. Even from forty feet away, Ron sensed an animal attraction that caused his breath to grow ragged.

What the hell is a classy-looking broad like that doing in a joint like this? Ron watched her intently as she moved through the room, his curiosity growing. She appeared to be searching for someone in particular; then, spotting Ron, her gaze intensified, and she started in his direction. *What does she want with* me? He adjusted his tie (the only one he possessed) and stepped down off the wooden platform. *What the hell, might as well introduce myself.* He made his way toward her, and they met in the middle of the room.

"Welcome," he said in a loud voice. "It's nice of you to join us." *What a bunch of crap,* he thought. "I'm Brother Ron...and *you* are?"

"Winona. Winona Stepp," she said, smiling and extending her hand.

Nice smile, thought Ron. He couldn't help noticing the firm, young bosom, barely concealed beneath her pale blue blouse; the top two buttons open and somewhat inviting. *Nice tits, too.*

"So nice to have you with us," he said, taking her hand in his, and holding it a bit longer than he ought to have, enjoying the feel of her soft skin against his own calloused palm. "What brings you out on such a nasty night, anyway?" *God, I am so full of shit.* The whole thing had the feel of a high stakes poker game, with the opponents making small, exploratory bets, feeling each other out.

"Actually," she said, "I was just curious."

Curious, my ass, he thought. *This broad* wants *something.* If nothing else, Ron was the quintessential skeptic—a predisposition that had served him well in prison.

"I was doing a bit of last minute shopping and I saw the lights on. Please don't take this the wrong way, but...is this...a church?"

Was she for real? *Okay,* he thought, *I'll play along.*

"Well, it sure as heck is, Little Lady," said Ron, affecting his best John Wayne drawl.

Winona blushed, and started to apologize. "Oh, no, I didn't mean to say—"

"No, no," interrupted Ron. "It's cool. I was just being a smartass. I just meant that it might not *look* like much of anything, but it isn't because we're not trying." It had been a long time since he'd talked to a female—let alone one as attractive as this one. He let his imagination wander.

As if reading his mind, Winona said, "I was wondering if you could use some help.

Here it comes.

"You know, decorating, or...cleaning...you know...whatever..."

"Well, we probably could," said Ron. "But, we don't exactly have anything in our...uh...budget for—"

"You keep saying 'we,'" said Winona. "Do you have a partner?"

"A *partner?*" Ron laughed. "Not a chance. I'm afraid it's just me and my shadow." He feigned a soft shoe dance step, and then made an exaggerated bow. Owing to the wear and tear of prison life, he looked considerably older than his actual age of twenty-five, and certainly carried himself in a way that belied his true persona, that of a con man. Then Winona revealed her hand.

"How'd you like to have one?" she asked.

"One *what?*" asked Ron.

"Why...a...*partner,* of course," replied Winona. "That's what."

Ron coughed, his voice catching in his throat. He never expected this. "Are you serious?"

Winona's face seemed to change; the softness disappearing along with her smile.

"I most certainly am," she replied. "It doesn't take a genius to see that *you* need *me* as much as *I* need *you*." She had a full house, "aces over," and she wasn't backing down.

"How do you know—"

"I know *everything*," she said. Do you *really* think I just wandered in here? I've been asking around about you for over a week. FCI Talladega, wasn't it?"

Shit. Now what do I do? Ron could feel his hands growing clammy. *I don't need this shit.* "Okay, what do you want?" he asked.

"Not much really," said Winona. "I just want to be part of your little side show. That's all. I left my old man a couple of weeks ago, and I've been staying with a cousin over in Schuylerville. But, she hasn't got two nickels to rub together; and besides, her old man's a drunk just like mine. He might get tired of beating up on her and start hitting on me. I sure as heck don't need that."

"So you figure you'll just join up with me, huh?"

"Well, I wouldn't put it quite that way; but, sure, why not? Besides, it might be fun." She leaned against Ron, letting her breasts rub against his chest to reinforce her position.

It sure would, thought Ron. He had to admit, though, that he was a bit perplexed, considering the way her classy looks contrasted with her actions. *Damn.* He never was any good at figuring out women. *Now what should I do?*

"Well, what do you say? Deal?" Winona's eyes danced with desire.

"Let me sleep on it."

"Better yet," whispered Winona into his ear. "Why don't *we* sleep on it?"

So, they did. And that's how it all began.

14

Roscoe, NY

I stumbled a bit, splashing water as I went, and managed to exit the stream without killing myself. I breathed a sigh of relief as I stepped onto dry land, and then stared back across the water through the rain, just barely able to see the rock ledge on the far side of the stream. From where I stood it was all but impossible to make out the shape of the rattlesnake without the aid of binoculars— and I'd be damned if I wanted a closer look at the reptile. I looked around self-consciously to see if anyone had witnessed my clumsy retreat (thankfully, no one had) and smiled at my foolishness.

"Fuck! Double fuck!"

I began making my way back to the Jeep, any thoughts of trout long replaced by visions of what *might* have happened on the water.

Fifteen minutes later, after loading my gear into the back of the old Wagoneer, I slammed the tailgate shut, and was soon happily headed home to a cup of hot chocolate, some bacon and eggs, and the comforting arms of my wife, Valerie. The trout would wait for another day—and it was beginning to rain.

When I reached the house, Val was already busy in the kitchen preparing a special chicken dish for that evening's dinner. School was closed for the summer, and Val, free of her daily routine as school nurse, was enjoying the cooking, baking, and gardening that brought her the most pleasure in life. If left to my own devices, I was perfectly content to have meatloaf every night, but Val made a point of trying at least one new dish a week. In fact, she was as devoted to the Cooking Channel as I was to fly fishing and chocolate. It wasn't that I wouldn't *try* new things—because I would; I just preferred food with which I had a longstanding relationship. However, in every other aspect, our likes and dislikes meshed perfectly, and our marriage was as solid as a rock.

I gave Val a glancing peck on the cheek as I passed by, and continued on to my study where I stashed my fishing gear in the cedar-lined closet I had constructed especially for that purpose. My hands were still shaking, and I took a deep breath before returning to the kitchen.

"How come you're back so soon?" asked Val. "Fish not biting?"

"Nah. I just got bored," I lied. "Besides, it's raining again. What a surprise, huh?"

"Why'd you *really* come home so early, honey? Something wrong?"

I could feel the blood rush to my face. I felt like a ten-year old kid, caught with my hand in the cookie jar. Married life did that to a man, especially if he had a good marriage—and mine was; it was the best. Val always saw right through me. And, I wasn't about to perpetuate a falsehood. "I'm sorry, honey. Actually, I got scared..."

"Because of what happened on Cathy's Creek?"

I remained silent. She was referring to the corpse I had found the last time I fished my preferred spot.

"Come here," said Val, moving to meet me halfway. She placed her arms around me, snuggling close and whispering in my ear. "It's okay, honey. *Really* it is."

I hugged her back and gave her a kiss on her neck, causing goose bumps to erupt on the surface of her skin. "That's *not* what it was," I said, a bit defensively. "It was a...well...it was a snake."

"A *snake*?" Val pulled away, holding me at arm's length, looking me up and down, as if she expected to find some sort of visible evidence of the encounter. "Were you bitten? Are you okay?"

"*No*, I wasn't bitten. Do you think I'd be standing here now if I got bit?"

Val frowned. "Duh. Okay, okay; so shoot me. I wasn't thinking. What kind of snake was it?"

"A damned rattlesnake—"

"A *rattlesnake?*"

"Yeah. It scared the crap out of me." I looked down at the floor, fidgeting with embarrassment.

"Oh, Matt. No wonder you came home so early." Val pulled me to her, squeezing me tightly. Then, laughing, she pushed me away. "Poor Matt. You can take the boy out of the city, but you can't take—"

"Yeah, yeah. Okay. So, I'm afraid of snakes. How about making me some breakfast?"

"Sure thing, Steve Irwin," Val quipped. "One breakfast, coming right up!"

I frowned melodramatically, and then Val remembered.

"Oh, damn," she said. "I forgot. He got killed, didn't he?" She was referring to the television naturalist who had died several years ago in a freak accident involving a stingray. The spine at the end of the ray's tail had entered the TV personality's heart, killing him on the spot. It was a sad end for a beloved individual. I had been one of his most ardent fans.

"Sorry, Matt. I'll make you some eggs." Val handed me a cup of hot chocolate. "Here, honey, why don't you go into the living room and watch the news? Do you want bacon or sausage?"

"Both—and an English muffin." I headed for the living room, flopped down in the recliner, and flipped on the TV. I didn't care what was on: news, weather, sports—anything—as long as it wasn't a nature show, and definitely not one about snakes.

15

Scottsboro, WV—spring of 2009

"What would you think about using snakes?" asked Ron. He and Winona were lying in bed in Ron's doublewide. It had been nearly five months since they met. After an initial night of getting to know one another, the two had quickly agreed upon an "arrangement," and Winona had moved in with him, bringing with her a modest collection of possessions—mostly clothes. She had served as his "assistant" ever since. Ron's question caught her completely off guard.

"Snakes?" she replied. "What *about* snakes?"

"You know, using them in the act. It's a hell of a hook. It'd keep the suckers coming in like crazy. And, it'd sure up the take."

Ever since meeting the itinerant preacher, Winona had constantly referred to the church as his "act." Ron really couldn't protest either, because that was how he had always perceived the practice himself.

"I don't have a clue what you're talking about," said Winona. "What the hell do snakes have to do with preaching?"

"Haven't you ever heard of snake handlers?" said Ron. "Mostly, the Pentecostals do it. There's this verse in the Bible about handling serpents—poisonous ones—that says it's supposed to be holy. It's a big deal. They dance around, stomping their feet, speaking in tongues, and passing around rattlesnakes and copperheads. I saw a documentary about it once. I wouldn't be surprised if it goes on right in this area."

Ron could see goose bumps forming on Winona's arms.

"I don't really care," she said. "I absolutely *hate* fucking snakes," she said. "They really creep me out."

"Oh, hell; they're not that bad," declared Ron with a smug tone to his voice. "I used to play with snakes when I was a kid—not poisonous ones, of course. Mostly garter snakes."

Winona stared at him, incredulously. "You did?"

"Yeah, sure; all the guys did. Hey, you know all that crap about snakes being slimy and stuff?"

"Yeah."

"Well, it's a bunch of bull. They're as dry as sand. They just look that way because of the way the light reflects off their scales."

Winona sat quietly, as though puzzling something out.

"So what do you think?" prodded Ron.

"I think you're nuts. Aren't you afraid you'll get bit?"

Ron shrugged his shoulders. "Sure. I guess so. But, from what I saw in that movie, won't nothin' happen as long as you believe."

"Believe what?"

"In the power of the Holy Ghost. That's what protects ya."

"Oh bullshit," whispered Winona.

"I'm serious. It says so right in the Bible."

Winona sat up straight, the covers slipping from around her neck, and exposing her breasts. "And you really believe that crap?"

"I know it sounds crazy," said Ron. "But I've seen videos of those people. If you saw them, you'd believe it, too."

"I don't think so."

Ron reached over and stroked one of Winona's breasts, and then the other, burying his face in her flesh. "Maybe you're right, baby," he cooed. "Instead of playing with snakes, maybe I'll just play with these."

"You're serious, aren't you? About the snakes, I mean," said Winona, pushing Ron away. "You think people will give all kinds of money when you break out the snakes. You think it'll put them in the right spirit I guess. Is that what you think?"

Ron grew quiet. Apparently, Winona had struck a chord.

"Something like that," he said. "It's *all* about the money. I remember seeing people in those films pulling out their wallets and giving everything they had to those preachers."

Ron stared intensely at Winona, and he thought he could almost see the wheels spinning inside her head as she processed the information.

"Hmmm," she said. "If *that's* the case, maybe you *could* learn to handle the damn things. *If* the money's as good as you say it is. Better yet—maybe *I* could even do it." She laughed aloud at the thought.

"I don't really care *who* does it," replied Ron, "just as long as *somebody* does it. But, at least we ought to *think* about it. We'd probably have to move around a lot, though."

"Why?"

"Why do you think? Sometimes people get bit. The cops might show up. Stuff like that. But, think about it. It'd be a gas. I'll ask around. See if anybody knows where they do it."

A funny look came over Winona's face, and for a second Ron actually thought she might be considering the idea. "So, what do you think," he said, with a hint of a daring in his voice, "Should I check it out?"

Winona hesitated. "I don't know. I mean it's really kind of—"

"Just say you'll think about it. I won't do it unless you agree. After all, we're partners."

"Okay. I'll think about it."

"Good! I'll start asking around."

"Yeah, yeah...you do that," said Winona. "And maybe—*just* maybe—I'll consider it."

"Good. And right now I'll consider *these.*" Ron lunged forward, and cupped Winona's breasts. She giggled, and slid under the covers. Ron followed.

Forty-five minutes later, fully sated, with Winona sleeping quietly by his side, Ron slipped out from beneath the covers, put on his robe and slippers, and padded softly to the bathroom for a shower. As he let the hot water envelop his body, he couldn't get the thought of the snakes out of his mind—especially the part about the money.

The evil storm was gathering strength, and money was its driving force.

16

Roscoe, NY

That evening, I sat quietly in my study indulging myself in some Hersheyettes chocolate candies that I'd bought on eBay at a ridiculously high price (sometimes being a chocoholic got expensive). Resembling M&Ms (only *way* better) they are my favorites, but can only be found at Christmas, when a few stores carry them packed in miniature, plastic candy canes. *Worth every penny*, I thought, as I sucked the creamy milk chocolate from the inside of the hard candy shell.

I heard the phone ring, but before I could answer it, Val hollered, "I've got it," so I picked up my copy of *Rheimer's Anthology of North American Snakes*, and began thumbing through its pages until I found the entry for the Eastern Diamondback rattlesnake, and began to read:

> *Crotalus adamanteus* is the scientific name assigned to the eastern diamondback rattlesnake. The name *crotalus* comes from the Greek word *krotolon*, which means "rattle" or "castanet." The word *adamanteus* is most likely derived from the Latin word *adamantinus*, which means 'made of diamond," or more aptly 'having the qualities of a diamond." This would refer to the diamond-like shape of the patterns of the eastern diamondback rattlesnake.

These snakes are the largest of all North American venomous snakes, and widely recognized as one of the most efficient predators in the animal kingdom, having few peers able to match its ability to kill. Records show individual specimens attaining lengths of nearly eight-and-a-half feet, but more commonly, the snakes average between three-and-a-half feet and four-and-a-half feet, and can weigh as much as ten pounds. In 1953, a reward was offered for any specimen brought in measuring over seven-and-a-half feet, but the reward was never claimed.

Its colors consist of browns, olive-gray, brownish-yellow, or tan overlaid by a series of diamond-shaped (hence the name) markings, usually dark brown, or black in color, with cream or yellowish borders. The tail is usually a different shade from the body, and darker bands replace the diamond shapes. The head is broad and triangular, with a dark, almost black, stripe running diagonally through each eye. This stripe is bordered by distinct yellowish or tan stripes, much like the eye of a cat.

One other characteristic of this and other rattlesnakes is the large pit (heat sensitive) located between the eye and the nostril, used to locate warm-blooded prey or other predators—hence the name "pit viper." The diet of the eastern diamondback rattlesnake consists of small mammals such as mice, rats, frogs, and other small snakes. Occasionally, larger warm-blooded mammals like rabbits, or even housecats, may fall prey to its potent venom.

It is no coincidence that they are known as "cold blooded" killers.

As I studied the accompanying photographs and diagrams, I felt that familiar tingle begin to run up and down my spine. I closed my eyes, and was immediately "rewarded" with a vision of that morning's encounter with the subject of the book's article that caused me to open them just as quickly. "That's enough of that shit!" I slammed the book shut and simultaneously reached for another handful of candy.

"What did you say, Matt?" called Valerie from the kitchen.

I finished swallowing, and hollered back, "Nothing, Val. I was just talking to myself."

"Well, come in here and talk to *me*," she answered back. "I've got something I need to discuss with you."

I didn't like the tone of her voice.

"That was the radiologist's office on the phone. They said they saw something that wasn't quite right, and—"

"Well, what was it?"

"It's probably nothing," said Val. She was sitting at the kitchen table with a frown on her face, sipping on a cup of decaf. "But, I just wanted you to know what's going on."

While I'd been at work that day, Val had been over at the hospital in Monticello, undergoing her annual mammogram. Apparently, the technician performing the mammogram had seen something that looked a bit abnormal.

"He wants to do an ultrasound—first thing tomorrow morning."

"That fast, huh?"

"Well, you know how it is, Matt. They don't like to wait. When the technician said he spotted something 'unusual,' at first I thought he was referring to that cyst they found last year in my left breast. But, he said, 'No. It's something in the right one.'"

My mind flashed back to the previous year and the "false alarm" that had scared both of us nearly to death. Thankfully, everything had been fine, but I still felt like a jerk for not being there today.

"I'm so sorry, Val. I should have been there for you today."

"Oh, Matt, don't be ridiculous. It was just a mammogram."

I sat down alongside her and pulled her to me. She leaned her head on my shoulder, and I could feel the warmth of her body. I couldn't imagine what life would be like without her. "I'm really sorry, honey. I *totally* forgot. Do you forgive me?"

She looked up at me and smiled. But, I could see the tension in her face.

"Are you scared?" I asked, putting my arm around her.

"Not *yet*," she laughed.

"Well, do you *feel* like there's anything there—in the right one?"

"Not *really*. But, I couldn't feel that cyst either, remember?"

"Yeah, I do remember that now. Well, I think I should be there tomorrow, just in case—"

"I was hoping you'd say that. I'm not scared yet—not *really*—but I'd definitely feel better if you were there." Val pressed against me, and I squeezed her shoulder.

"Well, don't worry, honey. I will be."

I slept like hell that night, tossing and turning, and waking several times; my dreams were filled with images of hospital operating rooms, people in green gowns, surgical instruments moving hurriedly over a green draped form, and blood spraying in every direction. The last time I awoke, I was drenched in perspiration, so I got up and crept downstairs to make myself a cup of hot chocolate. For most folks, that would be a recipe for insomnia, but for some reason hot chocolate has the opposite effect on me. I spent the remainder of the night in the relative safety of the recliner in the den, mercifully undisturbed—and very much asleep.

In the morning, I could hear Val scurrying around the kitchen, and I remembered the appointment. I immediately got on the phone and called Nancy.

"Don't expect me until after lunch," I said, explaining the situation.

"Never mind that. If you get here, fine. If not, we'll survive for one day without you. And, tell Val everything's going to be all right."

"Thanks, Nancy. I will."

I hung up the phone, desperately wanting to share Nancy's optimism, but filled instead with a sense of dread. Nevertheless, I relayed her message of cheer to Val. We shared a hurried breakfast of scrambled eggs, toast, and juice, and then it was time to leave. I put my arms around Val and held her tightly to my chest. I could feel her heart beating furiously.

"It's going to be just fine," I said, unconvincingly.

Val smiled bravely.

We got into the Jeep and headed for the hospital. There wasn't much traffic, and there was even less conversation as we made the forty-minute drive to Monticello in virtual silence. I didn't dare let my thoughts stray to the negative possibilities of the day, but stayed focused on the blacktop in front of me. Once we were at the hospital, I parked the car, and then turned to Val. It seemed to me that her eyes had never looked prettier or bluer. "It *will* be, you know," I said, my own eyes focused unwaveringly on hers. "It will *be* okay."

"As long as I have you, Matt; that's all that counts."

I thought of the famous line from the movie, "Jerry McGuire," and smiled.

Together, we exited the car and walked through the doors of the hospital, into its cool, sterile interior and into a new chapter of our lives—which would never be the same.

17

Scottsville, WV—2009

It had been several months since Ron had mentioned the snakes to Winona. In the meantime, he'd done a bit of investigating. Not only were there snake handlers in the area, but there was an active "church" less than thirty miles from where they were living. A fellow he met at the town's only gas station had sketched a crude map for him, but warned, "Don't say a word to nobody. This shit ain't legal, ya know." Ron promised he wouldn't speak of it to a soul, and then promptly hurried home to tell Winona. "Let's just go and see what it's all about, okay?" he'd said, his voice filled with excitement.

Now, a week later, they found themselves in a rundown barn behind a weathered, white farmhouse, along with dozens of others, all of them "true believers," watching as the itinerant preacher named Father James finished up the "appetizer" part of the service, and prepared to move on to the "main course." Ron and Winona remained in the rear among the shadows, trying hard to be unobtrusive.

Individuals shuffled their feet anxiously, and the tinkle of tambourines could be heard above the murmur of the crowd. Someone struck a chord on a guitar, and yet another member of the group began to chant rhythmically in time to the instrument's cadence.

Gradually the entire congregation joined in, and their simultaneous activity reminded Ron of one of those old Western movies in which a band of Indians does a war dance around a bonfire, before attacking an unsuspecting wagon train.

Moving ever so slowly, the preacher reached down into a wooden box and gently extracted one of the reptiles—a rattlesnake—and carefully lifted it up and out of the container. Ron's breath caught in his throat; Winona pressed herself against him, and squeezed his hand so hard he thought it might break. He looked down at her, and their eyes met for a moment in an instant that was charged with a kind of primitive sexuality, something akin to what members of ancient civilizations must have experienced during ritual sacrifices.

Suddenly, a collective "Ahhhh" from the crowd broke the silence, and caused the couple to re-focus on the preacher in front of them. What had caused the reaction was his placing the serpent around his neck, where it now hung suspended, with its tongue flicking the air lightly, as though trying to collectively taste its audience. The gray-haired preacher, who appeared to be in his sixties, would alternately remove the serpent from his shoulders and hold it in his hand, and then return it to its resting place. Most of the younger people were swaying side-to-side, arm in arm, watching with a level of intensity that Ron and Winona had only witnessed at tent revivals.

With a glazed look on his face, the preacher reached down into the box with his free hand, and brought up another serpent; this one was a copperhead. Suddenly, he began to whirl slowly around in a circle, babbling incoherently in what most Pentecostals would call "tongues."   Now, most of the people with tambourines were banging them in unison, and the man with the guitar began playing a gospel song. Then, a banjo's distinctive voice could be heard alongside its six-stringed cousin. Before long, everyone except Ron and Winona was singing at the top of his or her lungs, clapping in unison, and doing a kind of stomping dance in place.

Watching the small crowd embrace the emotion of the moment, Ron could understand how mob mentality worked. *He* elicited this kind of response every time he gave a sermon before his congregation. Glancing down at Winona, it was obvious to him that she, too, was processing the entire experience and probably already exploring in her mind the various ways they could profit by it.

In the next few minutes, the activity was ratcheted up another notch, as the preacher began passing out snakes, one at a time, to other members of the assembly, until after a while there were nearly a dozen serpents undulating gently in the hands of both men and women of varying ages. At one point, Winona looked up at Ron and was amazed by how enthralled he appeared to be.

"Baby," she said. "Do you want to try it?"

Ron didn't move.

"*Ron,*" she said, a bit louder this time. "How about it?"

"What?" he said, dully. It was as though he hadn't heard a word she said. He appeared almost to be in a trance.

"I said, *how about it?*" repeated Winona. "Do you want to give it a try?"

But, instead of answering her, and without uttering a syllable, Ron moved away from her, quickly slipped past an elderly couple in front of them, and moved down next to a young female standing at the front of the crowd. The shapely blond was holding a small copperhead in her delicate right hand, with her eyes focused on the serpent as she watched its every move. Ron stood immediately to her right.

Then, before Winona could take a step, and to her great surprise, Ron did something that totally shocked her. Only, it wasn't at all what she had expected.

18

Monticello, NY

I watched with fascination as the technician moved the sound emitting probe slowly over Val's right breast, pausing ever so often to fiddle with one of the myriad dials on the surface of the device's control panel. A tightly coiled wire ran from the machine to the probe, and for a moment I was reminded of the snake I had encountered the day before. Then, the technician's hand stopped, the probe hovering over a particular spot on Val's skin, just to the right of the nipple.

"There," he said. "Right there. Do you see it?"

I stared hard at the negative image of Val's breast showing on the screen above her head. I could see the white outline of her breast, with the tangle of veins showing as white spider-web like lines. But, I didn't see what the technician saw.

"What am I looking for?"

"It's not very large. Probably less than a centimeter." He pointed to what looked like a tiny, black image of the sun, with a ragged corona surrounding it. "Do you see how irregular the edge is?"

Okay, I thought, *so the edge is irregular. What does that mean?* "Is that bad?"

"It's probably a just a *fibro adenoma*—a benign tumor," said the technician.

I realized we were talking "around" Val, as if she weren't even there. I reached out and rubbed her shoulder. "Sorry, honey. I didn't mean to ignore you. Are you doing all right?"

Val didn't answer, and it suddenly occurred to me that all her nursing experience was of no use now. She was in a complete fog, unable to process anything because it was just too close to home. But there was another possibility that made even more sense—especially knowing my wife as I did—and that was that she *was* processing, knew exactly what the implications were, and was frightened to death. My money was on the latter.

"I'm sorry," said the technician. "The significance is this. It's definitely not a cyst. If it were a cyst, the edges would be smooth; the mass would be round—like a perfect circle. But what I'm seeing is an irregular mass. Can you see that?"

"I g-g-guess so," stammered Val. I squeezed her shoulder harder.

"I think I'd like to have Dr. Morsky, our head radiologist, take a look. I'll be right back."

The technician left the room, taking with him what felt like every molecule of air. Val and I held our collective breath.

In less than five minutes, the technician returned, accompanied by a slightly portly man in his forties, with dull brown hair and a receding hairline, whom he introduced as Dr. Roger Morsky. "Now, I don't want you to be upset, Mrs. Davis," said the radiologist. "It's probably nothing—but, I think we should get a needle biopsy, just to be sure."

"But I thought *he* said it was benign," I whispered to Val, aiming my eyes at the technician.

"No, honey," she corrected me. "He said it was *probably* benign."

The technician nodded his affirmation.

"Well, there's no point in speculating," said Dr. Morsky, "We'll just get a biopsy and we'll know for sure. One good thing, though, if it is a cancer, it's a tiny one."

"What does that mean?" I asked. I could feel my eyes filling with tears.

"It means that it probably hasn't had a chance to go anywhere. Most likely it hasn't spread."

Well, well, I thought, it was all out there: the word "cancer," with all its horrid implications. *Hell, he's already talking about it spreading.*

"Do you think it *could* have spread?" I asked impulsively, immediately wishing I hadn't opened my mouth.

"Now, now, let's not go jumping the gun. We don't even know if it's malignant yet."

But it was too late. He couldn't fool us. We'd been through too much together. I could see from the expression on Val's face that she had reached the same conclusion as I had. It was cancer. All that remained was to find out how big it was, and if it had metastasized. Suddenly, I felt as though someone were squeezing my chest in a ferocious bear hug. I forced myself to take deliberate, even breaths, exhaling slowly through my lips. Val reached up from the examining table on which she lay and squeezed my hand reassuringly. Just like her, I thought—*her* comforting *me.*

"Well," she said. "We might as well get that biopsy done, don't you think?"

"I guess we don't have much choice," I replied.

"It's really a simple procedure," said Dr. Morsky, already preparing the biopsy equipment. "You'll feel a little discomfort when I give you a local anesthetic and that's all. And then, once you're numb, we'll take the biopsy. I promise, all you should feel is a little pressure."

* * * *

True to his word, Dr. Morsky finished the biopsy in less than five minutes, and Val didn't appear to feel any pain.

"Do you have a surgeon?" asked the radiologist.

Do we have a surgeon? Oh, yeah, and a hematologist or whatever you call those blood guys, too. I couldn't believe this was happening. "No, we don't," I managed to reply. "Can you recommend someone?"

"I'd be happy to. Tom Eisenhauer is a very good man. His office is over in Liberty. I can call and set up an appointment for Friday if you'd like."

Sure, I thought. *And, while you're at it, let's schedule a tune up, an oil change, and a tire rotation.*

"That would be fine," I heard myself say.

Val just nodded.

Neither of us said a word during the ride home, and I forced myself to focus on the Billy Stillwater homicide in order to keep from speculating about Val's condition. There was something peculiar about Billy's murder, and it really bothered me, but I couldn't put a finger on it. Then, it hit me. Why did the murderer have to hit Billy over the head? He'd already been forced to drink the Strychnine—probably at gunpoint—so why bash his head in? There was only one explanation: It had to be personal. There *must* have been a history between the two of them—or some kind of rivalry.

I needed to get back to the Twin Islands bar.

19

Somewhere near Scottsville, WV—2009

Ron turned to face the blond holding the copperhead and slowly reached out his right hand in her direction, the palm facing upward, beckoning her to give him the snake. Winona gasped, and as she watched, horrified, from a distance, the girl carefully laid the serpent across the fleshy part of Ron's hand, and the copperhead settled comfortably into its new surroundings. Winona methodically made her way through the small crowd toward her partner, her breathing measured and shallow.

As she approached him, Ron smiled ever so slightly, as if amused. Winona found nothing pleasurable in watching her man handle the deadly serpent. What had she been thinking? As if in silent response, Ron's smile grew even wider, and he permitted himself to make eye contact with Winona's wide-open, big brown eyes. For just a second, Winona detected that same sensation she felt when she and Ron first met; there was a rush of blood to her cheeks, and a flash of desire that moistened her femininity. In spite of the air temperature that hovered in the mid-eighties, she shivered uncontrollably, and had to wrap her arms around her shoulders to maintain control of her body.

Ron now held the snake in both of his outstretched hands; its full length of nearly four feet was distributed evenly between them, and it appeared to be almost asleep. The music had grown more intense, and the foot stomping and shouting was even louder. An elderly man with sparse white hair and even less in the way of teeth approached Ron and lifted the snake from Ron's hands, laying the serpent across his own shoulders in a single motion. Ron collapsed to the ground. In an instant, Winona was by his side, hugging him and whispering in his ear, "It's good, Ron. It's *good*. You were *wonderful*."

For his part, Ron appeared oblivious, with sweat pouring down his face, and his lips moving silently, his eyes glazed and unseeing. She had never seen him like this before. Maybe he *could* do this. They'd make a fortune, she thought.

Ron stirred to life. "Did you see me?" he asked Winona. "Did you *see* me?" She thought he was like a small child, showing off his school project on Parents Night. "Yes, baby," she said. "I saw you. I saw you." Together, they made their way to the rear of the barn.

As the two huddled together and watched, the serpents were returned to their cage. Immediately, several young people carrying waste baskets moved through the crowd soliciting donations, many of which appeared to be quite generous. When they had finished the collection, they brought the overflowing containers to Father James, who disappeared with them out the side door of the barn. In a few minutes, he returned, picked up the box of snakes, and departed. Apparently, that signaled the end of the service, for immediately folks started filing out the front door of the barn.

Winona could hear the sound of car and truck engines being started, along with the echo of slamming doors and shouted goodbyes. One by one, the cars and pickups disappeared into the night, until at last Ron and Winona were completely alone inside the barn. Without warning, all the lights went out, and the interior of the barn went dark, so the pair stepped outside into a light rain, with Winona unsure what they should do next.

Next, the exterior lights were extinguished, and Ron and Winona were left standing with just the glow from the inside of the farmhouse illuminating the immediate area. They approached the house, climbed the two steps to the front porch, and Ron knocked gently on the wooden screen door. Winona held her breath, unsure of what to expect. Presently, the main door opened inward, revealing the preacher, clad in a white terrycloth robe. To her great surprise, Winona detected the sweet smell of marijuana smoke emanating from the tightly wrapped joint hanging loosely from Father James' lower lip. The aroma was one that she had come to know early in her life, and it signaled "welcome."

"So," said Father James, "I see I've piqued your curiosity. Well, don't just stand there. Come on in."

Winona waited for Ron to take the first step, and then followed him inside. She fully expected to find snakes slithering over the floor. Instead, the interior of the house was more spacious and far more ornate than she could have expected. The living room area was nicely appointed. High quality upholstery adorned the chairs and sofas, and rich brass hinges and handles accented the accompanying furniture. Thick carpeting covered the floor. It was obvious to her that the preacher's curious form of religion was not only rewarding spiritually, but materially as well.

"Was this your first time with the snakes?" asked Father James, offering the freshly lit joint first to Winona who declined, and then to Ron, who accepted eagerly.

"Uh huh," managed Ron through tightly clenched lips. He had inhaled the contents of the marijuana cigarette deeply into his lungs, and after holding the pungent smoke for as long as possible, slowly exhaled, filling the space around him with the depleted remains. He offered the joint to Winona, who, this time, unable to resist the familiar aroma, accepted it. Old habits were hard to break, she thought.

"It's not often that a first timer handles the snakes," observed Father James. "Had you planned to do it?"

"Not really," replied Ron. "Actually, the whole thing was Winona's idea. Wasn't it, baby?"

Realizing that no introductions had been made, Winona extended her hand toward the preacher. "I'm sorry," she offered. "I'm Winona. He's Ron. We heard about you from a friend."

"Father James," said the preacher. "Nice to meet you both."

With the formalities out of the way, the three of them found seats around the small coffee table, and conversation began in earnest, a freshly lighted joint traveling smoothly among them as they took turns speaking. Ron told Father James about his own "church," and his desire to begin using serpents to attract more attendees.

"It's not that simple," said Father James. "You'll have to be very careful. The law is doing its best to shut us down. *They* don't understand it, so they feel obligated to keep *us* from doing it. But, as long as there are believers, we'll be out there providing them with what they need."

Ron and Winona exchanged furtive glances. Maybe this was not for them after all, she thought.

"Of course, it helps if you're a believer," said Father James. "Do *you* believe, brother?"

Ron glanced at Winona before responding. "I think I do."

It was the second time that evening that he had caught her by surprise.

"Something came over me tonight," he continued. "I can't explain it. It was as if nothing could hurt me. It was as though I'd been born for this." Winona was bowled over. She had only known Ron for six months, but she sensed he was truly sincere. Never mind, she thought, so much the better. It could only help the "act."

Father James had picked up his Bible, and opened it to a page whose corners were dog-eared from use. He passed the book to Ron, indicating a highlighted passage with a finger stained by nicotine. "Read that. Maybe it'll make sense to you."

Ron started reading quietly to himself, moving his lips ever so slightly as went along. Winona rolled her eyes and pretended to pay attention. At last, he was ready. "Listen to this, Winona," he said. "Listen."

"*And these signs shall follow them that believe,*" read Ron. "*In my name shall they cast out devils; they shall speak with new tongues.*"

Father James was smiling his approval. Winona sat quietly, seeing dollar signs in her mind's eye.

"*They shall take up serpents; and if they drink any deadly thing, it shall not hurt them,*" continued Ron. "*They shall lay hands on the sick, and they shall recover.*" He closed the book and his eyes; remaining silent for several minutes. Winona had never seen him so serious.

"Well," she said at last, "that's that, I guess."

Ron said nothing. Neither did the preacher.

"So...uh...Ron," said Winona. "What do you think? Want to give it a try?"

Father James chuckled at her impertinence.

"When do you meet again?" asked Ron. "I'd like to be sure."

"Next week. Same time."

"I'll be there," said Ron. "Won't we, Winona?"

"Oh, yeah," she replied. "We'll be there."

And they were—every week for the next month.

20

Downsville, NY

There was a good crowd at the Twin Islands club. I didn't bother ordering a Coke this time, but went straight to the end of the bar and waited patiently for Donna to finish her "dance." A steely-eyed look from the bartender told me that his memory was sharp enough to recollect my last visit. A similar expression on Donna's face told me she wasn't looking forward to another conversation. When she had finished the last dance of her set, she climbed down off the bar, sidled over and plopped her ass down on the stool next to mine.

"So, Donna, how're things?" I asked.

She shrugged her shoulders non-committedly.

"Did you find yourself another Billy?"

"I don't know what you're talking about."

"Look, I really don't give a crap if you want to ruin your life by putting drugs into your body. But, a man was murdered, and I know you know *something*. So how about telling me who took Billy's place?"

Donna's eyes coolly scanned the interior of the bar, purposefully ignoring me. Suddenly, her face looked different, as if something—or *someone*—she had seen had scared her.

"What is it?"

"I can't talk. He'll know I told you."

"Okay, okay. I understand. Just make believe we're having a good time—laugh or something. I'll buy you a drink." I signaled fat Johnny, who took his sweet time in coming over. Good thing I wasn't on fire and he a fireman; if so, I wouldn't have stood a chance.

"Okay, so counting from the left, what number is he?"

"Three," she said, her voice barely audible. Her demeanor indicated a quiet resignation. There was no question that she was scared.

"Give the lady a drink, Johnny." I slapped a ten dollar bill on the bar top. "And, keep the change." I thought I detected the beginnings of a smile, but concluded it was just gas. A few seconds later, a loud belch confirmed my hunch.

I looked across to the other side of the bar and saw the guy Donna had indicated. He was a little on the pudgy side, about forty-years of age, and wearing a black, leather vest. He had a Harley Davidson "Do Rag" on his head, and a scraggily gray beard that looked like it hadn't been trimmed since it first appeared on his face. *A real winner*, I thought.

I whispered to Donna, "I'll wait until you start dancing again, okay? Then, I'll leave. That way it won't look like there's anything going on between us."

She smiled woodenly, and took a sip of her drink.

After Donna had resumed her uninspired gyrations, I slipped out the door and walked across the street to my car, where I waited patiently for about five minutes, until my guy came out of the bar. Searching to

116

his left, and then to his right, it was obvious to me who he was looking for. So, I made it easy for him; I honked the horn. Immediately, he started across the street, his stride long and purposeful. I got out of the Jeep and met him halfway.

"Looking for me?" I asked.

"Yeah. I'd like to ask you a question."

"Fire away," I replied.

"Whatta you want with Donna?" His eyes traveled up and down my body, sizing me up. I did the same, and concluded he wouldn't be a problem.

"Are you her new 'Main Man'?" I asked.

"What's it to you? It's none of your fuckin' business. Are you a cop?"

He moved closer. His breath smelled like a cross between vomit and a dead dog. I decided he was too far inside my comfort zone, so I pulled out my badge and stuck it under his nose. He glanced at the badge and shrugged his shoulders.

"As a matter of fact, I am," I said. "Now, why don't we start over again? What do you know about Billy Stillwater?"

"I know he's *dead*."

"And you're all broken up, right?"

"Fuck you."

"How well did you know him?"

"Well enough to know that he owed me money, and now I ain't gonna collect it." Then, the full impact of where I was going with my inquiries hit him. "Hey, wait a minute. You don't think *I* killed that dirt bag, do you? Hell, there's probably a dozen guys who—"

"Somebody did. And right now, you're at the top of my list. So, where were you the night he was killed?"

"Right here. Ask Johnny. He'll tell ya. I was here 'til three in the morning. Better still, ask Donna." His voice lacked conviction, but I guessed he was probably telling the truth.

"Maybe I will."

I put the second and third fingers of my right hand to my eyes, and then pointed them at the drug dealer. I guess he'd seen "Meet The Parents," too, because he smiled. So much for easy answers, I thought. He might be a scumbag, but he didn't kill Billy Stillwater.

The rain was falling harder now, and I decided I was wasting my time.

21

Scottsville, WV—2009, six weeks after meeting Father James

Winona and Ron were driving slowly down a deserted country road, about four miles outside of Scottsville, looking for a snake hunter named Skeeter Henderson. Father James had supplied them with the man's name, but not until he had been assured by Ron and Winona that they wouldn't be competing with him for parishioners. "If anybody can get you some snakes, it'd be Skeeter," he'd told them. "He's a good old boy, and he has a nose for them—especially copperheads."

Now if they could only find the guy.

Winona clutched a wrinkled envelope with the directions that Father James had hastily scribbled on it, and strained to read them in the dim light provided by the dashboard lights of Ron's ancient pickup truck. So far, the directions had been accurate. She squinted in an effort to see what came next. "Slow down a bit, Ron," she said. "It says here we should see a large white barn on the right, and then we need to turn up the dirt road that comes just after it." Ron eased off the accelerator and let the truck coast for a bit. "There it is!" exclaimed Winona. "Just like he said."

Ron passed the barn, and then made the turn, downshifting into second gear, gunning the engine, and pushing the pickup up the deeply rutted road that appeared to be taking them up a mountain. "It says to go about a half mile," said Winona, "and you should come to fork in the road." Dust, kicked up by the truck's tires, spread a cloud behind the vehicle that served as convenient camouflage.

"When you come to the fork in the road, bear to the right," continued Winona. "Then go about another quarter of a mile, and the guy should be waiting there with a flashlight."

The whole affair had the feel of a badly written movie, except that it wasn't—it was for real.

"There's the fork," said Winona. "You see it?"

"Yeah, yeah. I see it. I see it," said Ron, appearing impatient. "I'm not blind."

As Ron steered the truck carefully to the right, Winona said, "Watch out for deer." *That's all we need,* she thought, *nothing like hitting a damned deer in the middle of nowhere.* As if on cue, a large buck shot across the road, its eyes glowing red in the beam of the headlights. "Jesus Christ! Look out!" shouted Winona, as Ron slammed on the brakes.

"Holy shit," whispered Ron, as he watched the animal's bobbing white tail disappear in the distance. "A couple of seconds sooner and I would've hit the damn thing." He put the truck back in gear and slowly started forward.

"Wait," said Winona. "I think I see the guy." She pointed through the windshield at a figure off to the side of the road. "Pull over."

A man was slowly waving a flashlight back and forth about twenty yards ahead of them, its beam growing dimmer by the second. Ron shut down the engine, and turned off the lights. Instantly, they were enveloped by the inky blackness of the starless night. Frogs peeped rhythmically, and night birds chirped in chorus, as if offering some eco-friendly compensation for the lack of natural illumination. In the distance, a screech owl's cry shattered the quiet of the night, causing Ron to jump involuntarily.

As Ron and Winona exited the truck, the man extinguished what little was left of the flashlight's beam and walked quickly toward them—with a limp. He wore mustard colored, Carhartt brand coveralls, and a tattered, matching baseball cap scrunched down tight against his ears. In his mouth was a lit corncob pipe clenched tightly between what was left of his teeth. Although he appeared to be in his late forties, he was probably much younger, owing mostly to his lifestyle, which was undoubtedly hard. As he got closer, they noticed a burlap bag dangling from his left hand.

"Are those the snakes?" asked Ron.

The man nodded silently.

"Father James said you only take cash," said Winona coldly.

"Uh huh," said the man. "Twenty apiece. I can *git* thirty, but I ain't greedy. My wife gets the money, anyhow. Not me."

"What kind are they?" asked Ron. He was sweating profusely.

"These here is copperheads, but I got both," answered Skeeter. "Rattlers *and* coppers. Whatever blows your skirt up—ain't that right, lady?" He leered at

Winona, who ignored the implications of his remark, as if the two of them could possibly have *anything* in common.

"Uh, we thought we'd start with copperheads," she said. "Two, I guess. Right, Ron?"

"Yeah," laughed Ron. "Two should be plenty." He laughed again, but this time Winona detected a tinge of nervousness in his voice.

"Ya know how to feed 'em?" asked Skeeter. "It *ain't* like dogs and cats, ya know."

"Well, not exactly," answered Winona. "Could you show us?"

"Cost extra," said the man. "Mice ain't cheap."

Ron and Winona glanced at one another in silence. *Is this guy for real?* thought Winona.

Skeeter started to laugh; so hard, in fact, that his pipe fell out of his rotten mouth. As he stooped to retrieve it, he said, "I was only funnin' ya. I catch all the mice I need down there in the barn." He pointed to a small, rundown, red barn about a hundred yards back down the road. "Place is crawlin' with 'em. Follow me and I'll show you what to do."

The barn felt damp, as odors of mildew, straw, animal waste, and God knew what else wafted up into Winona's nose. Two mules shifted nervously in a stall at the far end of the building, unaccustomed to visitors, and agitated by the presence of the snakes that Skeeter carried in the burlap sack. Skeeter placed the sack on the ground, before turning on the flashlight and approaching the two animals. He stroked each one in turn across its backside. "Easy, boys. Easy," he whispered. "It's okay. They're friends. Come on, you two; say hello."

Oh, great, thought Winona. *Next thing you know we'll all be on Animal Planet.* She and Ron walked over and stood next to Skeeter, who reached into another burlap bag hanging next to the stall, and withdrew a handful of oats. "This is for Jodie," he said, as he placed his open hand up to the nearest mule's mouth, and permitted the animal to inhale the proffered food. "And, this is for Jamie," he said, repeating the ritual with the other one. When he had finished, he turned and started for the corner of the barn opposite the stalls.

"Let's see what we've got for the snakes," he said, as he stooped down and retrieved a small, wire mesh, live trap on the barn floor. It was tethered to the wall by a piece of rope and a nail, and attached to the trap with a small carabiner. Winona could hear a faint squeaking sound coming from the trap.

"Well, well," said Skeeter. "Look at what we got here." There were two field mice skittering around within the confines of the Havaheart trap. "Looks like we're in luck," he said. He unclipped the carabiner, and picked up the trap containing the two mice. He walked over to where he had left the bag of snakes, retrieved it and started for the barn door.

"Come on," said Skeeter. "I'll show you how to feed the snakes." He motioned for Winona and Ron to follow him outside. Around the back of the building was a small shed, its rotted wooden door hanging by one hinge. Skeeter maneuvered the door open, exposing a makeshift workbench with a large glass case sitting on its surface.

He didn't need to tell the couple what lay within it. A piece of plywood, just slightly larger than the opening of the case, sat atop it, weighted down by a pair of bricks.

"I don't like to keep 'em in the barn," said Skeeter. "Makes the animals too damned nervous." He reached out and turned the knob of an ancient, porcelain light switch, causing a low wattage bulb hanging above the bench to come on, barely illuminating its target. At first, it appeared that the case was empty, except for the newspaper lining its bottom, which was covered by quite a bit of straw and several rocks scattered about the interior. But, upon closer examination, the well-camouflaged body of a snake could be seen, lying in loose folds against the straw. Skeeter shown the beam of the flashlight onto the reptile, and the snake's tongue flickered eagerly in anticipation.

"Got company," said Skeeter.

Without warning, he removed the two bricks from the plywood, and lifted the board from the case. He undid the knot in the twine that held the burlap bag of snakes closed, and unceremoniously dumped its two occupants into the case, right on top of the other snake. There was a bit of commotion as the three serpents slithered around and bumped into one another, before settling into positions of relative comfort. After a minute or so, everything was calm. So effective was the camouflage of the three snakes that one had to strain to make out their presence.

"Okay, boys and girls," whispered Skeeter. "It's feeding time."

He picked up the wire mesh trap containing the mice, held it above the case, and opened one end, allowing the helpless rodents to fall into the glass case. Then, he quickly covered the top with the plywood board, and placed the two bricks back on its surface.

"Watch this," said Skeeter, a broad smirk spreading across his face. "It's better than NASCAR."

The two mice wandered aimlessly around the inside of the case, seemingly oblivious to the danger lurking within.

"Gotta be live ones," giggled Skeeter, pointing at the helpless rodents. "Otherwise the snakes won't eat 'em."

Ron and Winona stood nervously behind Skeeter, watching at a comfortable distance.

"Does it take long?" asked Ron.

"Just watch," replied Skeeter. "You'll see."

Slowly, one of the copperheads slithered toward the mice, and then, in the blink of an eye, shot its head forward and bit one. Instantly, the mouse began to twitch, its legs flying akimbo as it staggered around for ten or fifteen seconds, before collapsing on its side, its life nearly ended already. The other mouse wiggled its whiskers as it skittered back and forth, bumping into its dying mate, and into the sides of the snakes. Just as had happened before, one of the other two snakes quickly struck the second mouse. The mortal ballet repeated itself, as the little rodent stutter-stepped and cake walked around the floor of the case before finally collapsing like its dead counterpart, its legs pointing to the sky.

"Okay," said Winona, "but, when does it—"

"Shhhhhhhh," whispered Skeeter. "Just watch."

Slowly, the first snake approached the mouse it had bitten, nudging it with its head before opening its mouth, and engulfing the head of the rodent. As Ron watched in horror, the copperhead unhinged its jaws, allowing them to spread to nearly double their width. Then, methodically it began to engulf the lifeless rodent, bit by bit, by moving its upper jaw forward first, and then following with the lower half. Before long, the only evidence that the mouse had ever existed was the tip of its tail hanging out of the snake's mouth like an obscene, gray tongue—along with the large lump it had formed within the snake's body. From start to finish, the whole process had taken less than three minutes. In that time, the snake's eyes had never moved, while its mouth appeared to smile perpetually, as if delighting in its task.

The other snake finished up a minute or two later, leaving the third snake without a meal.

"I should have something for that other one in the morning," said Skeeter with a laugh. "Takes 'em a while to digest, ya know."

"How often do you feed them?" asked Ron.

"Oh, 'bout once a week or so," replied Skeeter.

"Say, you wouldn't mind letting us have the two that just ate, would you?" asked Winona.

Ron laughed aloud. "Always the penny pincher, huh?"

"No," sighed Winona. "I just figured they'd be easier to manage—while they're...you know...digesting."

After Skeeter had carefully separated the two sated snakes, one by one, from their still hungry neighbor, and placed them in the original burlap bag, he tied the string around the end, and offered it to the couple. Winona reached out and took it from him.

"Pay the man," she ordered Ron.

Ron pulled out his wallet, peeled off two twenty-dollar bills, and gave them to Skeeter, offering to shake the man's hand. But the snake trapper turned quickly away, muttering over his shoulder, "damned amateurs," and started up the road toward his truck.

"What'd he expect," asked Ron, looking at Winona, "a tip?"

"Probably expected you to give him something extra for the bag," she replied.

"Yeah? Well, screw him. Twenty buck apiece is plenty."

As they watched the man walk away, Winona couldn't help but notice his limp.

"Hey, Skeeter," she called. "Where'd you get that limp?"

Skeeter stopped, and then turned around to face the couple. He smiled widely, exposing a mouthful of rotten teeth. "Where do ya think?" he replied with a laugh.

The couple said nothing, but Winona shivered involuntarily.

"I'd be careful, if I was you," said Skeeter, before he turned away and continued down the road toward his truck.

"Let's get out of here," whispered Ron, taking Winona's arm and steering her back up the hill toward their vehicle. As they walked slowly back to the truck, the two made an odd couple, what with Winona carrying the bag of snakes, and Ron humming a Bruce Springsteen tune.

As for the burlap sack containing the two snakes, once it was placed in the bed of the truck, it could have been mistaken for just about anything—anything *except* for what it was.

Evil drove away into the night.

22

Liberty, NY

It was a Thursday. Just as Val had expected, the biopsy came back positive, and now she pondered her options. Hopefully, the cancer had not spread beyond the small, pea-sized tumor itself, and had not affected the so-called "sentinel nodes," those lymph nodes just beneath the breast, under the armpit. Dr. Eisenhauer had patiently described the surgical options, and based upon his experience had recommended a simple lumpectomy if at all possible.

"We believe in breast conservancy," he counseled. "I can't see any good reason for a mastectomy. There's no indication that the cancer has metastasized, and unless we find otherwise, why go there at all?"

But, the final decision as to a lumpectomy versus a mastectomy would belong to Val—unless it had spread. She had read about women who had opted for an immediate double mastectomy—even when the cancer was confined to a single breast—to eliminate altogether the possibility of a recurrence. In Val's mind, they were foolish (but in her heart she understood how they felt). For a split second, when she had first learned of the cancer, she had even considered having it done herself—before dismissing it out of hand. She felt guilty for being so judgmental. Her rationale was that there was *never* a guarantee that the disease would not reappear somewhere else, so why disfigure her body needlessly. A simple lumpectomy would almost certainly contain the cancer—provided, of course that she accompanied the procedure with the proper follow-up of radiation and drugs. No, she had thought. The choice was obvious. She would have the lumpectomy.

The "procedure" as Dr. Eisenhauer had referred to it, took place the following week. Everything went as expected, and Val was released from the hospital the next morning. A few days later, she and Matt returned to the surgeon's office for a follow up examination. What concerned Val most was whether she would need "chemo." She hated the thought of having to wear a wig. One of the things Matt adored about her was her beautiful hair; and she loved having him run his fingers through it whenever they kissed or made love. Naturally, he told her that it made no difference whatsoever.

"It's *you* I love, Val, not your hair," he'd said.

It was so "Matt." It was no wonder that she was so crazy about him.

"You'll need eight weeks of radiation, five times a week," said Dr. Eisenhauer, "but you won't start for another five or six weeks. Luckily, there's a radiological facility right here in the adjoining building, and since you're not working right now, there's no reason why Dr. Smathers, our radiology oncologist, can't just schedule your daily treatments each day at your convenience."

At my convenience, thought Val. *There's that word again. Oh, God*, she thought, *there's nothing convenient about it at all.* She wished it were just a dream. Now *that* would be convenient.

"There are different types of breast cancer," Dr. Eisenhauer explained. "What you had was ductal carcinoma *in situ* or DCIS as we refer to it. It's the most common type of non-invasive breast cancer." At that point, Val started to cry softly. Just the mention of the word "cancer" terrified her.

"But, that's the good news," Dr. Eisenhauer quickly added. He had a wonderful way of explaining things; and his enthusiasm, even when talking about cancer, made Val less apprehensive than she might have been with another doctor. "Ductal means that the cancer started inside the milk ducts," he continued. "But *in situ* means 'in its original place.' DCIS is called "non-invasive" because it hasn't spread beyond the milk duct into any normal surrounding breast tissue—and that's great news. We removed all the sentinel nodes and biopsied them. There were three in all. And each one was benign. There *was* no spread."

Matt listened attentively, storing every bit of information, so that later, alone in the privacy of their home, he could explain it to Val in a way that would make sense to both of them.

Thank God for Matt, thought Val. *What would I ever do without him?*

"DCIS isn't life threatening," Dr. Eisenhauer continued, "but having DCIS can increase the risk of developing an invasive breast cancer later on..." The rest of his words were a blur; lost in space as far as Val was concerned. Matt could listen. That was his job. He was good at that. But, she refused to hear another word, and that was that.

The radiation treatments would begin in early July.

23

Scottsboro, WV—March 2010

Six months had passed since Ron and Winona had acquired the snakes. In the beginning, they had taken turns feeding them. Winona had searched the Yellow Pages for pet supplies, and found a Pet Smart in Martinsburg that sold white mice. Rather than having to make a regular trip to purchase the rodents every time the snakes needed to be fed, she had bought a dozen the first time she visited the pet supply retailer. The helpful clerk had given her detailed instructions on how to maintain the mice, and even instructed her in whispered tones (for fear of being overheard by the store's owner) how to breed the little rodents, provided of course that Winona promised to purchase all her future supplies at that particular store.

With the help of Skeeter, the collection of serpents had grown to an even half-dozen: three copperheads and three rattlesnakes. Ron wasn't handling snakes at every service, but it was evident that he was becoming increasingly more comfortable with the whole process.

A package had just arrived via UPS, and Ron was busy unwrapping it.

"What've you got, baby?" asked Winona.

"Something I picked up on the Internet," said Ron. "It's for the show."

He held up a small, white plastic container with a tamper-proof lid.

"What is it?" asked Winona.

"Guess."

"Hell, Ron, I don't know." She smiled wickedly. "Is it an aphrodisiac?"

"What a one track mind," laughed Ron.

"Well, what *is* it?"

"It's Strychnine."

"*Strychnine?* What the hell do you need *that* for?"

"Relax. It's *okay*," said Ron. "I've been reading up on it. The Pentecostals drink it sometimes during their services. It all has to do with the part of that passage in Mark XVI that talks about the serpents. Anyway, I went online and got it from some outfit called AgriSearch. I told them I was a farmer, and I needed it to kill rats. Hell, I didn't even have to pay for shipping. All I need to do is dilute it enough and—"

"What?" said Winona. "You'll only die a *little*?"

"No! It's safe. I swear it."

"Look, *handling* the snakes is one thing," she said, "but drinking poison...well...that's something you really ought to think about."

"I've *already* thought about it. How will folks believe in me if I don't do it *all?*"

It appeared that Ron was poised to test his belief system to the max, and Winona had reservations. After all, things were going well and the money was really rolling in.

"Look, Winona," he said, changing the subject, "I've been thinking. Maybe we should consider moving."

"Moving?"

"Yeah."

"But, why?"

"Because I've got a bad feeling. I'm afraid something bad is going to happen," said Ron.

"What could happen?"

"I don't know. Somebody might get bit."

"So what? If it happens, we'll just deal with it. I don't see why we have to *move*."

"I just think it's time," said Ron.

So far, Ron's instincts had been pretty good. If it hadn't been for him, they'd still be nickel and diming it, barely making ends meet. As things stood, they were making more than enough to get by; in fact, they had even managed to accumulate a little nest egg. But, he couldn't convince Winona about moving.

"People get bit," she said. "It happens all the time—and *you* know it."

"But not to *us*," said Ron. His voice had an edge to it. "Anyway, I'm still going to try the Strychnine," abruptly changing the subject.

"It's your funeral," mumbled Winona.

"And what's that supposed to mean?"

"Never mind. Don't pay any attention to me."

In the weeks that followed, Ron drank the Strychnine twice without suffering anything more than a headache. A website put up by a Pentecostal church in Jolo, West Virginia, had apparently provided him with the proper measurements for the amount of Strychnine one could safely ingest. A warning on the site emphasized that it would not be held responsible for any injury or death that might occur as a result. But, oddly, it wasn't the Strychnine that caused a problem. It was an incident that occurred when Ron's worst fears concerning a possible snakebite were ultimately realized. The irony *was* that the accident didn't occur during a worship service at all. It took place many miles away— and it *wasn't* an accident.

Evil was about to make its presence felt.

24

Roscoe, NY

"You know, Matt," said Nancy, between mouthfuls of Moo Shoo Pork, "we really could use more help on the force."

"Fat chance," I replied. "I'm lucky to have Rick, Pete, and Bobcat."

Nancy frowned at the omission of her name.

"And *you*, of course," I quickly added. " We can't forget about *you*. What would I ever do without you."

Nancy smiled her approval.

When I took over as chief, it had just been the three of us: Bobcat, Rick, and me—until Pete Richards came on board at the beginning of the year. He was my "Number Three" now, behind Rick and Bobcat. Pete had joined the force after the town council reluctantly acquiesced to the continuous lobbying by both the mayor and me. It should have been a no-brainer, since anyone with a high school diploma knew it was damn near impossible to maintain an around-the-clock presence on the job with just three fulltime officers. But, funds were scarce, and the council members answered to the ballot box. So, I wasn't particularly surprised when they only signed Pete to a single-year contract—disappointed, perhaps, but not surprised. After that, well, they'd "just have to wait and see how it goes." Now, with another murder on our hands, it didn't take a genius to see what the future held—*unless* we could find our man, Pete would be nothing but a memory by year's end.

Pete and I had met as PBA representatives back in the city when we were both new to the NYPD. It was a curious friendship, since other than our being cops, we had little in common. I was a staunch Republican, unabashed about my conservative views; Pete was a "Card Carrying Libertarian," content to live without any government interference at all, and willing to let *you* live any way you wanted to—as long as what you did was legal. He was tall—about six-two—with a wiry build that belied his status as a black belt designee in karate. He had a full head of straight, blond hair with a touch of strawberry to it, punctuated by a cowlick that stood straight up in the back, like that of a seventh grader. But his most striking feature was a pair of piercing blue eyes. Pete had a way of looking at you that was totally disarming, almost as if he could see right through you. He was a good cop, and if you crossed the line, he'd hunt you down "like the dirty dog that you are," (as he was proud of saying). In twenty-two years on the force, he had received seven citations for bravery. I had one—the citation I received for being dumb enough to get myself slashed by a serial killer.

There *was* one thing Pete and I had in common— sort of; we were both fishermen. However, I was a *fly* fisherman and he was a *meat* fisherman. My motto was "Catch and Release." Pete's was "Catch and Fillet!" Often times he would say, "You catch 'em and I'll cook 'em," when we would join one another for the annual PBA "head boat" outing out of Sheepshead Bay. The quarry we pursued in those days was bluefish, neither scarce nor hard to catch. When it came to trout, however, and their elevated status as true game fish, Pete respected my point of view and never teased me about my fly-fishing passion. So, when I finally got the go-ahead from the council to add a man, I just naturally thought of him.

Sipping my Oolong tea, I studied Nancy from a distance. She had been most helpful ever since I had joined the force, and I didn't often dismiss her advice out of hand.

"I know you've got something up your sleeve," I said, considering her comment about more help. "What kind of *help* are we talking about?"

Nancy had on a dark gray, self-tailored woolen skirt, which was pleated at the waist, and extended to just below her knees. A white, ruffled, short-sleeved blouse with a three-button placard front completed her outfit, which gave her the dignified look she sought. On her feet were black Mary Jane flats, the only shoes she ever wore, along with a matching black, patent leather belt. She was the epitome of grace and style.

"Well, I was thinking about a couple of auxiliary members; kind of like what they have over in Walton."

"And I suppose you've already looked into how the whole thing works, right?"

"Uh huh," replied Nancy. "It won't cost a penny. The state foots the bill."

These types of small town goings on were still new to me, coming as I did from a big city police force, where everything was either connected to politics or tax increases—or both.

The next day, I called Ray Berger, the police chief over in Walton, to inquire about his auxiliary help.

"It's not like I want to add a dozen officers or anything like that," I said. "It's just that I could use an extra body or two. We've had a rash of break-ins lately, and I've got nobody to keep an eye on those businesses."

"Well, I don't know exactly what you have in mind," replied Ray . "But we use *our* auxiliary volunteers more for things like crowd control on Fourth of July, church traffic, you know, high school graduation, stuff like that. I *suppose* you could use them as night watchmen. I never thought of that. Anyway—"

"Actually, Ray , I was more interested in how you *fund* something like that. I don't have to tell you what it's like over here with the mayor and council. Trying to get an extra dime out of this bunch is like trying to get a sixty-yard field goal out of a forty-yard place kicker. It just can't be done."

"I know what you mean," laughed Ray. "But, really, there's not much to worry about in the way of funding. It's all strictly *voluntary*. Actually, they raise the money themselves with things like hoagie sales and flea markets. Our volunteer organization supplies each member with a uniform and an insignia—that's it. The rest of the stuff—things like walkie-talkies, flashlights, pepper spray—they buy themselves, or it's donated."

"Do they carry firearms?

"Ours don't," replied Ray. "But, some organizations do, but then they run the risk of all that liability shit; and who needs that, right?"

I pondered the prospects in silence.

"Anyway," continued Ray, "I've got a number for the state association if you need it. That'd be Region Three."

"I'd appreciate that, Ray."

I grabbed a pen and jotted down the number as read it to me over the phone.

"Oh, yeah," said Ray. "There's one more thing."

"What's that?"

"We run background checks on 'em through NCIC and CLEAN."

"Yeah, I figured that."

"Anyhow, I hope that helps. Let me know if you need anything else."

"Will do, Ray. Thanks."

"Don't mention it."

After hanging up the phone, I sat mulling over my options. Should I talk to Harold first, *before* I called the state organization? Or, should I contact the state first, get all my ducks in a row, and *then* speak to the mayor? Forewarned is forearmed, I decided, so I called the state.

A half hour later, just as I was finishing up with the state representative, Nancy padded into my office, and stood waiting patiently until I was through. After I hung up, she spoke.

"So, was I right?" she asked, a smug smile on her face.

"About what?" I was determined to play our usual game.

"The auxiliary." (Only she pronounced it *auxilirary*, as many of her generation often did).

"Yes and no," I replied.

"What's that supposed to mean?" She obviously wasn't impressed with my non-answer.

"Well, *yes*, as in they *do* have an auxiliary—"

"Told you so," said Nancy.

"And, *no*," I continued, "as in the *state* doesn't pay for it."

"Oh." Nancy appeared genuinely surprised. "They *don't?*"

"Nope. They don't." It was my turn to be self-righteous. I played it to the hilt; crossing my arms in front of my chest, and leaning back in my chair with a broad smile across my face.

"Then, who—"

"Who *pays?*"

"Come on, Matt," said Nancy. She was losing her patience. "I don't have all day. *Who* pays for it?"

I looked to my left, and then to my right. I leaned forward in my chair and whispered, "Get this. Because they're volunteers, *they* pay for themselves."

"No kidding," replied Nancy.

"I guess that's what happens when you're a cop 'wannabe,'" I replied. "You're willing to do anything—even if it means paying for it yourself. Actually, the auxiliary organization buys their uniforms and insignias with money they raise from fund raisers and donations. But, the volunteers pay for everything else out of their own pockets."

"That's fantastic!" said Nancy.

142

"But first, we've got to *start* an auxiliary—and that's where you come in."

"Oh, no," protested Nancy.

"Oh, *yes*. But, first I've got to talk to Harold."

"Good luck with that one," Nancy quipped.

"*Au contraire.* It's an election year; remember? And, anything that Harold can take credit for—that doesn't cost the town money—is an idea he'll listen to. Take my word for it."

"Hmmm," said Nancy.

"And, if you're lucky," added Matt, "maybe *he'll* do it all by himself."

"Now you're talking."

25

Scottsboro, WV—June 2010

The snake's Latin name was *Crotalus horridus,* but it was mostly referred to by its common name: timber rattlesnake. Because it was only a year or so in age, this particular snake wasn't very large—just twenty inches or so—as members of its species often grew to lengths in excess of five feet. And its distinctive rattle was barely developed after only having shed its delicate, paper-like skin twice. But even when it first wriggled out of its elongated, white, leathery shell, its venom was as potent as a viper twice its length or more, and it was already capable of inflicting a lethal strike to a small rodent or whatever unfortunate mammal it might encounter. Millions of years of evolutionary imprinting had equipped it with the necessary behavioral patterns needed to give it at least a marginal chance of survival, including heat sensitive pits on either side of its bony head, and a forked tongue capable of detecting the slightest molecules of scent in the air.

Because it was a cold-blooded animal—as all reptiles are—it didn't mind when, early that morning it had been placed within the dark cool confines of the metal rural mailbox that sat atop a wooden post, a few hundred feet from Chester Rawlings ancient, whitewashed farmhouse along Hightower Road. It had no sense of anger or displeasure, no ability to reason or question why it had been placed there; it only knew that it was cool and dark. The letters and assorted flyers delivered the previous afternoon felt neither pleasant nor uncomfortable beneath its scaly, parchment-like body; they were of no concern.

As the morning turned to mid-day, the sun began to warm the interior of the metal container holding the rattlesnake, and the serpent sensed a slight increase in its own body heat as well, since it was a cold-blooded creature whose temperature mirrored that of its surroundings. By noon, the sun's rays had made the confines of the mailbox somewhat uncomfortable, and the snake, sensing its vulnerability, began to vibrate its juvenile rattles as a sign of its displeasure.

Early that morning, Melinda Rawlings kissed her husband, Chester, on the cheek, noting at the time how "absolutely unbearable" his whiskers were becoming.

"Chester," she admonished him, "If you don't start shaving regular again, I'm going to have to start thinking about leavin' you."

She wasn't serious, of course; she'd never leave the man with whom she'd spent the last sixty-five years for something as trivial as his failure to maintain a smooth complexion. He was the love of her life. But, she didn't mind complaining about the situation.

"I'm going to pick you up some of those new throwaway razors with all those blades—and some 'real' shaving cream so you can throw away that damn antique."

Chester still insisted on using a brush, a mug of soap, and an old-fashioned straight razor to shave—whether he needed it or not—once a week at most.

Everyone at church knew that Melinda had been planning this outing for weeks, and she was anxious to pick up her friend, Dina, and make an early start to the day. The two were headed for the assembly of retail outlets located on the outskirts of Martinsburg, and they wanted to be there when the doors opened. Even though they were nearing eighty, the two women still enjoyed the rush they got from encountering a good bargain. Besides, if they departed early enough, they could stop first for breakfast at the Denny's on the edge of the mall. Chester would have a fit, she thought, if he ever saw her eating a Grand Slam, but that would be Dina's and her little secret.

She climbed into the sparkling, white Honda Accord sedan that Chester had bought her last fall, and inhaled deeply to fully appreciate the scent of the fine leather upholstery that he had insisted upon adding to the purchase "just for my honey." Chester was certainly no spendthrift—he still drove a weathered '83 Ford pickup—but after working like a dog for decades to become the successful farmer he was, he was finally financially secure enough to feel comfortable spending some of his hard-earned money. As was usually the case, he chose to spend it on his wife.

Melinda lightly tooted the horn as she passed the mailbox, waving automatically out the window. She turned left onto the oil and stone road that led toward Dina's place, and pressed down hard on the accelerator, leaving a trail of dust in the air. If the day went as planned, she wouldn't be back until after dinner. Chester would be thrilled, she thought. He loved to plop his feet up on the recliner and watch the Orioles on the new flat screen TV the kids had given him last year for his eightieth birthday. Mildred smiled at the imagery, and drove on to meet Dina.

It was just past noon when Chester decided to wander up the driveway to the mailbox. He wore blue, denim coveralls over a light, long-sleeved cotton shirt. Ever since retiring, it was his custom to wait until the following day to retrieve the mail—not because he was lazy, but just because he could. Due to his poor hearing, which was declining on a daily basis—"Chester, for God's sake get a hearing aid!" Melinda would often say—he was unaware of the soft buzzing sound emanating from the metal mail receptacle. So, when he reached inside to retrieve yesterday's mail, the reflexive strike of the rattlesnake came as a complete shock to his eighty-year old body.

"What in the world!" At first he thought he'd been stung by a wasp or a bee, but when he examined the back of his hand and saw the distinctive double puncture marks, he knew what had occurred. The forward motion of the strike carried the snake's body out into space, where it lost its momentum and dropped silently into the collection of carefully planted flowers at the base of the mailbox post. In a matter of minutes, it had slithered away, never to be seen again.

Chester cursed to himself, and reached into his back pocket for the handkerchief he generally carried there. Pulling it out with his good hand, he attempted to roll it into a cord so he could tie it around his arm. It should have been an easy task, but his rapidly beating heart and shallow breath were making it a daunting challenge. *Maybe if I go sit down on the porch,* he thought. He stumbled down the gravel walkway, not caring that he was kicking the fresh pea stone onto the surrounding lawn. *Oh, Holy Ghost,* he prayed, as he often did in church, *protect this sinner.* He thought of Brother Ron, and wished he possessed the preacher's faith. But, he, Chester Rawlings, was a sinner, and God had no time for him. He staggered onto the front porch, and collapsed into the wicker rocking chair, the force of the impact toppling the chair backward. "Melinda!" he cried out—just before he lost consciousness and collapsed on the porch.

Melinda Rawlings was humming along with the music from the radio as she pulled into the driveway. It was just barely light, and as she passed the mailbox, she was a bit surprised to see it open and what appeared to be mail scattered around its base. She pressed the remote control to open the garage door, pulled the Honda to a stop inside, shut off the engine, and pulled the lever to open the trunk. Gathering her day's treasurers up in her arms, she managed to slam the trunk shut with her elbow, hurried to the side door, and rang the bell.

It had seemed a bit odd that there had been no lights on inside the house when she pulled up, but when

Chester failed to respond to the second ringing of the doorbell, Melinda grew even more suspicious. *Where is he?* She rang for a third time, and then, exasperated, she used her key to let herself in. The house was eerily quiet—and dark.

"Chester!" she called. No answer. Now, she was scared. She rushed through the house calling, "Chester! Chester!" But all she heard was the sound of her own voice. Melinda ran to the front door, opened it, and stepped outside.

When she found her husband on the porch, he was barely alive, and she knew something was dreadfully wrong with him. At first, she thought he might have suffered a stroke. She felt his face. It was clammy—and hot. Then, she noticed his right hand. It was swollen to twice its normal size, and was nearly black. When she saw the two puncture marks in the skin, she knew right away what had happened. This was no stroke. She got on the phone immediately and called 911. "My husband's been bitten by a snake," she cried. "I need an ambulance right away!"

It took less than twenty minutes for the EMTs to arrive, and they immediately started Chester on an IV drip to combat his worsening dehydration. But it was a forty-minute drive to the nearest hospital in Martinsburg, and by the time they administered the first dose of antivenin, he was already unconscious. He remained in a coma for nearly three days, before a massive seizure finally put an end to his suffering. In the meantime, a police investigation concluded that what had happened was that Chester had dropped a piece of mail by the mailbox, and in the process of retrieving it from the ground had been struck by the snake, which was probably hidden among the plants at the base of the post.

It was the obvious explanation—or at least that's how it appeared.

Evil has a way of obscuring the truth.

26

Roscoe, NY

Wayne Sabolewski's hearing before Judge Holscher went as expected, and he was released into the custody of Frank Merritt, the social worker over at the rehab center in Monticello. I decided to have Bobcat run him over there, while I talked to our esteemed mayor about starting a police auxiliary.

To my surprise, Harold was less receptive to the idea than I had hoped he would be. He'd agreed to meet me at the diner, where I thought we'd have a civilized conversation over a hot drink. But, when I arrived I was surprised to find him standing outside on the landing in front of the entrance door. It was raining.

"Jesus, Matt," he said. "I just got the council to go along with the new car, and now you want me to hit 'em up again? What's gotten into you?"

Apparently, in the time it had taken me to drive over to meet him, he'd soured on the proposition, and needed more convincing before he could buy into it. We were barely sheltered from the rain by the slight overhang, and I was hoping he'd suggest going inside, but he wasn't in an inviting mood.

"Oh, come on, Harold. You and I both know that we're woefully undermanned. Besides, there's virtually no cost involved at all. How am I supposed to solve murders around here if I can't even keep the drug addicts from knocking over the laundromat?"

What I was saying made perfectly good sense, and it was obvious that Harold was at least willing to consider the idea, but as usual he needed to find his own way to arrive at the proper conclusion.

"Oh, okay, I'll think about it. But, I'll need some time. Send me some paperwork on it, and I'll get back to you."

"Not a problem. I'll have Nancy drop it off."

"Now, let me get the hell out of this damned rain."

"Thanks, Harold."

"For what? I haven't done anything yet."

"No, but you will."

I smiled wickedly at the mayor, who grimaced in response.

"Screw you," he replied.

"Screw not, lest ye be not screwed," said I.

It was a stalemate—as it usually was.

27

Scottsboro, WV—2010

Naturally, Ron was called upon to preside over Chester Rawlings' funeral service, held at a small family cemetery on the Rawlings property overlooking a small pond. The grievers numbered several dozen, including numerous members of the Devoted Church of Jesus with Signs Following. It was a simple service, but thanks to Ron's efforts, one that appeared to bring comfort and solace to all who attended it.

Several weeks later, after a regular Sunday service, Chester's widow approached Ron just as he was heading to the small office behind the church's makeshift stage. She was carrying a white envelope, which she handed to him.

"This is something that Chester wanted y'all to have," she said quietly, handing the envelope to Ron and looking at Winona.

"What is it?" asked Winona.

"It's just some insurance money that Chester left behind. He wanted the church to have it."

Ron appeared shocked, and for a moment was unable to speak. "I never expected anything like this," he finally managed to say.

"Well," said Mrs. Rawlings, "Chester thought you folks had made a big difference in our lives, so he named your church as beneficiary. I guess he done it pretty recent, 'cause I didn't find out 'til just the other day, when the lawyer told me about it."

"Well, we're most grateful, Melinda," said Winona. "And I promise we'll put it to good use."

Mrs. Rawlings adjusted her hat, and gave Ron a light peck on the cheek. "He *really* liked you," she said, and then started to walk away. Then, she stopped, looked back at the couple, with a curious expression on her face. "It's kind of funny, don't you think, that he got his self killed by one of those snakes?"

Winona nodded.

"Guess God works in mysterious ways," sighed Melinda, "Just like my mother used to say."

"I guess so," said Ron.

Winona just smiled.

That evening, back at the trailer, Ron opened the envelope and looked at the insurance check. It was made out to Winona and him for fifteen thousand dollars.

"Can you believe that? Fifteen thousand bucks, right out of the blue."

Then, he again brought up the subject of moving, only to Winona's apparent surprise, he had changed his mind.

"I hate to leave these people," he said, "especially now, after what happened to Chester and all."

"I'm not so sure, baby," said Winona. "I think you were right in the first place. Maybe it *is* time to go."

"But, I thought you said—"

"I know, Ron. But that was *before* this happened," said Winona. "Now, how long do you think it'll be before word gets out and the authorities start snooping around and pointing fingers at us? I think you're right. We *should* go."

"But, why would they suspect *us* of anything? There was no mention of the snake in the obituary. Besides, these people *need* me here. I don't see any reason at all to leave."

Whether it was a case of naiveté or just being stupid, Ron's resistance to Winona's suggestion was steadfast.

"Look, baby," said Winona. "There's another reason to move on."

"Like what?"

"Like, for instance, there's *no* possibility of growth here. These people are tapped out."

Ron furrowed his brow, and reflected upon the truth. He had to admit that "donations" at the church *had* started to decline. Perhaps Winona was right. After all, the lease for the little storefront church was due to be renewed in two weeks, so what better time to leave than now.

"Maybe you're right," he said softly. "But let's at least stay until the lease runs out, okay? It's only two more weeks."

"Sure," said Winona. "Besides, I've got some loose ends to tie up before we can go. Two weeks should be fine."

Ron got up from his chair, and walked over to the refrigerator. He opened the door, took out two cans of beer, and popped them open.

"Here," he said, handing one to Winona, "Here's to bigger and better things."

Winona smiled, clinked her can against Ron's, and replied, "Bigger and better." She took a hard swallow. "Damn, that's good."

"So," said Ron. "Where do you want to go?"

"Far from here; that's for sure," answered Winona. "Maybe Pennsylvania. What would you think about that?"

"That sounds okay to me."

"Good. We'll pray on it."

Grabbing Winona's hand, Ron yanked her to her feet and pulled her toward the trailer's tiny bedroom. "Come on," he said. "I know just the place."

Once inside, Winona removed her shoes, undid her jeans and kicked them off in one motion, and flopped down on the unmade bed, as beer from the open can shot into the air. She lay on her back with her legs splayed wide apart and her eyes nearly closed.

"Come here, preacher man," she whispered. "Kneel and pray."

Ron immediately assumed the position. Before long, the worship service had begun, and to anyone passing by in the night, the cries of "Oh Jesus," coming from inside the trailer might well have been mistaken for actual prayers.

But, Evil knew better.

28

Roscoe, NY

About six weeks had elapsed since the murder, and we were no closer to finding Billy Stillwater's killer than when we first started. I had all three of my patrolmen following up on any tips we received, including a phone call from a farmer's menopausal wife who insisted that she murdered Billy to keep the school children safe. A quick check with the husband confirmed that she had been home the night of the murder.

The truth was that we had virtually nothing to go on, and had made absolutely no progress. Just as with the homicide cases we were assigned back in Manhattan, if a crime wasn't solved within the first forty-eight hours, the chances of a successful conclusion decreased with every passing day. It was beginning to look as though Billy's killer would probably go undiscovered. I couldn't say that I was *real* upset, but I wasn't about to quit, either.

I had just spent the last three hours with Pete Richards, the two of us trying to make sense of the clutter of information scattered across the surface of the white board I had erected in my office. I might just as well have had Einstein's Theory of Relativity up there for all the good it was doing. On it were several names, among them those of the victim, Billy Stillwater, a known Meth dealer, and Wayne Sabolewski, his last known client. But, I'd checked with the owner of the diner, who verified Wayne's alibi, so I could probably take his name off the board. Then there was Donna, the dancer at the Twin Islands. She, too, had an alibi, but might still know something. For the time being, I left her name with the rest.

When we searched Stillwater's trailer immediately following the murder, I was surprised to find a framed high school diploma hanging on his bedroom wall with the name Stepp, rather than Stillwater as his last name. Apparently, Billy was a "Son of the South," with Beaumont Regional High School, in Jefferson County, Alabama as his alma mater—a distinguished member of The Class of 1991. Wouldn't *his* classmates be proud! Talk about your quintessential incongruity; here was a Meth dealer, no doubt selling drugs to underage kids, yet boasting of his own graduation from high school. It made no sense. But, after a career as a New York City homicide detective, nothing surprised me anymore.

I contacted the Jefferson County authorities and found that Billy had legally changed his name to Stillwater (his mother's maiden name) when he had turned eighteen, which explained the name on the driver's license. However, the name on his birth certificate was Stepp, the same as his deceased father. The records also showed that he had a sister, Winona, who was just slightly more than a year older than he was, but there was no record of her ever having changed her name. My guess was that when his parents divorced, the old man had left with the daughter, leaving Billy and his mom to fend for themselves—which really pissed off the son. By changing his last name to Stillwater he had effectively separated himself, once and for all, from both his father *and* his sister.

There was no record of any aunts or uncles—so there was no one to even claim the body. More likely than not, Billy's body would be buried in a Potter's Field after a specified waiting period, during which it would remain in the morgue. Apparently, the record keeping in Alabama was about on a par with that of New York State..

Also written on the white board was the word "Strychnine," the murder "weapon," which was a *real* mystery in itself. And that was it; that was all we had. Not very much information with which to solve a murder, I thought. Disgusted, I left Pete to ponder the clues, after deciding my time would be better spent at the library—*if* I could get there before it closed. It was a Wednesday evening, and the one night of the week that the library remained open until nine o'clock.

Just past eight-thirty, I made my way slowly through the cramped aisles of the book stacks that occupied the limited space assigned to the Roscoe Public Library. It wasn't even a freestanding edifice, but merely a five-hundred square foot adjunct to the ancient, wooden VFW hall, designated by a hand-painted sign that hung next to that of the building's principle occupant. It used to be worse. In the past, residents of the little fishing village were forced to avail themselves of the county facility in Monticello, whose location required more than an hour's drive round trip. Only the most devoted readers were up to the journey, so it came as no surprise that there was rampant support when the current mayor proposed the present arrangement.

Unfortunately, now, three years later, that accomplishment remained the only significant one of an administration with less than a full year left in its term. The addition of a new patrol car would greatly alter that legacy—at least for me. But that was a subject for another day. Right now I was searching for something interesting to read during my spare time.

A hand lettered sign affixed with cellophane tape to the top shelf of one of the stacks proclaimed "New Non-Fiction," and I stopped in front of it to peruse its contents. A book down on the bottom shelf caught my eye: *Salvation on Sand Mountain: Snake Handling and Redemption in Southern Appalachia* by Dennis Covington. It wasn't a large book, not more than two-hundred-and-fifty pages at most, but its title intrigued me. I bent down to pick it up. Immediately, a twinge in my lower back reminded me of my chiropractor's advice to always bend my knees—rather than bending from the waist—but it was too late, and I stood there quietly massaging the bottom of my spine until the pain subsided. I squatted back down (as I should have done the first time), removed the book from the shelf, stood back up, and began reading the inside flap of the front cover. It was touted as "a story of snake handling and strychnine drinking, of faith healing and speaking in tongues."

Strychnine drinking? I pored over the pages. Maybe this was what I'd been looking for? The book went on to describe how one man's search for his roots had resulted in "spiritual renewal." There were all kinds of details of how the author had covered the sensational murder case of Glen Summerford, pastor of the Church of Jesus with Signs Following, who had been accused of attempting to kill his wife with rattlesnakes. The author had "felt the pull of a spirituality that was to dominate his life for the next several years," said the promotional blurb. It went on to say that he had even attended snake-handling services throughout the south, and how he "eventually took up snakes himself."

The last bit of information proved to be too much, and I closed the cover and returned the book to its place on the shelf. "Hey, Margaret," I called to the young librarian who was busy re-shelving books in the next aisle, "Got any new books on fly fishing?"

Margaret mumbled something sarcastic under her breath, and then replied in a soft voice, "You know, Chief, fishing isn't all that folks around here care about. Have you thought about broadening your horizons a bit?"

I just smiled. "Just tell me what section they're in, please, Margaret; I'll find them myself."

"It's seven, ninety-nine, Chief—and we close in twenty minutes."

"Thank you, Margaret."

Twenty minutes later, I left the library with about as disparate a pair of books as one might find: the book about the snakes and drinking strychnine by a southern journalist; and *Sex, Death, and Fly-Fishing* by John Gierach. I chose the former for its possible informational value, and the latter for the levity I would no doubt require after reading the former.

God, I hated snakes.

29

Scottsboro, WV—several months after the Rawlings funeral
Ron took Winona to the library in Martinsburg, and using the computer's search engine, investigated a number of small towns further up spine of the Appalachians, before settling on a town in Pennsylvania along the I-81 corridor called Black Mountain, near the infamous coal-mining town of Centralia.

In 1962, a garbage dump fire had ignited an underground vein of coal from a strip mine outside that town, and that fire continues to burn to this day. Most of the town's residents were forced to move, and their legal battle with the various authorities garnered national attention when it was the subject of numerous books.

Ron and Winona settled on Black Mountain because of its proximity to Interstate Highway I-81 and nearby Harrisburg, the state capitol. Had they known about the history of its neighbor, the little town of Centralia, it's doubtful they would have ever made it their destination. But, choose it they did, especially when they found that an abandoned church building located a stone's throw from Centralia could be rented for next to nothing from a local bank hungering for *some* form of income from the foreclosed property. Even better, Black Mountain was located in the heart of the Pennsylvania coal-mining district, and its marginally educated workers would make excellent disciples for

163

Ron's Devoted Church of Jesus with Signs Following. It was a no-brainer.

The day they left Scottsboro it was raining, a possible precursor to what lay in store for them in Pennsylvania. The snakes were safely ensconced in two heavy Plexiglas cases, their steel mesh tops secured with small padlocks hooked through overlapping metal hasps. A heavy burlap drop cloth covered the two cases as they made their way north, along with the rest of the couple's meager possessions, in the confines of the small U-Haul trailer they had rented for the move. It didn't hurt any that nearby Harrisburg was an official drop-off point.

The church itself was not much to look at, with its peeling, white paint and crooked spire, but it did have one big advantage: there were living quarters attached to it at the rear—*and* they'd been able to rent it on a month-to-month basis, which suited them both just fine. Inside were about two-dozen rows of pews, divided by a center aisle. They guessed it would hold around a hundred worshippers when full. Getting it filled would be a challenge they welcomed.

The first thing they did upon their arrival was to decide on a place to store the snakes. There was a small outbuilding in the rear that had probably served as a makeshift stable at one time that was just perfect. The other thing they did was drop off the trailer in Harrisburg and order several hundred posters, which they planned to tack to every bulletin board, abandoned building, and well-positioned signpost within a ten-mile radius of the church, announcing their first church service

Next, they tackled the accumulated dust and dirt within the church building itself. It took three days, but at last the place was presentable, and they could look forward to the first Sunday's service.

Standing in the outbuilding as he fed the snakes on the second day, Ron noticed that the floor of the shed seemed particularly warm—hot, in fact. When he mentioned it to Winona, she just laughed it off. "Maybe it's Hell Fire trying to get out."

"Then, I smite thee, Satan!" exclaimed Ron in a loud voice, with a theatrical flourish of his hand.

Had the two of them been familiar with the town's history, they might not have been so quick to dismiss the analogy.

30

"Hi, honey," I said, as I rushed into the house, past Val, who was just finishing up in the kitchen, and into my study, carrying my treasure trove of books. "How'd the radiation go?" It had been about five weeks since Val's lumpectomy, and today she had had her first treatment.

"Okay, I guess," sighed Val from the other room. "At first it was a little scary getting under that huge machine. But the girls were really nice, especially the young one; I think her name was Marsha."

I put the books down on my desk, and went back into the kitchen to join my wife.

"I'm sorry, Val," I said, giving her a kiss on the cheek. "I don't know what I was thinking. Come on; sit down and tell me all about it."

"There's really not that much to tell."

"Did it hurt?"

"Oh, no. Not at all."

"Well, what did it feel like?"

"Actually, I didn't *feel* anything. It was weird, really. First, they made all these tattoo-like marks around my breast. Want to see?"

"Why not."

Val pulled her blouse out from under the waistband of her skirt and lifted it up, exposing her breasts. I felt a huge twinge of guilt, looking at the dark red scar that indicated where the tumor had been removed just to the side of her right nipple. I'd have given anything if it could have been me rather than she who had to endure the surgery. Surrounding the scar was a series of tiny little marks, drawn in black ink. I leaned over and kissed her breasts, first the good one, and then the "bad" one.

"So what's with the tattoos?"

"Well, they don't want to irradiate any more of the good tissue than necessary, so the marks help them to keep the radiation focused exactly where it should be."

"Makes sense to me."

I placed my fingertips as gently as possible on Val's right breast, and traced the outline of the tattoo marks. Immediately, a ridge of goose bumps erupted along the path my finger had taken along her flesh. "Hmmm," I teased. "Something's still working, huh?"

"Matt!"

"Oh, Val. I'm so sorry. I didn't mean anything."

I took my wife in my arms and squeezed her tightly, wanting desperately to make it all go away, and praying that soon it would. I held her like that for several minutes, before letting her go.

"It'll be okay," she sighed. "Hey! It looks like you've got some reading to do. I'll be upstairs when you're finished."

"Okay. I won't be long."

"Love you," she said, over her shoulder, as she disappeared up the stairs.

"I love you, too," I whispered.

By the time I had finished reading the "snake book," it was well past midnight, and I had gleaned everything I needed to know about snakes *and* strychnine. When I slipped into the darkened bedroom, Val was fast asleep. I undressed quietly in the bathroom, brushed my teeth, and then climbed into the bed, spooning myself around her from the rear, and immediately drifted off into a dreamless sleep. Love does that.

31

Black Mountain, PA—Christmas Eve 2010

"Brother, Sisters, God is *watching* us. God is watching *you* every *second*, every *minute*, every *hour!* He *knows* what's in your heart. He *knows* what's in your thoughts. And He won't *accept* lip service. It isn't *enough* to get down on your knees every night. It isn't *enough* to read the Word of The Lord each evening from The Holy Bible. Jesus demands *more!*"

Ron was in fine fettle as he delivered his weekly sermon to the members of his congregation in a driving, hypnotic cadence that held them spellbound like rubes at a carnival. He'd been preaching now for nearly two years, and the results of his hard work and practice were evident in his nearly perfect delivery.

Tonight, since it was Christmas Eve, Ron wore his finest navy blue, gabardine suit, black patent leather shoes and tailored white shirt, along with a forty-dollar silk tie (tied in a perfect Windsor knot by Winona, who kissed him hard on the lips before sending him out before his flock). He looked every bit the successful country preacher he had become. As his late father used to say: "If looks could kill, son, you'd be in jail." Ron smiled to himself every time he thought of those words— and a glance at any available mirror only reinforced his belief in their veracity.

Ron was fully engaged with his audience as he continued speaking, raising and lowering his voice to suit his rhetoric. He could sense the connection he had made with these people over the last few weeks.

"The Lord God *compels* us to believe," he whispered. "The Living God *demands* that we honor and obey his commandments. But we fall short, don't we?"

A few "Amens" echoed among the audience.

"But, we keep on *trying*—and we keep on *failing*. And why? And why? And *why?*" The last "why?" exited his mouth as a scream. "Because, we're *weak!* Because we're *mortal!* Because," he sighed, "we're sinners."

A few more "Amens" rattled around the church.

"So, how can we show *Him* we *truly* believe? *Not* just by prayer—although pray we must. *Not* just by devotion—although devoted we must be. *Not* by speaking *His name*—although speak it we must. We show him we believe by *doing!* That's right, by *doing.*" Ron's voice dropped to a barely audible whisper. "And *what* do we do?"

He stood completely still and stared out at the men and women in the audience. Although he'd never heard of the Socratic method, Ron was one of its finest unwitting proponents; and as such he waited quietly for an answer to his question that he knew would never come. Feet shuffled and bodies wiggled anxiously in the hard wooden pews. But, there was no answer forthcoming. It was up to him to provide it.

"Brothers and sisters," he shouted, "what we *do* is written. It is *written* in Mark 16: Verse 18."

He held his copy of the King James Version of The Bible aloft, waving it hypnotically back and forth, back and forth. In unison, every head of every person in the congregation followed the proffered book as it moved in space.

"Read with me, brothers and sisters. Read it together."

Collectively, the worshippers turned to the enumerated verse in their Bibles and followed Ron as he read aloud.

"And these signs shall follow them that believe," he read slowly. "You *do* believe, don't you?" he asked. There were a few murmured replies, but not nearly enough to satisfy his purpose of working the crowd into frenzy. "I said, you *do* believe don't you?" he repeated, only this time there was a distinct edge to his rising voice and the response was correspondingly loud and convincing. "Amen," he muttered.

Someone in the audience echoed the sentiment.

Ron smiled and closed his eyes. Then, taking a deep breath, he motioned to a young man in the rear of the church who immediately began to strum softly a succession of chords on a battered guitar as a young woman accompanied him with the soft taps of her tambourine.

Ron continued speaking. *"In my name shall they cast out devils; they shall speak with new tongues."*

An elderly gentleman in the front row, dressed in coveralls and a checked shirt, began shaking, throwing his arms into the air and emitting a guttural sound that resonated deep within his chest cavity. What he spoke sounded like words, but the words were unintelligible. He was speaking "in tongues." The guitar player increased the pace of his strumming, as did the tambourine wielding young lady.

Ron's voice grew louder and more insistent as he spoke the words that many had come to hear: *"They shall take up serpents; and if they drink any deadly thing, it shall not hurt them; they shall lay hands on the sick, and they shall recover."*

A multitude of resonant voices haltingly joined in with Ron's and finished reciting the final words in unison with the preacher. Ron placed the Bible on the scarred, wooden lectern in front of him and moved out from behind it.

This was the moment; this was the time. Men and women whispered nervously among themselves in anticipation of what was to come next. The man in the coveralls continued to babble incoherently, oblivious of the stares of those around him. He was in another place, another time altogether, and his face was contorted as if in pain. Beads of perspiration rolled down his weathered face, mixed with the tears that were pouring from his half-closed eyes.

Ron nodded his head at the musical accompanists in the back of the building, and instantly they ceased their playing. The result was a dramatic silence punctuated solely by the haunting sound of the old man speaking in his alien language. The effect was surreal. Turning his head toward the curtain behind him, Ron called out softly, "Sister Winona, bring them forth."

A hush fell over the crowd as from behind the curtain out she came, dressed in a simple black dress that reached to the floor. Her hair was arranged in a braid atop her head, with a simple, white barrette holding it in place. In her arms she carried a rectangular Plexiglas case with a wire mesh cover affixed by hinges on one end and secured by a hasp lock on the other. A single, small, variegated rattlesnake lay inside, loosely draped over several small rocks. Winona held the case aloft and turned slowly from side to side, displaying its contents to the congregation, which issued a collective "Ahhh" in response.

The guitar player began strumming softly again, and the tambourine came to life in the hands of the young woman. Ron approached Winona and whispered something in her ear. Without hesitation, she carefully undid the hasp lock and opened the hinged top to the case. The crowd "Ooh'd and Ahh'd." Slowly and deliberately, Ron reached his left hand into the case and gently slid his fingers beneath the snake's belly. The reptile flicked its forked tongue nervously and shifted its weight ever so slightly, permitting Ron to slowly slip his other hand beneath it and lift it from the confines of the case. Rolling his eyes upward so that only the whites showed, Ron raised the snake in front of him so everyone could see it. It was a routine he had perfected back in West Virginia. Whispers of disbelief flooded through the audience. Ron walked down the center aisle, displaying the viper to the curious but cautious few who dared to lean out for a closer look. Winona followed closely behind, with the empty case held in front of her.

When he had reached the rear of the church, Ron turned and slowly made his way back to the front, then carefully placed the snake back into the case. Winona closed the cover and secured it, as Ron dropped his hands limply to his sides and stood alongside her with his eyes closed tightly, obviously spent. Perspiration dotted his forehead, and Winona extracted a handkerchief from a shallow pocket on the side of her dress and gently patted the moisture away. All the while this was taking place, the old man in the front row continued his unintelligible speech. Suddenly, just as it appeared he might go on forever, he stopped and sat down abruptly, slumping against the hard back of the pew.

Ron's voice broke the silence. "Brothers and sisters, tonight it was *I* who handled the serpent. It was *I* who answered the question. It was *I* who showed my faith in the Holy Ghost. But it's not just up to *me*; it's up to *you*. For if *you* believe—*truly* believe—*you, too,* will show that the Holy Ghost moves in you—as he does in *all* of us—by demonstrating with your actions what *you* believe in your hearts." There were "Amens" and "Hallelujahs" whispered and shouted among the worshippers.

"And now, let us celebrate the birth of the Baby Jesus with song," said Ron, nodding to the rear of the church.

In response, someone began strumming the chords to "O Holy Night" on a guitar, as a tambourine added its pleasant sound to the mix. Ron started singing the words, and soon the congregation joined in. Next, they sang "O Little Town of Bethlehem," followed by "Silent Night."

When the last strains of the final hymn had disappeared into the night, Ron announced, "Merry Christmas, everyone! Go in peace. I hope you'll be particularly generous with your offerings this evening, and continue to support our efforts with your prayers. Thank you, brothers and sisters, for making our work possible. Amen and hallelujah. I hope to see you all next Sunday."

With a slight bow, Ron turned to Winona, and taking the Plexiglas case containing the snake from her, quickly exited behind the curtain. Winona picked up a woven, wicker collection basket and made her way down the center aisle as eager worshippers dropped whatever they could into the receptacle, which was soon filled to overflowing.

After the service, as Ron and Winona were straightening up in the rear of the church, one of their church members, Walt Witkowsky, appeared in the doorway that separated the office from the body of the church. He was a retired coal miner, and his wife, Nadia, was suffering from an inoperable brain tumor, and had very little time left to live. Over the last several weeks, Ron and Winona had spent numerous evenings with the couple, praying over Nadia, and comforting her soon-to-be widower.

"Well, I don't think it'll be very long now," sighed Walt. "She hasn't known who I am for the last two days." His eyes were red-rimmed, most likely from crying, and he appeared to Ron to be struggling just to maintain his composure.

Ron stopped what he was doing, walked over, and placed his arm around Walt's shoulder. "I'm so sorry, Walt. I really am. Nadia is a good woman, and I know she'll find peace with the Lord."

"There's something I wanted you two to know," said the old man. "I've decided to make your church the beneficiary of my life insurance policy. Actually, it was Nadia's idea. When she's gone, there'll be no one but me, since we don't have any children, and—"

"Now, now, Walt," said Winona. "Let's not go talking about anything like that. The church is doing just fine. You shouldn't be thinking about anything but Nadia."

"Well, maybe so, but I just wanted you to know. Like I said, it was Nadia's idea. About two weeks ago, she made me promise—before she got so sick."

Winona and Ron embraced the old man from either side.

"Why don't we pray?" said Winona.

"I think that's a good idea," replied Ron. "Shall we?"

The three of them joined arms, bowed their heads, and stood that way, arms around each other, for several minutes, praying silently.

"Praise the Lord," said Ron. "His will be done."

"Amen," said Winona.

"Amen," mouthed Walter.

Nadia Witkowsky died three days later.

A week later, Ron drank Strychnine for the first time during a service at the Black Mountain church. The night before the notable event, Winona knelt alongside her man as the couple prayed for the Holy Ghost to protect Ron as it was written in the Bible that It would. Ron's eyes were pressed tightly closed and he seemed almost in a trance as he offered up his prayers to God and the Holy Spirit. Winona peeked at him through her clasped hands and marveled at the intensity with which he beseeched God's blessings and protection. He *really* believes, she thought.

At the following night's service, she held a glass with trembling hands as Ron confidently poured a small amount of the Strychnine crystals into the water in full view of the congregation. Then, as he held the glass aloft, she watched in amazement as he recited the now familiar passage from Mark 16, Verse 18, and slowly drained the contents of the glass. He coughed a few times, and Winona held her breath, feeling certain (as she always did when he tested his faith) that surely *this time* she would see him collapse and die before her very eyes. But, to the congregation's and her continued amazement, Ron did not collapse; nor did he die. Instead, he proceeded to call for the snakes.

Winona found herself caught up in the magic of the moment, and hurried behind the curtain to retrieve a Plexiglas case containing two small rattlesnakes. The worshippers were going wild, singing and rejoicing, their voices threatening to drown out the sound of the accompanying guitars and tambourines. She gingerly opened the top of the case and offered its contents to

Ron. Without hesitation, he reached in first with his right hand, and then with his left, and withdrew both snakes from the container. She'd never seen him so confident.

More than twenty minutes elapsed as Ron toyed with the serpents, at times even bringing one and then the other within inches of his face. Finally, he indicated to Winona that he was through, and she quickly knelt and retrieved the empty case from the floor and held it firmly in front of her as Ron returned the snakes to their familiar surroundings. Exhaling through pursed lips, Winona carefully closed the mesh top and quickly secured the hasps.

That evening's contributions were the highest they had been since Ron and Winona moved to the small mining community, and Winona knew that for the next few months or so the money would continue to pour in. But eventually donations would begin to deteriorate, and before long Winona would have to convince Ron to move elsewhere.

32

Roscoe, NY—July 14, 2011

Val was into the first full week of her radiation regimen, and although it tired her somewhat, she was relieved to find that she was able to keep up with her housekeeping, and still have enough energy to prepare most of the meals. Hopefully, by the time school was back in session in the fall, she'd be able to resume her full time nursing duties. Matt insisted that he help out, and took over the laundry, and vacuuming, but Val drew the line at him cooking, by explaining how preparing his meals was something she just "had" to do.

She was seeing Dr. Radford once a month, and while initially unsure about her new oncologist (she could scarcely believe she had one), she now found him to be an engaging man with a marvelous bedside manner. He had a curious habit of curling his feet beneath his posterior as he sat in his chair making notes in an impossibly small handwriting that she found delightful.

Her initial meeting with the oncologist had posed more questions than it had answered, and had Matt not been there to listen and digest every bit of information, Val would most certainly have been lost. It wasn't that she didn't understand the technical terminology, because she did. She just wasn't in a state of mind to process it.

As always, she trusted her husband to be there for her when she needed him most; and he was.

Right away, the oncologist had ordered a sophisticated lab test to determine whether chemotherapy would be of any value. Based upon the results, he and Val would decide together how best to proceed with her treatment. Today Dr. Radford was explaining how her tumor had been identified as having estrogen positive receptors. In essence, what it meant was that estrogen, a female hormone, was responsible for the tumor's origin. The drug he was advocating was Tamoxifen, and it would work by shielding Val's healthy breast cells against the harmful effects of estrogen, which would ordinarily bind with those cells; in doing so, the Tamoxifen would deny her breasts the ability to produce another tumor. In theory, it was a wonderful plan; in reality, it would depend greatly upon Val's tolerance to the drug, which had numerous side effects.

One of the side effects that Val noticed right away were the cramps in her legs that were so severe they caused her to wake in the middle of the night, screaming in pain. Fortunately, relief was delivered by a simple regimen of a glass of quinine water, suggested by Dr. Radford, taken every evening before retiring. It was going to be a long slog, and Val was glad she wouldn't have to face it alone. Matt was the best friend she had and the only one with whom she felt safe. He was her knight in shining armor. She only hoped that his armor was sufficient enough to protect them both.

33

Black Mountain, PA

Nadia Witkowsky had been in her grave exactly three weeks, and Walt had spent most of that time completely alone. Aside from his weekly visit to the church, his days were filled mostly with prayer and meditation in the dark confines of his four-room home. Without his beloved wife, there just didn't seem much point in living, and he was sinking deeper and deeper into despair. After another unremarkable day, he climbed the stairs to his lonely bedroom, got undressed, and slipped beneath the covers of the painfully empty bed.

That night he was visited by his wife's spirit in a dream. She scolded him for not moving on with his life. "God helps those what helps themselves," she had admonished him. "You make the most of what time God gives you, Walt Witkowsky." When he awoke the next morning, he couldn't remember much more than that of the dream, but it was enough. He determined he would honor his wife's wishes.

After breakfast, Walt decided to wash and wax his pickup truck. He waited until noon, however, when the winter sun was at its highest, before starting. He poured a capful of Turtle Wax car washing soap into a plastic bucket, and filled it three-quarters full with hot water from the tap, before using the outside hose to generate a healthy layer of foam.

When he'd finished washing the red, 2002 Chevy Silverado, he decided to pull the truck back inside the garage where he could take his time waxing it without freezing to death. The sun was waning, and the temperature had dropped considerably; after all, it was still winter. The Witkowsky house was the solitary residence on its stretch of Rural Route 27. The nearest other home was over two miles away at the intersection with Meadow Lane. So, Walt was somewhat surprised when he heard the sound of a vehicle approaching, and then slowing, before it pulled into his driveway, coming to a stop in front of the garage. He laid down the towel he'd been using and stepped outside.

"Well, what brings you out here?" he asked of his visitor.

"I just wanted to check to see if you'd changed the beneficiary designation on that life insurance policy yet."

Walt thought the question was a bit strange, but he answered anyway as was his nature. "Sure did. Just the way Nadia wanted me to. Did it the week after she died."

"That's good. Really good," said the visitor. "So, it looks like you've decided to move on with your life."

"Yep. Nadia came to me in a dream last night."

"You don't say?"

"Uh huh. She said 'God helps those what helps themselves.' So, I thought I'd start by cleaning up this old truck."

"Well, I'd say that's a good idea. Why don't I give you a hand?"

"Oh, you don't have to do that."

"No, no, I insist. You go ahead. I'll be right back. I just want to get my jacket."

Walt turned his back to the visitor, climbed inside the cab of the truck, and began spraying Armoral on the vinyl surface of the dashboard. A moment later, something landed atop the dashboard with a thud, right near his face. It was a copperhead snake!

"What the—"

"Sorry, Walt," said the visitor. "I just had to be sure."

Instinctively, Walt used his left hand to swipe the reptile away, and was rewarded by a painful bite to his extremity. He rubbed the back of his hand, which was quickly swelling, and his mind overflowed with unanswerable questions. "But, why?" he managed to ask, before the heart attack began—along with the pain.

"Why not?" came the reply.

Walt grabbed his left arm, which was hurting something awful and beginning to grow numb, and fumbled with his right hand inside his pants pocket in a desperate attempt to retrieve the nitroglycerine tablets he always carried. But as he pulled them from his pocket, the cap came loose and the pills tumbled to the floor of the cab and he collapsed against the steering wheel. Instantly, the horn began to sound. Calmly, the murderer carefully retrieved the copperhead, got back into the vehicle parked in the driveway, and drove away, with the sound of the blaring horn fading in the distance.

Evil left the way it had come—without a trace.

Because of the odd circumstances of Walt's death from the snakebite and subsequent heart attack, there had been an intense investigation launched by the state police and the insurance company, but eventually, it had been concluded that it was just a case of unfortunate coincidence. Of course, there was no tangible evidence connecting Walt's death with Ron or Winona, other than the insurance policy. For that matter, there was nothing to even cast suspicion on anyone else connected with the church. Eventually, the church and its members were cleared completely. Because of the investigation, however, it was several months before the proceeds were released.

It was early in April when the check finally arrived in the mail, Winona held the financial instrument in her hand and studied it carefully. It was a cashier's check issued by Reliable Life Indemnity of Le Grange, Illinois, and drawn on First Chicago Bank. The amount was fifty thousand dollars, and it was made payable to the Devoted Church of Jesus With Signs Following.

Winona didn't show the check to Ron, because she knew he'd want to cash it right away and pour the money back into the church to demonstrate to the parishioners just how sorry he and Winona were about Walter Witkowsky's untimely passing, especially coming right on top of the death of the man's wife only two months earlier. Since the church's checking account only required an endorsement by one of the two signatories to cash a check, Winona decided to do so using just hers. The next morning, she went to the bank and cashed it, but only deposited fifteen thousand in their joint account, while placing the balance of thirty-five thousand in an individual savings account that she maintained under her own "real" name. What Ron didn't know would never hurt him. To Ron, the fifteen thousand would appear like a fortune, especially since he was unaware of the face value of the life insurance policy. With no particular knowledge of banking procedures, he preferred instead to let Winona handle "those things," as he referred to financial matters. In fact, ever since the move, Ron had shown less and less inclination to worry about money, and more concern instead for the welfare of "his flock" as he referred to the collection of coal miners and their families that frequented the church.

Ever since the miner's death, Ron had ceased handling the snakes. As a result of that and the worsening economy, donations had dwindled considerably. And, although there was still sufficient money in the checking account to carry them for a month or so, Winona knew the money wouldn't last forever.

"I cashed Walt Witkowsky's insurance check today," she informed Ron that evening over dinner. "I still can't believe how much money he left to the church—to us, actually."

Ron popped another tater tot into his already full mouth and followed it with a swallow of beer. "I didn't know it had come. How much was it anyway, ten thousand?"

"No," answered Winona. "It was *fifteen!* Can you believe it?"

"He was a good man," said Ron between mouthfuls of food. "That money will be a big help to this community. I've been thinking we could start a hot meals service, once or twice a week—to help out some of these people who are out of work. And, maybe we could do a lunch thing for the kids."

"And maybe we could just take the fifteen thousand and move somewhere else," replied Winona. "What would you think of that idea?"

Ron put down his fork, took a swallow of beer, and leaned back in his chair. He stared hard at Winona with a curious look on his face. "Why is it that every time we get a little money you want to move? These people *need* us."

"Maybe they need *you*. But they sure as hell don't need *me*. I'm sick of this place."

"But, why?"

"Because I just *am*, that's all. You said it yourself; the air stinks, the water stinks, and there's coal dust on everything. We should leave; that's what I say."

"And what about our plans to get married?"

Ron had made an informal proposal right after they had arrived in Black Mountain, but hadn't mentioned the idea since. Now, he hoped to use it to his advantage. "Have you forgotten about that?" he asked.

It was Winona's turn to stare. It was what she did whenever she had no answer for one of Ron's questions.

"Well?"

"Well, what about it?" Winona replied. "If I marry you, I'll just be stuck here in no man's land with a bunch of loser coal miners."

Then, she had an idea.

"I'll tell you what. If you'll agree to move, I promise I'll marry you in the next town we settle in. Deal?"

Ron hesitated. Just like in a prison poker game, she had called his bluff.

"We'll make a new start—as Mr. and Mrs. *Ronald Trentweiler*. There, now wouldn't that be a nice way to begin a marriage? In a new town?"

"Let me sleep on it. I really have mixed feelings— not about marrying you, of course, but about leaving these people. Give me a day or two, okay?"

"Okay. But if the answer's 'no,' I might have to think about moving on without you."

Ron frowned. Winona came up behind him and wrapped her arms around his shoulders. She bent down and whispered into his ear, "Oh Ron, you know I'd never do that. Honest. But I really do hate it here. Please say we can move, *please*."

"Wel-l-l-l," he replied. "I guess we could make a pretty good start with fifteen thousand bucks in our pockets, couldn't we?"

"You bet we could."

"Okay. We'll do it. But, on one condition. We have to pick a place we both agree on. That's the deal. Okay?"

"You bet your sweet ass," sighed Winona, planting a wet kiss on the side of Ron's neck. "You're the best, baby, the absolute best."

"And you're a pain in my ass."

That night Winona lay in bed alongside Ron, listening to him snore, unable to contain her excitement at the prospects of getting out of Black Mountain after nearly two years. Finally, around two in the morning, when she could stand it no longer, she pulled the top sheet of the bedding between her legs, and pleasured herself with thoughts of a former lover until, at last, she squeezed out a weak but sufficient orgasm and fell into a deep, dreamless sleep.

Tomorrow, she'd help Ron pick their new home.

34

Roscoe, NY

It was late in July, and I was sitting quietly in the back of the Roscoe Diner, sipping from a cup of hot chocolate and reading a copy of the *Binghamton Press* that I'd found on the seat. I quickly scanned the national headlines on the front page, then worked my way through the pages towards the back until I came to a small article with the headline "Authorities Rule Out Foul Play In Snake Death." I folded the paper lengthwise, and then again from top to bottom, just as the myriad of straphangers did every morning in the New York subway system as they read their daily copies of the *Wall Street Journal* on the way down to the financial district in lower Manhattan. I read the article deliberately, absorbing every detail:

> "BLACK MOUNTAIN, PA—After a nearly three-month investigation into the death of a seventy-eight-year old, retired coal miner, Walter Witkowsky, State Police officials in Columbia County have concluded that circumstances surrounding his death were merely "unusual coincidences," (to quote an unnamed source) and not evidence of foul play. Witkowsky died in January of this year from a heart attack apparently caused when a poisonous snake struck him while he was detailing his pickup truck in his garage. An autopsy revealed puncture wounds on the man's hand as well as traces of copperhead venom in his bloodstream. State police

speculate that the reptile may have been inadvertently trapped inside the garage, and at some point bit the man while he was at work on his vehicle.

"A trooper responding to a report by a passerby of a horn blowing continuously found the man, a recent widower, slumped over the steering wheel of his truck. Efforts to revive him failed, and he was pronounced dead at the scene. At the time of the incident, no foul play was suspected. However, when authorities learned that the victim belonged to a small Pentecostal church in nearby Centralia, rumored to dabble in the practice of snake handling, suspicions were aroused, and an investigation was launched into the man's death. A family attorney revealed that Mr. Witkowsky's church, the Devoted Church of Christ With Signs Following, was the beneficiary of a life insurance policy owned by the deceased. However, members of the church insisted that the pastor of the church, Ron Trentweiler, had been exceptionally involved in caring for Mr. Witkowsky's late wife prior to her recent death, and praised him as a true friend to the members of the congregation. A spokesperson for Reliable Life Indemnity indicated to investigators that it is not unusual for a widow or a widower with no children, to name a church as beneficiary of a life insurance policy. The same spokesperson said that Mr. Witkowsky had changed the beneficiary designation immediately following his wife's death."

I took a look at the date on the newspaper and laughed; it was April 30, 2011.

"Hey, George," I said, in the direction of the diner's ubiquitous owner. "Don't you have any current newspapers around here? This one's three months old, for crying out loud."

190

George laughed. "I don't know, Mr. Matt," he said in his heavy Greek accent. "I guess some fisherman left it there. What's a matter? You got plenty of money. Why don't you break down and *buy* a new one once in a while?"

"Very funny. Very funny."

I took another sip of my hot chocolate and shook my head. My detective instinct told me that there was more to the story than met the eye. I made a mental note to contact the Black Mountain, Pennsylvania police department as soon as I got back to headquarters. I was curious whether or not the church in question also used Strychnine in its services. It was a long shot, but maybe there was some kind of connection there that might provide some direction in the Billy Stillwater case. After all, Black Mountain was less than a hundred-and-fifty miles from Roscoe.

I swallowed the remainder of my drink, picked up the newspaper, and made my way to the cashier. Outside, a fine rain was beginning to fall. By the time I reached my Jeep, it was pouring.

Evil was moving closer.

35

Black Mountain, PA—April 12, 2011

It was the day after Winona told Ron about the insurance check, and he woke up early, with the conversation they had the night before still fresh in his mind. Only today he wasn't so sure about getting married. He kept thinking about what the guys in prison used to say whenever the subject of marriage was broached. "Why buy the cow when the milk is free?" Maybe they had a point.

As far as Winona's proposal to move was concerned, Ron concluded that she was probably right after all. It was time to go. Walt Witkowsky's death seemed to have taken the bloom off the Black Mountain rose. And, even though the State Police had pretty much cleared the couple of any suspicion in Walt's death, staying in the small town no longer held the appeal it once had before the tragedy. Winona was definitely right. He turned to wake her, and was surprised to find that her side of the bed was already empty. Wandering into the kitchen, Ron half expected to find her having breakfast. But, the kitchen was dark and deserted.

"I'm in here," called Winona from the living room.

Ron followed the voice to its source.

"Ever been to Cooperstown?" asked Winona.

She was sitting on the couch, clothed in a bathrobe and slippers, her body hunched over the coffee table, studying a map of New York State.

"Do you mean Cooperstown, like in the Hall of Fame?"

"Yeah. That's right. You like baseball, don't you?"

Ron had to admit baseball was his favorite sport by far. While in Talladega, he'd frequently dreamed of pitching for the Florida Marlins, the southernmost team in the major leagues, and striking out the final batter in the final game of the World Series—against the hated Yankees.

"Sure I like baseball," he replied. "What about it?"

"Well, why don't we go there?"

"Where?"

"Cooperstown."

"Well, for starters," said Ron. "What will the people in our church think? Won't it look a little suspicious if we just up and move away—especially after we just got the insurance check and all?"

"Who cares what they think. It's not our fault that Walt died and left us the money. Right?"

Ron hesitated.

"Right?" repeated Winona.

"Yeah. I guess so, but—"

"But nothing! We're moving, and that's it."

Three days later they settled on a place called Treadwell, New York, just outside Delhi, the county seat of Delaware County. A comprehensive study of real estate websites revealed that home prices and rental rates in and around Cooperstown were sky high and totally out of Ron and Winona's price range. Cooperstown was, in Winona's words: "*Ex-pens-ive* with a capital *E*."

On the other hand, Treadwell, because it was located about an hour away from the baseball Mecca, was not a tourist trap, and as a result was definitely within their price range. Besides, reasoned Winona, it was close enough that Ron could visit it whenever he desired. And, after all, how much closer did he need to be? Ron agreed. So, they rented a U-Haul trailer, loaded it with their meager belongings, and headed for their new home. The snakes rode in boxes in the back of the pickup, covered by a tarp, and oblivious to their destination.

Evil was on the move.

36

Roscoe, NY

It turned out there was no Black Mountain police department. In fact, the nearest law enforcement agency of any kind was in Wilkes Barre, about twenty miles away, and it was a Pennsylvania State Police Barracks. The desk sergeant on duty was Roger Vogel, and he answered my call on the first ring.

I explained that I was investigating a murder in my jurisdiction and that the cause of death had been determined to be Strychnine poisoning.

"No shit!" exclaimed the officer. "That's a new one on me."

I explained that I had read an article in the *Binghamton Press* about a man being bitten by a snake and dying from a heart attack over in Black Mountain, along with the fact that he had been a member of a Pentecostal church that practiced snake handling. The sergeant said he was familiar with the story, but he didn't know anything about the church itself.

"I'm thinking there might be a connection between that death and our murder over here in Roscoe," I said.

"What makes you think that?"

"Well, I read in a book recently that some of these churches not only handle poisonous snakes, but drink Strychnine as well."

"And you want to know whether they drink Strychnine at that church in Black Mountain, right?"

"Right."

"What'd you say the name of the church was?"

"I didn't. But, it's the Devoted Church of Jesus With Signs Following. Are you familiar with it?"

"Nah," replied the officer, "but that's no surprise. This is Bum Fuck, USA. Every two-bit town has at least three churches in it. Some of them have only ten or fifteen members. Anyway, I'm afraid I can't help you on this one," replied officer Vogel. "We don't have much to do with those folks over in Black Mountain. But I'll tell you what I *can* do for you. I can check with some of the boys here, see if they know anything, and get back to you. Would that be okay?"

It wasn't the answer I'd hoped for, but what could I say?

"Sure," I replied. "That'd be fine. I'd really appreciate it."

I gave him my phone number and hung up.

I called information and asked for the phone number of the Devoted Church of Jesus With Signs Following in Black Mountain, Pennsylvania. I wasn't too surprised to find that there was no such listing.

"Well, thanks, anyway," I said to the operator.

I placed the receiver back into the cradle of the phone.

"Nancy," I shouted, "I think I'm going to take a ride over to Pennsy. Check out that church in Black Mountain."

"What time will you be back?" shouted my secretary from her office.

Rather than continue the shouting match, I tiptoed down the hall from my office to hers as quietly as I could. The door was open and Nancy was sitting with her back to me. I crept up behind her and whispered in her right ear, "It's about two-and-a-half hours each way, so I probably won't be back until dinnertime."

She jumped straight up and the top of her head crashed into my chin, causing me to bite my tongue.

"Oh, Matt," she cried. "I'm so sorry. You startled me. Are you okay?"

Exaggerating my injury and affecting a lisp, I replied in a pained voice, "That'th awright, it therves me right for thneaking up on you. I thould be okay with a couple of thtitches."

Nancy rolled her eyes.

"Men," she sighed. "You're all just little boys at heart."

As I started for the exit door, I called over my shoulder, "Would you give Val a call and tell her I'll be late?"

Before she could answer, I quickly dashed outside into the parking lot, and as I did a blast of rainwater hit me in the face.

Jesus, it's still coming down, I thought. *Will it never end?*

37

"Not much to look at, is it?" said Ron. He and Winona had just finished inspecting the inside of a rundown farmhouse, easily over a hundred years old, which stood on a ten-acre parcel of rolling land at the end of a dirt road. Now they were standing in front of the place with a local realtor, discussing its viability as a rental.

The white, painted house had a small, utilitarian front porch with a glider on it, actual working shutters on the windows, and a modest barn out back. The owner had installed a plywood floor and heat, in the hope of renting the structure separately. The out building was important, thought Ron; they'd need that for the services. They had already looked at four other rentals that morning, but this one was by far the best of the lot. With its isolated location, well out from the nearest town of Delhi, it would provide the privacy that they would need for their church and its unusual practices.

The realtor, a woman named Susan Maybin, in her fifties, wore a tailored, pale gray, business suit, and spoke in an affected "folksy" manner that seemed to appeal to the majority of her clients, most of them from New York City. She shaded her eyes from the sun and studied Ron's face carefully. "Well, considering what the owners are asking for rent, I'd say it's a palace—*if* you get my drift."

"We'll take it," said Winona, a bit prematurely to suit Ron's liking.

"But *only* on a month-to-month basis," he quickly added, making sure the woman understood who was in charge. "We tend to move around a bit, and we don't want to be tied down."

"Minimum they'll accept is a six-month lease—*then*, you can continue on a month-to-month." The woman inserted a stick of gum into her mouth and began chewing angrily.

"That'll work," answered Ron. "We're staying in a Motel 6 over in...what's the name of that town, Winona?"

"Oneonta?" she replied.

"Yeah; that's it—Oneonta," affirmed Ron. "How soon can you have the lease ready for us to sign?"

"I can do it right now," replied the Maybin woman, pulling a multi-page document from her attaché case. "And, you could move in tomorrow."

The realtor removed the gum from her mouth, folded it carefully into its paper wrapper and put it in her purse, then extracted a ballpoint pen.

"I'll just...change the terms...right...here," she said, using the pen to cross out one set of words and insert the corrected terminology. "There, now if you'll just sign right *here*, and initial those changes, I'll take it over to the owners and have them do likewise; then, you can pick up your copy and a set of keys at my office, first thing tomorrow morning."

"Sounds good," said Ron.

He took the lease from the realtor and quickly initialed and signed it, then handed it back to her. "What time does your office open?"

"Nine, sharp. Oh, and of course I'll need a check for the first two months rent."

"Will you take cash?" asked Ron, removing a number of crisp, one-hundred-dollar bills from his wallet. "We haven't opened a checking account yet, and—"

"Cash will do just fine," said the woman, nearly yanking the proffered currency from Ron's hand. "I'll write you a receipt. To *whom* shall I make it out?" Suddenly, it seemed her speech pattern had changed from that of a country bumpkin to one of "all business."

"Make it out to the Devoted Church of Jesus with Signs Following," said Ron.

"Cute," said the realtor, scribbling the receipt and handing it to Ron.

"That way we can deduct it off our taxes," added Winona, with a smile. "Even *God* can use a little help in the financial department. Don't you agree?"

"I don't know about that," replied the realtor. "But *these* folks can certainly use a little religion. That much I *do* know. What kind of church is that, anyway? Baptist? Methodist?"

"Pentecostal," replied Ron.

"Oh. Well, we've never had one of *those* around here, but I don't think people will care much about that, as long as you can pick their spirits up. If you know what I mean."

"Oh, I *do.* I sure do."

That's not *all* we'll pick, thought Ron, as he watched the realtor's car disappear out of sight.

38

The ride to Black Mountain was an easy one. It would have been a nice one, too, if it hadn't been for the rain. As I drove along the Quickway, on my way east to pick up- I-81 South at Binghamton, I was amazed at how high the rivers were. The Beaverkill was near the top of its banks—and even over them at its junction with the East Branch of the Delaware River. Further along, at Deposit, I looked upriver along Route 10 to where the West Branch was spilling over the Canonsville Dam, above the now submerged concrete weir on its way downstream to the junction at Bard-Parker Pool in Hancock. This area of the Catskills depended heavily upon these rivers for its economic survival, and if the rain didn't break soon, most of the employees of the lodges and fishing camps would be filing for unemployment. And, I thought, if I didn't make some headway on my murder case, the same fate might await me. I pressed harder on the accelerator. I felt sure there were answers waiting for me in Black Mountain.

It was after two when I exited I-81 and followed the narrow, two lane road west until at last I saw a small, green sign on the side of the highway that read: "Black Mountain." I looked around for signs of civilization, but all I could see were a couple of fast food joints. I pulled the Jeep into the parking lot of a Burger King. The aroma of charcoal-broiled beef (or whatever it was that they put in their burgers) assaulted my nasal passages, reminding me that I hadn't eaten a bite since seven that morning. For a fleeting second, my doctor's admonitions about my diet passed through my mind—then, just as quickly, passed out—and I pulled the Jeep into the drive-through lane of the fast food restaurant, compromising just a smidgen by leaving off the cheese and ordering "just a hamburger, no fries." Then, I quickly added, "And give me a cup of hot chocolate, would you, please?"

A teenaged voice tinged with sarcasm issued through the metal speaker. "I'm sorry, sir, but we don't *serve* hot chocolate in the *summer*. Would you like coffee, instead?"

I couldn't resist the challenge. "Nope. I don't *drink* coffee. Just give me a cup of ice water, okay?"

"*Okay*," replied the metallic voice. "But that *will* be twenty-five cents. One cup of ice water, coming up!"

Smart-ass!

After I'd finished eating, I sat quietly in the Jeep, planning my next move. I'd checked a road map before I left the office, and I knew that if I followed this particular road, I should come to some semblance of a town. Sure enough, within a few minutes I spotted a group of storefronts clustered together on either side of a two-block section of the road. This must be Black Mountain, I thought. *Big deal.* I pulled the Jeep to the curb in front of a second-hand shop that appeared to be out of business. That wasn't a good sign. To its left, there was a hardware store with a "Closed" sign hanging in the window; but judging by the dust clouding the glass, I guessed that it should have read "Vacant," which is exactly what it was. A pharmacy, immediately to the right of the thrift shop was also "Closed." I was getting a bad feeling about Black Mountain.

I turned and crossed over to the other side of the street, where there was a rundown bar and grille that had a painted banner advertising "All Nude Dancers" stretched across its shallow roof. Although, it, too, was closed, I felt certain that it was definitely *not* out of business, unlike the other two shops that definitely were. That left a pawnshop—long ago abandoned—and a laundromat, which, surprisingly was not only still in business, but open as well.

The door of the establishment was propped open with a brick, and as I walked inside I was immediately aware of a loud "thump, thump, thump" sound coming from the rear. I observed a young woman in her early twenties, dressed in tattered blue jeans, a stained black tee shirt, and flip-flops, asleep in an orange, plastic backed chair; apparently she was oblivious to the ear shattering noise that I now recognized as coming from a clothes dryer in the rear. Upon further examination, I found that said dryer only contained a pair of sneakers and a dress; hence the noise emanating from its confines, as the sneakers within reluctantly acceded to the pull of gravity with each rotation of the enameled drum and dropped down to its bottom with a resounding thump.

Looking up and down the row of washing machines and dryers, I concluded that the woman was the laundromat's only occupant, and exercising great care, I leaned down and gently tapped her on the shoulder. She didn't budge. I tapped again, a bit more firmly this time, and she roused slightly, readjusting her position in the chair. She was still asleep.

"Excuse me," I said in a loud voice, "I was wondering if you could help me."

The young woman sat up with a start, her eyes open wide, with a look that indicated she wasn't aware of where she was or who was speaking to her.

"I hate to bother you, but I'm trying to locate a particular church."

She shook her head rapidly from side to side, almost as though she were trying to clear literal cobwebs from it, and then appeared to come fully awake.

"I'm sorry," she said, "I was asleep."

No shit.

"I hate to disturb you, but I'm looking for the Devoted Church of Jesus With Signs Following. It's supposed to be here in Black Mountain, but—"

"They moved," she said.

"Excuse me?"

"I said they *moved.* The people that ran it. About two months ago."

Shit. "Well, do you think you could tell me how to get to the church anyway?"

"Won't do you any good," she said, yawning wide enough for me to notice that she was missing several teeth. "There's no one there. Them and their snakes are history."

"So they *did* have snakes?"

"Well, *I* never saw 'em, but that's what everybody else said."

"Do you know where they went?"

The girl shook her head. "Are you a cop?"

Now I knew she was *really* awake.

"Yeah," I replied. "But, not from here. I'm from over in Roscoe. Over in New York State."

"Oh. Well, what are you doing here?"

Awake and *nosey*, I thought. I ignored her inquiry.

"So, can you tell me how to get to the church?"

"Oh, sure," replied the girl. "And it's *Centralia.*"

"*What* is?"

"The *church*. The church is in Centralia—*not* Black Mountain. That's if you can call Centralia a town. It's pretty much abandoned. Just go that way (she pointed west with a bony finger) until you come to the railroad tracks. As soon as you cross over, make the next right, and follow that road for about a half mile until it bends around to the left. The church is right there—at the end of the road."

"Are there any houses near it?"

"A couple."

"Anybody live there?"

"Of course."

"Good. Thanks for the information. I'll let you get back to sleep. Sorry to bother you."

"No bother."

I turned and started for the door.

"Hey mister!"

I turned to face the girl.

"Can you spare some change?"

I smiled. Some things were the same no matter where you went. I walked over, pulled a five-dollar bill from my wallet, and handed it to her.

She frowned, handing the bill back to me. "Don't ya have any change?"

I looked at her, puzzled.

"For the machine," she said. "The *washing* machine."

Maybe I was wrong after all.

39

Treadwell, NY—late April 2011

The house and barn had required a bit more fixing up than Ron and Winona had planned on, but after nearly two weeks of backbreaking labor, they were at last ready to begin preaching again. One of those "Insty-Print" copying places had delivered the handbills they ordered within the three-day, guaranteed time limit, and they had placed one on every windshield of every vehicle they could, in each strip mall parking lot between Treadwell and Cooperstown, along Route 28 to the northeast, and south to Roscoe, nearly thirty-five miles away. Along the road, they saw signs for the Hall of Fame in Cooperstown, and Ron made Winona promise that soon they'd visit the famous landmark. They made no mention of snakes in the flyer, but instead used the code words "Pentecostal," "Mark XVI," and "speaking in tongues" to convey the essence of their emerging congregation.

In addition to the flyers, Ron decided to accelerate the growth of his church's membership by running several small, discrete ads in local, free newspapers, because he knew from experience that country folks pored over every square inch of these "penny savers" in search not only of discount coupons, but local news and announcements as well.

The first week's service saw only a handful of attendees, but the following Sunday, there were over three-dozen eager worshippers, several of whom brought musical instruments. The service itself wasn't particularly noteworthy, but afterwards, as the people filed out of barn, an older couple stopped to speak with Ron, and what they had to say gave him great hope that, indeed, he'd chosen just the right area to establish a permanent church.

Their names were Eleanor and Everett Jones, and Ron estimated their ages to be well into the eighties. She was dressed in a traditional, two-piece woman's suit of very good quality wool, beige, and a lavender, ruffled blouse, open at the throat. On her feet were closed-toe, black leather shoes with little bows and just a hint of a heel. Her legs were covered by taupe-colored, support stockings, and a modest string of freshwater pearls lay against her wrinkled, age-spotted neck.

Mrs. Jones had a full head of white hair, notable for its lack of blue coloring, which she wore in a braid. Her husband was tastefully attired in a dark blue, three-piece, pinstriped suit, also of wool, and a pale blue shirt with button-down collar. His tie was a classic, red and white, regimental stripe, held in place with a pearl tie tack. His shoes were black oxfords. He was mostly bald, except for a faint trace of thin white hair that ran from above his ears and around the back of his head, almost like a half-halo. Both stood ramrod straight, a testimony, no doubt, to a life filled with honest labor and good care. The only sign of infirmity between the two was a small, flesh-colored hearing aid, buried deep within the confines of Mr. Jones's left ear.

"We've waited a long time for a young man like you to come to Treadwell," said Mrs. Jones. "Most folks in our area worship mostly in Catholic or Protestant churches. A *true* Pentecostal church is hard to find."

Ron smiled.

"We were just wondering when you might get to Mark 16: Verse 18," said Everett Jones with a barely perceptible wink. "The Holy Ghost has been absent from these hills for many years, if you know what I mean."

Ron knew the man was referring to the snakes, but as always, he had to be careful in introducing the practice to a new congregation. Still, there was no doubting the man's interest.

"Would you and Mrs. Jones care to join us inside the house for a cup of coffee—or tea?"

"Why, thank you; I'd love a cup of tea," said Eleanor. "Everett only drinks coffee—black, with 'no sugar, no cream, no nothin',' to quote him."

"Well, we've got both—coffee *and* tea, that is. It won't be any trouble at all," said Winona, who stood quietly to the side, as Ron guided the couple in through the back door of the farmhouse and into the kitchen. She waited until the three of them were inside, and then closed the door. "I'll put some water on," she said, filling a blue enameled teapot with cold water from the tap. "Is instant coffee, all right, Mr. Jones?"

Everett nodded his approval.

"Good. Ron, why don't you show Mr. and Mrs. Jones into the dining room, and I'll bring everything in in just a minute."

Five minutes later, the two couples were seated around the small, drop-leaf dining room table, sipping on their beverages and taking turns in the conversation, which eventually got around to the subject of the snakes.

"You know," said Everett, "we had one preacher here about thirty years ago who handled snakes, but he left after only a year or so when his wife got bit by a rattler."

"Darn nice young fellow," offered Mrs. Jones. "We hated to see him go."

"Was it just his wife getting bitten that caused them to leave?" asked Ron.

"That and the sheriff from over in Delhi," chimed in Eleanor. "He told him, flat out, that if he didn't leave right away, there'd be trouble. So he left."

"We were wondering about that," said Winona. "Usually, we try to keep everything as quiet as possible— you know, so we don't have any trouble with the law."

"Well, you needn't worry yourself one bit about that here. *That* sheriff's gone, and the new fellow who took his place is one of us. Lived here all his life—*and* he's a Pentecostal."

The talk continued for an hour or so, before the Joneses excused themselves, saying they needed to get back to their farm to feed their animals.

After they'd left, Ron remarked to Winona that perhaps they had finally found a home.

"Could be," she replied. "Could be."

It seemed to Ron that his partner was pre-occupied, and more than a little distant.

"What's bugging you?"

"Nothing."

"Bull*shit*. I've known you long enough to know when something's on your mind. What is it?"

"It's nothing—honest."

"Then why are you so...I don't know...agitated?"

"I've been thinking about Black Mountain."

"What about Black Mountain?"

"You know; the investigation."

"The investigation's over," laughed Ron. "Besides, they said there wasn't any problem."

"But what if—"

"Just forget all about that. We're *here* now. Black Mountain is history. Besides, I think this might be just the place." A small smile spread across Ron's face. "After all, you *did* promise me that if we moved, you'd—"

"Yeah, yeah, I know," said Winona. "Hey," she said, obviously attempting to change the subject, "why don't we take a ride over to the Hall of Fame? You said you've always wanted to go there. This is as good a day as any."

"Oh, okay," said Ron, with a shrug. He'd have to wait for another day to bring up the subject of marriage. It was obvious that Winona wasn't in a mood to talk about *it*.

Besides, evil had *other* plans.

40

Centralia, PA

The girl's instructions were perfect, and I soon found myself at a cul-de-sac, staring at what was once probably a fine, country church, with a spire containing an ancient, forged iron bell within. Now, unfortunately, it was just one more abandoned building among many in an area in desperate need of economic repair.

Parking the Jeep, I silently climbed the several steps in front of the church, and stopped before a pair of glass-paneled, wooden doors that were padlocked shut; not that it mattered, because, judging by the overall appearance of the church, I doubted there was anything inside worth stealing. There were no signs of life, so I wiped the dust away from one of the glass panes and peered inside. All I saw were empty pews, a few folding chairs toward the rear—and more dust. There was a small stage up front, and behind it a blank wall with a faint outline of what must have been a large cross on it, now gone.

I turned, walked back down the steps, and made my way around to the back of the building, where there was a small, one-story residence, undoubtedly built to house the clergy and his family. Out of habit, I knocked on the door and waited patiently for someone to open it. After half a minute, I realized how foolish I'd been, and attempted to open it myself. To my surprise, it was unlocked.

"Hello," I called, before stepping inside.

There was no reply.

Like the church itself, this building, too, was also deserted.

I poked around the premises, but found nothing other than a few discarded newspapers and an abundance of mouse droppings. At least *something* was making use of the edifice.

I closed the door behind me, walked back past the church and out into the street, stopping alongside my Jeep to survey the neighborhood—*if* one could even call it that. In total, there were seven houses on the street. To my right were four, to my left, several more. I chose the second home on the right, mainly because it was the only one on the street that had a vehicle in its driveway.

Simultaneously as I stepped onto the front porch, the weathered front door opened to reveal an elderly woman in a wrinkled, black, dotted Swiss housedress, accompanied by a small girl, doubtless her grandchild, who was dressed almost identically.

"May I help you?" she asked.

The kid clung to her side and looked up at me with an innocent smile. The look on old woman's face was far more constrained.

"I was looking for the pastor of the church, but it seems as though—"

"They're gone."

"I can see that. I was wondering if—"

"You the police?"

"Not really," I lied.

It wasn't *really* a lie—more of a half-truth—since I had no official standing in the state. But, I figured I'd get more information if the negative baggage generally associated with law enforcement were not attached to my inquiry.

"I'm with the mortgage company," I said.

Okay, that *was* a lie, but a harmless one, I rationalized.

"Hmmph!" said the old woman. "I figured there was *some* reason those folks took off so quick."

"How long would you say they've been gone?"

"Oh, probably a couple of months by now, I'd guess."

"I don't suppose you'd know where they went, would you?"

"Not a clue."

The little girl had separated herself from her grandmother and gone inside. Now, she returned to her side, clutching a ragged doll. I stooped down to her level and admired her playmate.

"Does she have a name?" I inquired.

"Come on, child," hissed the grandmother. "You don't need to be talking to any strangers—especially some man from the bank."

"Okay, okay. You win. I *am* a policeman—but *not* from here, okay?"

I extracted my credentials and held them up for the woman to see.

"I'm from Roscoe, over in New York State. I'm just trying to track something some information."

"About the preacher?"

"Not exactly. But, I was hoping to *talk* to the preacher about something that might help me with a case back home."

"Well, you should have said so, right off."

"I'm sorry about that," I apologized, "but, most people aren't too eager to discuss their neighbors with the police."

"Well, who says *I* am?"

"Was the preacher alone, or did he have a family?"

"Don't know. There was *two* of 'em, anyways. That's all I know—him and some woman. I *guess* she was his wife."

"Well, that's something. Is there anyone who might know where they went?"

"I doubt it. One day they was here; next day they was gone."

"Do you have any idea *why* they might have left?"

"Probably had *somethin'* to do with that feller got bit by that snake and died."

"Mr. Witkowsky?"

"Uh huh."

"Were you a member of the church?"

"I *was*—that is until they started handling them snakes, and drinkin' that poison."

"Strychnine?"

"I don't know what you call it, but it was *some* kinda poison."

"So they *definitely* drank Strychnine," I thought aloud. "Is that what you're saying?"

"If *that's* what you call it. Then, *they* drank it."

"*Who* drank it? Did any of the church members drink it?"

"Just *him*, as far as I know—just the preacher. But, I stopped goin' there once that stuff started, so I really can't say."

I stood quietly, looking from the grandmother to her offspring. If this woman knew anything of substance, she certainly wasn't going to tell me. But, at least I'd learned part of what I needed to know; finding out where the couple had gone would have been a bonus.

"Well, I certainly appreciate your time," I said.

I reached into my pocket and extracted the five-dollar bill that the girl in the laundromat had refused.

"Here," I said, offering it to the little girl. "Maybe you can put this toward a nice doll house for your friend."

She immediately grabbed it and ran inside, shouting "Thank you," over her shoulder.

"Now what'd you have to go and do that fer?" said the old woman. "*Now* she'll think it's hers to *keep*."

"It is."

"The *hell* it is. *We* can *use* that money."

Boy, things must really be bad here, I thought. I reached into my wallet and pulled out a ten spot. "Here; *this* is for you. I *really* appreciate your—"

Before I could finish the sentence, the old woman yanked the bill out of my hand, stepped inside, and slammed the door behind her. The sound of the lock being turned in the cylinder assured me that she was finished talking. It was time to head for home.

This time, however, evil was *ahead* of me.

41

Walton, NY—four days before Billy's murder

A pale yellow piece of paper was lodged beneath the windshield wiper blade on the driver's side of Billy Stillwater's pickup truck. The vehicle sat in the rear of the parking lot that surrounded the Walton Diner, one of the true, old-fashioned diners remaining that had a traditional, stainless steel exterior. The diner was Billy's favorite place to eat breakfast on a Sunday morning, and he'd just finished wolfing down a whopper: three egg omelet, a double rasher of bacon, English muffin, and two cups of coffee. He belched loudly as he approached the truck, removing a roll of Tums from his pants pocket, and popping several into his mouth. Better late than never, he thought.

Walking over to the pickup, he removed the handbill from the windshield, unfolded it, and studied its contents carefully. The first words that caught his eye were "Pentecostal" and "speaking in tongues," which is exactly what they'd been designed to do. Immediately, his head swam dizzily, and beads of cold perspiration ran down from his forehead, along his neck, and onto his chest, quickly soaking the front of his shirt. The palms of his hands were sweating, too, and he had to clutch the door handle to keep from falling to the pavement. He climbed inside the cab and collapsed against the back of the bench seat. In seconds, he was transported back to a time in his life that he'd spent over a quarter of a century trying to forget. He was a child again; in fact, he was exactly nine years old...

...It was a Sunday evening in Alabama, just outside Birmingham, and his mother had brought his younger sister and him to "church" to see his father, known simply as Brother Richard, preach for the very first time. It wasn't *really* a church in the truest sense; there were no wooden pews, no steeple—not so much as a bell. In fact, there wasn't even a building. His mother had always told him that his daddy was "special," that he was a Pentecostal preacher; but Billy wasn't quite sure what that meant. He only knew that whatever it was, it wasn't legal—at least that's what his mama said. That was why they always met in crazy places like this, and they were always "a few steps ahead of the law," as his mama liked to put it. "The only place where it's legal for your daddy to do what he does is Jolo, West Virginia, and we ain't hardly goin' there."

The site of tonight's assembly was a clearing, deep in the woods on a mountainside, where Billy's dad had parked a trailer that served as his portable headquarters. There was a wooden stage (at least that's what it looked like to young Bill), with a crowd of mostly college-aged young people and a few older folks gathered around it. Raynette, Billy's mom, held his hand tightly, along with that of his sister, as the three of them waited for their father to begin the service.

"You pay attention," his mother said. "Your daddy don't do this every time, and I expect it's 'bout time you seen it for yourself."

"Don't do *what*, Mama?" asked Billy. He'd always known his father was doing something "different" out in the barn behind their farmhouse, but he'd never been allowed inside to see. Whenever his daddy went out to preach, he'd always carried a wooden box from the barn to his truck before leaving for church.

"Hush, child. Just watch."

Billy was filled with a sense of dread. Whatever it was that his father carried in that box, Billy didn't know, but one thing was certain: it couldn't be good. Why else would they be out there in the dark, in the middle of nowhere? He squeezed his mother's hand tightly, holding his breath, with eyes closed, as he waited quietly for heaven knew what. His sister, too, was silent.

Presently, Billy could hear the sound of his father preaching. There was a good deal of emotion coloring his voice, which grew louder on occasion to emphasize a point, and then lower—almost to a whisper—as if to draw the crowd closer. After a while, there was some singing, followed by the sound of his daddy speaking in some foreign language. Billy guessed this was the "speaking in tongues" part that his mama had told him about. Then a growing restlessness filled the small crowd of worshippers, and Billy opened his eyes just the tiniest bit to see what was causing the disturbance. His father was standing over the wooden box, which had been placed on a folding table. People were whispering to one another, and some were making strange sounds, much like his daddy had been making.

Suddenly, a hush spread over the group of worshippers. Billy opened his eyes all the way and saw his father opening the lid of the box. A soft buzzing sound was coming out of it. It sounded to Billy as if someone were shaking a box of rice; that was the kind of dry, rattling sound it made. He watched, enraptured, as Brother Richard slowly reached his hand down into the box, his eyes staring intently at whatever was inside.

And then, at last, Billy knew what all the fuss was about.

42

Roscoe, NY

It was late. Bobcat sat quietly in his Nissan Pathfinder, across the street from the Roscoe Diner, watching carefully as a steady stream of customers paraded in and out of the restaurant, which remained open 24/7. Most were tourists, hurrying in to use the bathroom or to pick up a container of coffee and a buttered roll to hold them till the next destination on their itinerary. But, a few were locals, mostly ne'er-do-wells, drunks, and drug addicts. It was well past midnight, and Bobcat's tour of duty had officially ended with the change of time to *ante meridian*. He often remained "on the job" beyond his appointed hours, hoping against hope for something to occur that would propel him into the good graces of the mayor and council, and remove the stain from his record.

The container of coffee that sat on his dashboard had long ago lost any trace of warmth, but he continued to sip from it absentmindedly as he maintained his vigil, watching the entrance to the diner through the light drizzle that had been falling continually over the last week. He didn't know exactly what he was looking for, but he felt certain that he'd recognize it when it came along. Somebody killed Billy Stillwater, he thought, and at some point, as sure as God made little green apples that person would undoubtedly occupy a stool or booth in the Roscoe Diner—and Bobcat aimed to be there when he or she did.

A tap on the driver's side window of Bob's SUV startled him, causing him to nearly drop the container of coffee. When he turned in the direction of the sound, he was greeted by the smiling face of Don Brann, the owner of the Grime Be Gone laundromat, who was squatting beside the vehicle, peering through the rain covered window of the Pathfinder. "What's goin' on?" he asked.

"Jesus, Don," barked Walker, rolling down the window. "What's going on is that you could've got yourself shot; that's what."

"Sorry. Didn't mean to startle you."

"Well you damn sure did."

Then, realizing the harshness of his tone, Bobcat grinned sheepishly and apologized. "Sorry, Don. I shouldn't have yelled at you."

"It's okay. My bad."

It was an awkward moment, and Bobcat struggled to think of something else to say. "What are you doing out so late?" he added finally. "Everything okay?"

"Everything's fine," smiled Don. "Ever since that Sabolewski kid got caught, things seem to have calmed down. I was just working on my books and watching a Mets game. I guess the time just kinda got away from me."

"Well, good. That's good—really—I mean about things being okay." More awkwardness. Bobcat wished Don would just go away.

"So...any luck finding out who killed Billy Stillwater?"

"Not yet, Don. But it's only a matter of time. We'll catch him."

"Not *like* Roscoe, you know," said Don. "People getting murdered and all that stuff. Always been a peaceful town."

"Yep."

The conversation was becoming strained. Bobcat decided to end it. "Look, I hate to run, Don," he said. "But I promised the old lady I'd get home as soon as my shift ended."

Walker looked at his watch, and then up at Don. "Shit! I should've been home an hour ago. Sorry, man. Gotta go."

He reached over and turned the key to start the engine, slipped the shift lever into drive, and being sure he was clear of Don, stepped on the accelerator and drove off, leaving the man standing alone in the night. Bobcat hated to lie to people, but he just hadn't felt comfortable talking about a murder case to someone who wasn't in law enforcement. It wasn't good procedure.

As he drove slowly through the streets of the little town, he mulled over the facts of the unsolved homicide case. He had to admit that he didn't envy Matt's situation one bit. Most people in the area were just happy to be rid of Stillwater, and probably secretly wished that his murderer would get away with the crime. It was just like the Mafia, reasoned Bobcat. As long as the Italians killed one another and didn't hurt anyone else, who cared? Nevertheless, he thought, he wouldn't mind helping Matt solve the case. On a whim, he decided to ride over to the crime scene and look around.

The wooden sawhorses blocking the access road to the fishermen's parking area had been removed several weeks ago, as had the crime scene tape surrounding that section of the lot where Billy's truck had been found. Most local residents, aware of the crime, were pretty much staying away, but occasional visitors from out of state, intent upon getting away from the crowds that frequented the more popular pools on the main stem of the Beaverkill, continued to seek the solace that the upper river's waters provided.

Bobcat pulled out the big, four D-cell battery flashlight from his glove box, switched it on and got out of the Pathfinder. He walked down the narrow path that led from the parking area to the water, and then started downstream along the river's shoreline. If there was any evidence at all in the area, chances are it would have washed downstream. The continual rain that had plagued the area since early April had kept the river full, but it hadn't rained for several days, and the water had receded slightly, exposing a bit of the rocky, river bed. As he walked, Bobcat moved the flashlight side to side in a slow, sweeping motion, the bright beam illuminating the landscape almost as well as the natural light of the sun.

About two hundred yards downstream from where he had started, something caught Walker's eye. It was light reflecting off some kind of glass object that appeared to be caught between some rocks and some brush in a back eddy. Each time a small wave of water would hit the object it would jiggle ever so slightly, causing it to reflect the luminescence from the flashlight back at Bob. He stepped into the water, and made his way to the source of the reflection. Being careful not to disturb the water, he stooped down and peered closely at the object that had caught his eye. It was another flashlight, and not too different from the one he was carrying. Actually, it was nearly identical—except for the color. Bobcat's was stainless steel; this one was made of aluminum, with a matte black finish. No doubt it was the cracked glass lens that had reflected the light and caught his attention.

Taking a handkerchief out of his pocket, Bob picked up the flashlight by its end, being careful not to touch the smooth plastic sides that he hoped might contain a fingerprint or two. Perhaps this was the object that had been used to bash Billy Stillwater's head in. He carried the flashlight back to his vehicle, put it into an evidence bag. He'd show it to Matt first thing in the morning. At this point, it was *only* a flashlight, but it might be a clue—and, more importantly, a start down that long road to solving Billy Stillwater's murder.

When he first showed Matt the flashlight, the Chief had immediately logged its description, the time and date of its collection, and Bob's name into the evidence record or, in this case, the "murder book," so there wouldn't be any chain of custody problems.

"You know," said Bob. "If you think back to that wound on the side of Billy Stillwater's head, it's not too hard to imagine that this might just be what they used to hit him. This fucker could really do some damage."

"My guess is that it's been in the water all this time," said Matt. "And if that's true, then it's pretty unlikely that there's any trace of blood left on it that could connect it to Billy—much less to whoever hit him with it."

Bobcat digested what Matt said, but had an idea of his own. "You're probably right about the blood and the fingerprints. But, I'll bet that if we compare the flashlight's shape against the dimensions of the wound on Stillwater's head, it'll tell us whether or not it was the object that the killer used."

"That's a good idea," said Matt. "I'll get Pete Richards to run it over to the forensics lab in Monticello. If it's a match, we'll put it into evidence. Who knows, at least we'll have *something* to confront a possible suspect with."

Around four o'clock, Pete returned with the flashlight and the news; it was a mixed bag, but mostly good. Not only did its shape match the outline of the wound on the deceased's skull, but the lab also discovered a tiny bit of flesh with some hair, trapped in the housing of the on-off switch, which undoubtedly came from Billy's scalp. It would take five-to-seven days to get the DNA results back, so they'd have to wait until then to be absolutely sure. On the downside, there were no usable fingerprints. No big surprise there, thought Bobcat, since anyone determined enough to use Strychnine to kill someone would probably have thought to wear gloves. But, they were still making some headway—thanks to him—and that was encouraging.

43

Walton, NY—less than three days before Billy's murder
Billy was still thinking about that first time, back in Alabama in 1984. The memories were so real that he could reach out and touch them...

...His father, "Brother" Richard, lifted the mature, timber rattlesnake from the wooden box with his right hand, supporting the belly of the serpent with his left, and held it aloft for everyone to see. Billy sucked in his breath, and felt his heartbeat triple its pace inside the small cavity of his little boy's chest. He had never been so terrified—yet fascinated—in all his young life. Part of him wanted to flee; and yet part of him wanted to get closer. All the while, his father moved the snake rhythmically from side to side, displaying the creature as though it were some kind of precious treasure.

"Come on, children," said his mother. "Let's get you two up closer, so's you can get a better look."

Billy's mama began walking toward the front of the assembly, leading her son and daughter gently by their hands. Young Bill followed, stiff-legged, never taking his eyes off his father—and the snake. His sister, on the other hand, ambled forward without fear. In less than a minute, they had reached the stage. His father and the rattlesnake were less than five feet away. The serpent swayed to and fro, its forked tongue flicking the air in a twittering manner that reminded Billy of a small bird flapping its wings in an effort to get airborne. Only this wasn't a bird; it was a deadly rattlesnake, and it frightened Billy to death. Just then, the reptile turned sharply in his father's hands and made a hissing sound in Billy's direction. It was almost as if it were staring with its lifeless eyes directly at the little boy. Billy felt something warm and wet on his leg, and looking down, saw to his horror that he had wet himself.

"Mama," he cried, looking up at his mother. "I want to go home."

Billy's mother looked down at him, and then at the widening stain across the front of his trousers. "Now look what you gone and done. You done wet your pants." His sister turned, stared at him, and then laughed.

Billy closed his eyes and wished with all his might that he were invisible. But, when he opened them again, he realized that his wish had not come true. Instead, he could feel the eyes of his younger sister upon him, as she continued to stare at the widening stain.

"Billy wet his pants," she said, pointing at his crotch and laughing even harder.

Billy wished again that he were invisible—or, better yet, dead. And the more he tried to will himself to be invisible, the harder his sister laughed.

The rest of the evening went by in a blur, but one image was burned forever into Billy's memory. At some point during the service, his sister actually took hold of the snake and paraded around fearlessly with it, pushing it in the direction of those curious enough to come close. And as she did, she would turn and stare at Billy, mocking him, almost as if to say, "See. I'm not afraid like you."

The next morning, when he awoke, Billy remembered the events of the night before, and hoped, perhaps, that the whole thing might have been nothing more than a dream. He breathed a sigh of relief. That was it, he thought, it *was* just a bad dream. But, to his horror, when he entered the kitchen for breakfast, he found that his dream had turned into a full-blown nightmare. Someone had taken a Polaroid picture of the event, and there, fastened to the kitchen wall with a thumbtack, was a photograph of his sister holding the snake. But, what made it even worse was that in the background of the photo, clearly visible, was the image of Billy—with the dark, incriminating stain of shame upon his pants. At that moment, he swore to himself that he'd get even with his sister if it were the last thing he ever did.

By the time Billy was fifteen, his father's relationship with his sister had morphed from one of simple paternal affection to a bizarre bond that was at the very least unnatural—if not downright unholy. In many ways Winona had become her father's supplicant. Often times the two would disappear into the barn, and not emerge for hours, the pretext always being their common affinity for the snakes; something Billy would "never understand," according to his father. Sounds of giggling and muffled chatter would give way to noises more sensual in their character. Once or twice Billy swore he actually heard his father moaning in that certain way usually reserved for those occasions when he would assault their mother while on a drunk.

As if to confirm his suspicions, Winona would openly taunt him upon returning to the house, sticking her tongue out and moving her hands seductively over her immature body in ways that left little to Billy's adolescent imagination. Occasionally, she would even go so far as to rub herself against him, flicking her wet tongue along his neck, testing his resolve to the fullest, while eliciting involuntary erections that only deepened his sense of shame. His father, in marked contrast, would pick up his Bible and immerse himself in its contents, as if doing so provided a valid disclaimer to his actual deeds. But Billy knew better—or at least suspected so. His mother's behavior was an enigma. If she knew—or even suspected—what was happening between her husband and their daughter, she never let on. Instead, she busied herself around the house, occupying her time with an endless array of tasks, consisting mostly of cleaning and more cleaning. To Billy, it was as if she were symbolically cleansing her soul.

But, there was more. His father drank incessantly; and, when he drank, he beat them—not Billy's sister, of course, just Billy and his mother. Afterwards, there would be the "loving," as his father called the making up process. In reality, there was nothing *loving* about it; it was more like passive rape, with his mother as the victim. Billy would lie in bed and listen as his father took out his rage on his mother, who would weep quietly in submission until the ordeal was over. Eventually his father would fall asleep, his snoring so loud that Billy could actually feel the paper-thin walls vibrating. Then came the familiar sound of the shower in the adjacent bathroom, as his mother stood beneath the running water, no doubt attempting to wash away her shame.

The next morning, it would be as if nothing had ever happened. At least that's the way it would appear to a casual observer. But Billy knew it was only a matter of time before something would occur that would change his life for the better; he just didn't know what that "something" would be.

44

Roscoe, NY

The ride back from Black Mountain had given me plenty of time to reflect upon a number of things, not the least of which was Val. Ever since her cancer surgery, she hadn't been herself. Oh, she still joked and kidded with me about things during the day. But now, when it came time for bed, she'd often remain in the bathroom with the door closed for an inordinate amount of time. It was almost as though she were avoiding me. And then, when she finally *did* exit, she'd immediately slide under the covers and turn off the light.

One of the things I'd always enjoyed most in the past was lying next to Val in bed, with our backs to one another and the soles of our feet touching. We'd both read books, the subjects of which were totally divergent, before one or both of us eventually tired and turned out the light. Then, it would be time to make love. But now, it was as if she didn't want me to see her or touch her at all. It was, wham, bam, into bed, lights out, and thank you very much. And I wasn't one bit happy about it.

We hadn't been away from Roscoe together in over six months, not since we'd traveled down to Newburgh to see Chris Freitag, my old partner at the NYPD, get married to Rita Valdez, the detective with whom I'd nearly been killed on my last case. Normally, I hated weddings, but this one had been special, since I was

Chris's best man; and Val and I had a really great time. In fact, it was the last time I could remember seeing Val happy.

The wedding was held on New Year's Eve, in a little Catholic church in New Windsor, just south of Newburgh. The date had been Rita's idea, to ensure that the couple could file their taxes jointly for the entire year. To my surprise, however, it was Chris who chose the wedding site, which was purely in deference to Rita's religious beliefs, since he was not a practicing *anything*, and would have been perfectly content to be married by a justice of the peace.

An American Legion hall hosted the reception, which was a real, down-to-earth affair, featuring a local band that accommodated both partners' preferences in music, including some Latin melodies for Rita and some '70s tunes for Chris—with a little Native American licks thrown in for good measure. Actually, they only played one piece of the latter, a kind of war dance that had Chris whooping and hollering in a mock tribute to his Mohawk Indian ancestry. The rest of the time they alternated between fox trots, rock 'n' roll, and Cha Chas. We danced and drank well into the New Year, before retiring to a nearby motel to sleep it off.

The following morning—or, mid-afternoon to be more accurate—the four of us got together for a brunch at one of Chris's favorite diners. But, not before Val and I had given the mattress a good run for its money prior to checking out of the motel. After the meal, there were handshakes, hugs and kisses, a mandatory "let's stay in touch," and then weepy goodbyes, as we all went our separate ways.

Now, as I headed toward home, I decided it was time to rekindle the old fires. We'd take a trip. But, where? What did it matter; I'd let Val choose. The important thing was to get away—and soon.

45

Billy sat in his pickup recalling the day when everything *finally* changed...

...It was 1992, and he was still living in Alabama.

"What do you mean Miss Hattie Godsey died and left you some money and now you got to split?" asked Raynette Stillwater.

Billy's father had just informed her that he was leaving—and taking their daughter with him. Billy could scarcely believe his ears. He'd never heard the name Hattie Godsey before, but apparently she was a member of the church who had died and left the proceeds of an insurance policy to his father. And now his father was going away. It was a miracle, thought Billy. His prayers had finally been answered. Along with Winona, he listened in silence from the living room, as the drama played out in the kitchen for what seemed like an eternity.

"I *know* what you did," he heard his mother say. "You *killed* that woman, didn't you?"

"You don't know nothin'. That woman died of a heart attack."

"Maybe so, but *you* had somethin' to do with it. I can just feel it in my bones."

Winona giggled, and Billy wondered what *she* knew.

"So help me God, Richard, I'll tell the police what you done."

"You won't tell nobody *nothin'*, or you'll never see that child again—and I *mean* it. Besides, who'd ever believe *you* over me? I'm a *preacher*, remember?"

Not a sound came from the kitchen for nearly a minute. Eventually, Billy heard his mother's soft voice.

"Okay, Richard," sighed Raynette. "You win. But I need some of that money—please. There's no way we can make it, Billy and me, without some of that money."

"Relax. I'll give you somethin'. Hell, I'll give you five thousand. And I'll send you a check every month."

That afternoon, Billy watched as Winona helped her father load their belongings into the trailer. Then he helped his dad hitch the ancient aluminum Coleman trailer to the pickup. The last thing to be put in the camper was the heavy glass aquarium containing the snakes. Billy stood back a good distance as his sister and father carefully carried the container from the barn and placed it into the rear of the trailer.

"Where will you go?" asked Raynette, as Richard climbed into the cab of the truck.

"Don't rightly know yet. But, don't worry, we'll be in touch."

Billy's mom squeezed her daughter with all her might and held on desperately before Winona finally pulled away and hopped up next to her daddy on the bench seat of the pickup. Automatically, without realizing what she was doing, Raynette closed the door behind her daughter as she had done countless times before. Only this time, it was final. She gasped as the reality hit home. But, it was too late. Richard threw the truck into gear and hit the gas.

As they watched the truck and trailer disappear into the distance, Billy stood silently alongside his mother, who held a handkerchief to her eyes to absorb the river of tears that flowed for her daughter. She surely wasn't crying for her husband; of that much Billy was certain. Neither he nor his mother would shed a single tear for him. Still, Billy's eyes watered a bit, too, but for a different reason—pure joy. He was glad to finally be free of his father—and the snakes.

A week went by before the first letter arrived. But, it wasn't from Billy's father, and the envelope didn't contain any money. It was a hastily-scrawled note from twelve-year old Winona, bragging childishly about how she and her father had arranged for Miss Hattie's seemingly innocent death. She said it was an easy way to make money, and that she didn't know why they hadn't thought of it sooner. Although Billy didn't know it then, the letter's contents would someday provide him with the means to finally extract his revenge for that awful night when his sister first made him know the meaning of shame.

Over the next couple of months, there were other letters, mostly chit-chatty in nature, but none with a return address to reveal the unlikely couple's location. Billy showed all of the letters to his mother—except the first one. That letter he kept to himself, stored in a secret hiding place.

From the start, Billy vowed to stay with his mother, but theirs was a constant financial struggle. They never, *ever* saw a dime of the five thousand dollars she was promised by her husband, and no checks ever came in the mail. Within a few months, they lost the house and had to move into a tiny apartment. The day Billy turned eighteen, he packed a cardboard suitcase with his few meager belongings and hitchhiked to the nearest Marine recruiting office to enlist. But, before he did, he went to the county courthouse and changed his name to Stillwater, his mother's maiden name. He wanted nothing more to do with his father.

Less than a month later, Raynette Stillwater committed suicide. Billy learned of her death when a high school classmate who had seen the obituary in the local paper, clipped it out, and sent it to him. By the time he received it, it was much too late to do anything but cry quietly at night in his barracks. Years later he would find out that she had hanged herself with a remnant of the dress in which she'd been married, no doubt an expression of her former feelings for her estranged husband.

Now, alone in the cab of his truck, Billy studied the flyer again, only this time he noted the time and place for the advertised prayer service. It was just two days away, on Tuesday at seven in the evening.

What if? Nah. It couldn't be. Or could it?

He decided to go find out for himself.

46

Oakdale, Long Island, NY

Val and I hadn't fished the Connetquot River in probably ten years, and as we crossed over the Throgs Neck Bridge and onto Long Island's Southern State Parkway, towards "The Quot," I thought back to the first time I took her there and introduced her to fly fishing.

When you fish the Connetquot, you don't really fish the whole river, but rather a "beat," or small section of water that's leased to you in four-hour increments for a nominal fee. The river contains numerous varieties of trout, including some sea-run browns, brooks, and rainbows, and because it's spring fed, it's always at an acceptable temperature. The fish are large and numerous (which is why I brought Val there in the first place). The fishery itself is actually part of a much larger recreation area formally known as the Connetquot River State Preserve, and it encompasses over 3,000 acres of land, which includes fifty miles of hiking, horseback riding, cross-country ski, and nature trails. Rumor has it that the entire preserve was once a private club, open selectively to Wall Street types at the turn of the century; when times got tough during The Great Depression, the state took it over for taxes. Whether the story is true or not is open to debate, but it lends itself nicely to a certain sense of blue collar satisfaction based no doubt upon class envy.

As far as the fishing that day was concerned, it had been a modest success; I managed to catch and release a half-dozen trout, while Val caught two. But what I remembered most about it was Val's courage. She was a city kid who'd never heard the word "fly-fishing" until she met me. But, she was a trooper, and there she was, waist deep in the water, encapsulated in bulky nylon waders, struggling mightily to learn how to false cast, mend line, and master all the other techniques that went with the sport. It cemented our relationship, and we'd married shortly thereafter.

Now, here we were, together again, headed for that very same spot—but, for a very different purpose. Instead of testing Val's courage on the river, we were attempting to mitigate the stress and strain that accompanied her battle with breast cancer by recapturing those carefree days when we first met. When we originally came here it was part of a single-day, round-trip marathon that ended late at night with each of us desperately struggling to keep our eyes open until our arrival home.

This time, we were older—and wiser—and had rented a room in a motel belonging to a nationally-known chain. Whatever fishing we did during this excursion would merely serve as a preliminary to the subtly disguised main event I had planned, which I hoped would take place after dark.

We arrived at the motel around noon, just in time to check in, grab a burger, and arrive at the river for our two o'clock reservation. I parked the Jeep in the gravel lot, and we quickly donned our waders, pulled on our vests, and assembled our outfits.

"Hang on," I said. "I want to take your picture."

"Oh, Matt, don't. You know how I hate having my picture taken."

"No picture, no fishy," I laughed. "Besides, I need this for evidence. None of the guys ever believe me when I tell them you fly fish. They think all we *ever* do is have sex."

"Well?"

"Oh, I just let them think whatever they want. *I* know the *truth*."

"Oh, you bastard!"

"Now, smile for the camera," I commanded.

Val struck several comic, pseudo-seductive poses while I snapped away with my outdated Konica 35-mm SLR camera. I still hadn't made the move to digital, but sooner or later I'd have no choice. I still remembered the shock I felt last June when I read that Eastman Kodak was ending production of Kodachrome, long considered the Cadillac of print film, but now just a dinosaur in the modern world of photography. It was only a matter of time before there'd be no film at all. I took a few more traditional shots of Val and stashed the camera in the waterproof bag I always carried in the back of my vest when I went fishing. One of these days I might catch a real trophy, and I wanted to be prepared. Although, truth be told, I'd never taken a single picture of *any* of the fish I'd caught. Maybe this time would be different.

The scar from Val's surgery had healed nicely, but I was concerned that the effort of false casting, again and again, might cause her some discomfort, especially in light of her ongoing radiation treatments.

"Honey," I suggested, as we approached our section of the river, "why don't we just fish nymphs, today. That way you won't have to cast too much."

Val frowned, and I realized immediately that I had just negated the whole purpose of the trip—to forget about the cancer for a day or two. The tumor had been in her right breast, adjacent to her casting arm. I just wanted to protect her.

"Sorry, sweetheart. My bad. Do whatever you're comfortable with."

The kick is up; it's headed toward the goal posts, and it looks good. No, wait, it's wide left. I'd blown it again.

"I think I'll start with a Prince," I said, extracting one of the nymphs tied with a Peacock herl body and two white, goose biots along its top. I kept the flies in a special "no lead" fly box that I kept for the Connetquot and places like it that prohibited the used of lead weight in the flies used in their waters. All the nymphs I tied for the "Quott" had Tungsten bead heads to supply the weight required to get them down into the trout's feeding zone. As with everything associated with fly fishing, the beads were priced as though they were made of platinum, and I always tied the flies on carefully with an improved clinch knot. For some reason, the goose biots were particularly attractive to brook trout, although no one really knew why.

Out of the corner of my eye, I watched as Val tossed some free line onto the water, and then made a roll cast, landing her fly forward into a feeding lane between two large rocks. A hooded merganser duck treading water above us was also watching, and while I knew the species were fish eaters that wouldn't hesitate to scoop up a trout, I still enjoyed seeing the beautiful, red-headed females whenever I was fortunate enough to spot one.

"Nice roll cast, sweetie. What've you got on?"

"Wouldn't *you* like to know," said Val with a smile. "I'll tell you *after* I've caught my first fish."

"Well, *duh*, that's no fun. Okay, how about first one catches a fish gets to decide where we eat?"

Val knew exactly where I was headed with my challenge. The last time we had come here, we had eaten in a restaurant recommended by a fellow officer, which had turned out to be a dump (I should have considered the source). We'd both suffered upset stomachs afterward and had vowed to avoid the place at all costs.

"You're on," she answered. "And no cheating."

"And *no* coffee for you after dinner," I added. "That's *no* coffee, *no* caffeine, no matter what. I don't want you keeping me up all night. "

"Actually, that's kind of what I had in mind," giggled Val.

"Oh, *really?*"

"Well, yeah...I thought maybe we'd have a couple of frozen Margaritas and then we'd...well...you know..." Val's face turned crimson red at the thought of her private desires. At that moment I loved her more than life itself.

It had been quite a while for both of us, and just the thought of making love to her had me excited already. I'd have just as soon skipped the fishing and gone back to the motel, but there needed to be an order to things, so I refocused my attention to the task at hand.

"Good luck," said Val.

"I guess that all depends on what we're talking about, doesn't it."

Val smirked and stuck out her tongue. "You're such an asshole!"

"Watch it, lady. I'll call a cop."

"Big deal," scoffed Val.

"You'd better hope it is."

We still had nearly an hour of our allotted time remaining, but I could see that Val was beginning to tire. Even though she had restricted herself to the less strenuous roll casting, a paleness in her face showed me that she'd probably had her fill for the day.

"What do you say, Joan Wulff, had enough?"

"I should be asking *you* that question, don't you think?"

"*No mas, no mas,*" I joked. "Besides, I could really use one of those Margaritas."

Val had not only caught the *first* fish, a three-pounds-plus, sea-run brookie; but had also caught the most—six in all! I, on the other hand, had only managed to land two average-sized rainbows—neither of which jumped.

"I'll race you to the car!" shouted Val, already out of the water and staggering down the road in her waders.

I'd showered, and was just about dressed when Val summoned me to the bathroom. "Look, Matt. You can hardly see the scar."

Stepping into the bathroom, I looked her straight in the face and said, "What scar?"

We both laughed. She knew I was referring to a line from a scene in one of our favorite old Paul Newman movies, "Cool Hand Luke." In it, a fellow inmate inquires about a rather obvious scar on Luke's abdomen, asking innocently, "Hey Luke, where'd you get that scar?" Luke's response was the one that I had just repeated.

I stepped closer and cupped Val's right breast gently in the palm of my hand, inspecting the half circle of scar tissue that followed the gentle curve above and to the right of her nipple. Val was right; whereas previously the scar had been a bright, angry red, now it was more of a dark pink, and not nearly as tough in texture. I bent my lips to her breast and kissed the flesh softly, letting my lips drag across the tip of her now erect nipple. Val shivered, and almost immediately a field of goose bumps erupted across her breast.

"What do you say we get that dinner out of the way?" I whispered in her ear.

This time, her entire body responded.

"What dinner?" she sighed.

I pulled her to me and kissed her hard on the lips. Then, I slapped her on the ass. "Come on, hurry up and get dressed. I'm starved."

The restaurant Val had chosen was right on Nicoll Bay, where the Connetquot empties its spring fed waters into the salty brine of the Atlantic. We sat at an outdoor table, swilled our frozen cocktails and slurped down clams on the half shell, as sea gulls squawked noisily above us. After a delightful dinner of trout Meniere, scalloped potatoes, and an endive salad accompanied by a crisp Riesling, we headed back to the motel, eschewing a restaurant dessert for one more suited to the occasion. It was time to put the finishing touches on what had surely been the best day we'd shared in the last six months.

Later, as we lay silently next to one another in bed, savoring the results of our love making, each of us lost in our private thoughts, I placed my hand on Val's stomach and let it slide slowly up and over her rib cage to her surgically altered right breast. Using just my fingertips, I carefully massaged the scar that encompassed the lower right half of the aureole. I raised myself up and looked down at her beautiful face, marveling at the fineness of her cheek bones, the gentle curve of her nose, and the depth of color in her eyes.

"I love you, Val," I said, before engulfing her lips in mine with a kiss that physically imparted all that I felt in my heart and soul.

"I love you, too, Matt," she whispered.

In a moment, all that filled the space between us was the soft breathing of one and the ragged snoring of the other.

When we awoke, bright sunshine was streaming into the room between the narrow spaces on either side of the room-darkening drapes that seem to come as standard issue in every motel room in the universe. We showered and dressed quickly, packing our overnight bags in silence. It wasn't that we didn't have anything to say; it was more like neither of us wanted to be the first to disturb the magic of the night before. And that was fine.

Val popped in a Sinatra CD into the player on the dashboard of the Jeep, and we headed for home. As I drove steadily down the highway, my heart was alive again, and all the horror of the preceding months had been replaced by a feeling of optimism. That's funny, I thought. I didn't remember any duets on the album. Then I smiled. It was Val, singing along with Frank. She was actually singing—and she was happy.

I thought of George Bush on the deck of that aircraft carrier, with the now infamous sign hanging above him that read: "Mission Accomplished!" That sign might not have been quite appropriate then, but for me it expressed exactly what I was feeling at the moment.

A few minutes later, the first drops of rain struck the windshield.

47

Treadwell, NY—five hours before Billy's murder

Billy didn't want to arrive at the service *too* early, since he planned to lose himself in whatever crowd there might be to better observe without being observed. So, when he pulled his pickup onto the grassy parking area between the house and the barn, it was already seven-thirty. As he exited the truck and made his way toward the freshly-painted "church," he could hear singing coming from within—and it was quite inspired by the sound of it. Good, he thought. No one would notice him slip into the rear of the building.

The first thing Billy observed was that the man conducting the service was *not* his father. Of course that didn't mean his father wasn't still alive; he just wasn't at this place. *Hell, he could be anywhere.* But, still, Billy was a bit disappointed. It would have been nice to confront the old bastard after all these years; maybe kick his ass around a bit. He'd probably be about sixty, if not older, and surely in no condition to offer any resistance (much like Billy had been when he used absorb his father's beatings). No, thought Billy, it'd be fun to knock the old man around a little—settle a few old scores; maybe he wasn't in such hot shape, but he knew enough from his special forces training to teach his father a lesson or two.

The second thing Billy noticed was that the woman assisting the preacher bore a striking resemblance to his own mother. Sure, she was a lot younger than his mom; but the bone structure of her face was remarkably similar, and her hair was the same dark, chestnut color he remembered so well. The woman singing loudly alongside the preacher was none other than his long lost sister. She was older and definitely prettier now—and apparently a lot better off than he was—but there was no doubt about it; it was her. It was Winona.

Billy could scarcely contain his emotions, which were many and diverse. He was somewhat satisfied to have finally located his only living flesh and blood, yet mildly angry at the shameful childhood memories her presence evoked. Those feelings were just as valid and powerful today as they were then. But there was a third emotion at work. It was envy. And, envy was an awesome motivator. Here he was a drug dealer *and* user, broke and struggling; and there she was with her preacher man, the two of them doing just fine. Nice, white house; nice barn; probably lots of money— compared to him.

The way Winona looked at the preacher, there was no doubt that he was her "main squeeze." He was good looking, seemed to be a polished performer, and sported some pretty expensive clothes. Amidst Billy's confused emotions there now arose an overpowering thought. It pulsed and vibrated with its intensity. But this wasn't a time for jealousy, he thought. Jealousy was for losers. Instead of being a time for envy, this just might be the opportunity of a lifetime. If he played his cards right, he could not only take his revenge and bring the whole world crashing down around his little sister, but at the same time he could bolster his sagging resources.

After all, he still had "the letter."

48

Nancy stuck her head inside my office.

"I dropped off that proposal for the auxiliary program to the mayor this morning," she announced. "But, I wouldn't hold my breath if I were you."

"I won't," I said. "Actually, I'd kind of forgotten about it. But thanks for reminding me. At least we don't have to worry about the laundromat for a while. Who knows, maybe things will finally settle down to where we won't need the extra help after all."

"In your dreams," said Nancy with a laugh.

"Yeah, you're probably right. Hey, that reminds me. I dreamed about you last night."

"Oh you did, did you?"

Nancy, wet her index finger and dragged it along her eyebrow, which was arched provocatively high.

"Well, not exactly. I mean, the dream wasn't about you...but you were *in* it...sort of. You know how dreams are. They're almost always kind of jumbled, with details you can hardly remember."

"I wouldn't know. I've never had *one* worth remembering. Most of *mine* are about tall, handsome men—who *always* have wives."

"Well, maybe you shouldn't watch so much late night television before you go to bed."

"And maybe *you* should mind your own business."

I knew this conversation was going nowhere, so I punted. "Okay, okay. Point taken. My bad."

"So?"

"So what?"

"So, are you going to tell me about your dream or not?"

"Oh, it wasn't much of a dream."

"Then why'd you mention it?"

Why *had* I mentioned it? I wasn't sure.

"Well?" Nancy wasn't giving up.

"Okay, okay. Here it is. I'm sitting at my desk, leaning back in my chair with my feet up like this..." I leaned back and put my feet on top of my desk. "...and you come in with this enormous stack of papers and you plop them right down in front of me. I ask you what they are and you say they're forms from the county that I have to fill out and sign."

"Sounds okay so far," said Nancy with a broad smile across her face.

"But when I look at the first piece of paper it's all gobbledygook. And the next one is just like it, and so are all the others."

"Still making perfect sense to me."

"And you keep bringing in more stacks of paper and piling them up on my desk. And pretty soon, the top of my desk is filled up with papers."

"Uh huh. So what happens next?"

"Nothing."

"Nothing?"

"Yeah. My alarm goes off and I wake up."

Nancy frowned. "That's it?"

"Uh huh."

"Boy, you weren't kidding when you said it wasn't much of a dream."

"I told you so."

"Well, let me know when you have one that's worth hearing about."

"I'll do that," I answered, as I started walking toward my office.

"Oh, I almost forgot," said Nancy. "Something came for you this morning."

She left my office, and returned a minute later with an 8 ½" x 11" manila envelope with the familiar return address of the forensics lab in the upper left hand corner. A look of anticipation covered her face as she handed it to me and then stood there waiting for me to open it. I purposefully took my time turning the envelope over and over in my hands and examining its exterior carefully; as if by doing so I might glean some secret information it contained without opening it.

"Well? Are you going to open it or not?"

"Letter opener," I said, looking in Nancy's direction.

I put out my right hand as though I were a surgeon awaiting a fine, stainless steel instrument. Nancy took my cue and slapped the pearl-handled opener firmly into my waiting palm.

"Opener!" she shouted dramatically.

I inserted the blade carefully into the top of the envelope, then lifted it with a quick snap, tearing it cleanly. Holding it to my lips, I blew into it, forcing the sides apart, and removed its contents with my free hand.

"Looks like a lab report," I said dryly.

"And?"

"Well, let's see."

I held the report close enough to preclude Nancy from reading it, and let my eyes wander down the page. It stated quite simply that the DNA from the flesh and hair recovered from the switch housing of the flashlight that Bobcat had found was a perfect match to that of the deceased, Billy Stillwater.

"Excellent," I whispered.

"*What's* excellent?" asked Nancy, a touch of impatience in her voice.

"This report," I answered.

"Well I *know* it's a report. What does it say?"

"It says we've got the blunt instrument that put that crease in Billy Stillwater's skull. The skin sample matches perfectly."

"Now that *is* excellent," said Nancy. "So what are you going to do with that little tidbit?"

"Nothing...for now. But I'm sure it'll come in handy."

Just then, Pete Richards burst through the door to my office waving a piece of yellow paper in his hand. I was still enjoying the memory of the delightful weekend that Val and I had spent on Long Island, and wasn't prepared for what he had to say.

"Check this out. I was over in Delhi, picking up a new battery for my outboard, and when I came out of the Napa store, this was stuck under my windshield." He handed me the sheet of paper. "It's an advertisement for a Pentecostal church—the Devoted Church of Jesus with

Signs Following. But what *really* caught my eye was the reference to Mark 16: Verse 18."

I scanned the flyer, and sure enough, there was also a mention of "speaking in tongues." Further inspection revealed a place, date and time for the church's next meeting—and the pastor's name: Ron Trentweiler. Why did that name ring a bell? I wracked my brain trying to recall where I'd seen it before. Then it hit me. Trentweiler was the name of the preacher associated with the church I'd visited in Centralia that had been named beneficiary of the contested life insurance policy. Providence was shining its little light upon me just when I needed its illumination the most. The advertised church service was in Treadwell, at seven o'clock that Wednesday evening, just two days away. Maybe, at last, we had the break we needed.

I turned to Pete. "What are you doing Wednesday night?"

"Wednesday?"

"Yeah."

"Nothing I can think of. Janet's got a volunteer meeting at the fly fishing center, but I'm not doing anything. Why? What's up?"

"This flyer says there's a meeting scheduled for this Wednesday night, over in Treadwell. Want to take a ride? Do a little snooping around this church?"

"Absolutely."

"Good. Rick's on four-to-twelve, so we're covered here. I'll pick you up around six-fifteen."

I could scarcely wait.

49

Treadwell, NY—less than four hours before Billy's murder
Toward the end of the service, many of the older church members—including some of the women—took turns briefly handling the venomous snakes. They clogged to the rhythm of the guitar and banjo music, oblivious to the dangerous reptiles that lay in their hands. For their part, the snakes appeared oblivious to the hopping and wiggling of those that held them. One of the younger women appeared to slip into a trance, and threw herself down on the floor, shouting gibberish into the air and flopping around on her back like a fish out of water. The preacher, meanwhile, made a big show out of wrapping one of the serpents about his shoulders, and placing the snake's head less than a foot from his own. Billy had never seen anything like it—not since that day so very long ago. Although the sight of the snakes no longer threatened to weaken his bladder, it still made his flesh crawl, and he found the whole endeavor revolting to watch.

Winona, dressed in a simple but elegant, dark gray suit and lilac-colored blouse, just stood by watching—that is until the reptiles were returned safely to their case. Then, she immediately went into a frenzy of activity, moving rapidly among the worshippers, using a straw basket to collect donations from each one. Billy sat in the rear of the building with his hands clenched tightly in his lap, watching in amazement as his little sister raked in the contributions.

When the service concluded, he stayed in the back of the makeshift church and waited until all the worshippers had departed and the last vehicle had left the parking area. Satisfied that he was the only one remaining, he got up and began walking slowly toward the front where the preacher and his sister were busy straightening up. It wasn't until Billy had gotten within ten feet of the pair that Winona first noticed his presence.

"Can I help you, friend?" she inquired.

"That depends," replied Billy.

Winona's eyes narrowed suspiciously.

"I guess you don't remember me, huh?"

Winona studied the unkempt thirty-five-year old man standing before her, dressed in wrinkled jeans and a blue work shirt. "No, I'm afraid I don't. Should I?" It was clear to Billy that there was no sign of recognition in her eyes.

"Think hard," he said. "Think Alabama."

By now, the preacher had taken notice of Billy, and walked over and extended his hand. "I'm Brother Ron."

Billy took the preacher's hand in his own, shaking it firmly. "Billy Stillwater. Pleased to meet you."

Brother Ron turned to Winona. "Do you know this man, honey?"

Winona shook her head.

"Well, it *has* been a long time since we've seen each other," said Billy.

Winona squinted her eyes. Nothing.

"How's Dad?" he finally asked.

Immediately he detected a flicker of recognition in his sister's eyes.

"Is he still alive?"

"What's he talking about?" asked Ron. "Who is this man?"

"Tell him, Winona."

"He...well...he's...uh...my brother."

"Yeah, that's it," said Billy. "I'm her brother."

The preacher appeared shocked. "You never said *anything* about a brother. Is that true? Is he *really* your brother?"

Winona stood silent.

"Sure I am," said Billy. "But why *would* she mention me? She never wanted anything to do with me when we were kids, right, Winona? Did you tell your preacher friend about you and our Dad? I bet he doesn't know about *that*."

Winona sprang into action.

"Billy," she said, grabbing his arm. "Why don't you and I go outside and talk in private?"

Ron stood quietly by, apparently too perplexed to say anything.

Winona walked slowly toward the exit at the front of the church, pulling her brother with her. Billy glanced back at Ron, then at Winona, before following her out the door.

It was raining when they stepped outside, and Billy motioned Winona to his truck. Once the two were inside the vehicle, Billy wasted no time in getting to the point.

Did Winona's boyfriend know about her past? Did he know that she and her father were responsible for the death of Miss Hattie—*and* who knew how many others? He wanted money—ten thousand dollars to be precise— or he'd show Brother Ron the letter and put a stop to Winona's gravy train.

"What makes you think I have that kind of money?" asked Winona.

"Are you kidding? I might not be the brightest bulb in the package, but it doesn't take a genius to see that you and your boyfriend got a pretty good thing going for yourselves. And you know what? I don't really give a shit. I just want the money, and I want it tonight."

"Okay, okay. But how am I going to explain you to Ron? I told him I didn't have any family—and he believed me. Now he's going to start asking questions."

"That's *your* problem. Tell him anything you want. Tell him I'm your long, lost cousin. Hell, better yet, tell him I'm an old boyfriend. Yeah, that's it. Tell him you and I used to go together, and you owe me money from when we broke up."

Winona appeared to be considering Billy's suggestion.

"Hey," said Billy, "whatever happened to the old man? Is the son of a bitch still alive?"

"Daddy died about four years ago."

"Oh he did, huh?"

Winona nodded her head.

"Well, good. I hope the old bastard rots in Hell. How'd he die anyway?"

"Snake bit him."

Twice Bitten: A Matt Davis Mystery

"No shit?"

"No shit. But it was really his heart that did him in. He'd been bitten before, but this time his heart couldn't take it."

"Serves him right. Fuck him and the horse he rode in on."

Winona didn't say a word.

"Hey! What about life insurance? Did he have any kind of policy?"

Winona shook her head.

"Yeah. My ass. I'll bet he left you fixed just fine. Well, you just get me that money or I'll tell old Brother Robert, or whatever his name is, more than he'll ever want to know about his innocent, little sweetheart."

Billy gave Winona directions where to meet him later that evening, shoved her out the passenger-side door, and drove off into the night, leaving her standing in the rain.

50

I'd never been to Treadwell, but I'd seen signs for it when I'd traveled to Delhi to fish the West Branch of the Delaware where it ran alongside Route 10, outside Delancey. The water there contains a nice mixture of native browns and the occasional smallmouth bass. It's also easy to wade; it's a place I feel comfortable fishing alone. But, we were on a different kind of fishing expedition, and I scarcely noticed the water as Pete and I drove through what passed for the town of Hamden (lots of good pocket water), and rolled into Delhi, the Delaware County seat.

The flyer said the church was on Crowter Lane, off Case Hill Road. To get there, we had to make a left in town onto County Road 14, which connected Delhi to Route 357, a main thoroughfare leading to the Susquehanna River. Treadwell is more an "area," rather than a town. There's a general store and an elementary school across from a cemetery where Tupper Hill Road meets Case Hill Road, but no real "town." It's a place populated largely by "natives," who are fiercely loyal to their heritage and their way of life, which is dairy farming.

Lately, a few "city types" have bought tracts of land from the locals and built edifices more fitting to the title holders' financial status than to their surroundings. Thankfully, they are still a minority, although the modest influx of population *has* brought a disproportionate share of taxes to a region sorely in need of it, and even engendered a few businesses to spring up in support of the land owners' semi-nomadic lifestyle. Most of these newer homes are occupied less than a month or two out of every year.

The sun was still fairly high in the summer sky as we turned up Crowter Lane and bounced along the deeply rutted, dirt road toward the church, which, according to the directions, was situated on a dead end. There were open fields filled with colorful dairy cows all along the route, the property lines marked by electric fences. Each tract of land was serviced by a small, cookie-cutter farmhouse with a silo and compulsory henhouse, and occasionally, a chicken would dart across the road, reminding us to keep our speed to a minimum or face the consequences.

Just as I was growing impatient, I heard the faint sound of singing in the distance, and spotted a farmhouse ahead of us at the end of the road. Vehicles were strewn in every direction, but the concentration of pickups and cars were located on the grass between the modest, white building and a barn to its rear. I guessed that was where the service was being held.

I pulled the Jeep alongside a restored, black, 1950 Studebaker, shut off the engine and threw the transmission into park.

"Now, remember," I said to Pete. "Let me do all the talking. I'm mostly interested in finding out where these folks are from and whether or not they drink Strychnine."

Pete removed his Carhartt baseball hat, and I my plain, navy one, as we entered the barn. We'd both dressed casually in jeans and tee shirts in order to be as unobtrusive as possible, and it seemed from the looks of those inside the barn that we'd made the proper choice. Most of the occupants were older men dressed in dark suits, accompanied by women in plain, country dresses. But there was a small contingent of what I assumed were college students, both male and female, hanging out in the rear, and their apparel more closely mimicked ours. We smiled and nodded politely to a few, and made our way to a couple of empty seats in the very last row where we could observe without being noticed. Almost at the same time we took our seats, the singing came to a halt, and a practiced male voice shouted, "Amen! Amen! Amen!" It belonged to the preacher.

Billy Graham in his prime had nothing on this guy. He appeared to be about thirty, with brown hair worn stylishly long. He was dressed immaculately in a dark blue, pin-striped suit, the razor-creased trousers supported by a pair of bright red suspenders that matched his tie. On his lapel was a freshly-cut, red carnation, and gold cuff links adorned the French cuffs of his powder blue dress shirt. His shoes were traditional, black wingtips, polished to a dazzling shine. Next to him, seated on a folding chair was a woman in her early thirties, perhaps, with dark brown hair worn in a single braid. She was dressed in a simple, burgundy-colored shift and a pair of brown sandals.

It never ceased to amaze me how poor, hardworking farmers, coal miners, and other manual laborers held these "carny" types in such high esteem. Week after week, when searching for early morning fishing shows, I marveled at the professional preachers that dominated the television airwaves. And each one had a unique gimmick. There was one who cried as he played an assortment of honkytonk sounding hymns on a fifty-thousand-dollars-plus Steinway piano, and another who broadcast from a gigantic cathedral made entirely of glass.

"Brothers and sisters, I'm happy to see so many of you here tonight. I can feel the power of the Holy Ghost in our presence."

Amens and Hallelujahs echoed throughout the audience.

"It's not every evening we feel His presence, but when we do we are challenged. We are challenged in a way that few can understand, for there is another spirit that moves among us..."

Boos and hisses came from members of the congregation at the intimation of the Devil.

"...another spirit that taunts us and tempts us," continued the preacher. "It is not a *Holy* Spirit, but a demon cast in God's image who chose to challenge the righteous power of the Almighty, and was cast into the outer darkness. His name is Beelzebub!"

More booing and catcalling.

"Call him Beelzebub; call him Satan; call him the Devil. It matters not what name he's known by, for he comes in many guises and what we call him is not important."

I looked over at Pete and he rolled his eyes. I shook my head sharply, side to side, to indicate "don't do that," and he stopped. My sentiments were the same, but I dared not give voice to them. Not here. Not now.

The preacher continued. "If we let him, the Devil will try to steal our peace. We need to be vigilant and stout of heart. We must resist him with all our soul. As it says in I Peter 5:8,9, *'Be sober, be vigilant; because your adversary the devil, as a roaring lion, walketh about, seeking whom he may devour: whom resist steadfast in the faith, knowing that the same afflictions are accomplished in your brethren that are in the world.'*"

He was really rolling now, and continued on spouting Scripture for the next fifteen minutes or so, interrupted only occasionally when a member of the congregation felt so moved that he or she needed to stand and shout or cry out in genuine anguish. At any given moment, a half dozen or more worshippers waved their arms in the air, seemingly possessed by an unseen force.

Gradually, the tenor of the preacher's sermon softened, until at last he was back where he started—talking about the Holy Ghost.

"So, tonight, with the spirit of the Holy Ghost moving amongst us, enveloping us in His power, I believe it is time to see who amongst us can give himself completely to that which no man can understand, and no man can control. Are you with me, brothers and sisters?"

"Yes, Brother Ron, we're with you!" shouted an old man in front of me.

"His will be done!" cried another.

An assortment of amens, hallelujahs, and other intonations filled the hall.

Brother Ron held his hands up, palms facing the worshippers, and spoke in a slow, clear voice. "And it says in Mark 16, Verse 18, '*And these signs shall follow them that believe; In my name shall they cast out devils; they shall speak with new tongues; They shall take up serpents; and if they drink any deadly thing, it shall not hurt them; they shall lay hands on the sick, and they shall recover.*'"

Oh, shit, I thought, here it comes.

The woman who had been sitting on the little platform that served as a sort of altar, but who hadn't uttered as much as a syllable this entire time, stood up and walked swiftly to a door behind the preacher, disappearing from sight. When she returned she was carrying a glass case; in the case were about a half dozen snakes. There were several rattlesnakes, and the remainder were copperheads. Immediately, cold beads of perspiration dripped from beneath my armpits, my forehead grew clammy, and my stomach got that old queasy feeling I always get when in the presence of any kind of reptile.

Out of the corner of my eye I could see that Pete, unlike me, was totally unaffected; in fact, he seemed to be leaning forward in his seat in order to get a better look. The snakes seemed oblivious to one another. The rattlesnakes sat calmly, their bodies draped in loose coils, their tongues vibrating rapidly in an effort to capture any available scent in the air. By contrast, the copperheads were more active, slithering slowly around the inside perimeter of the case with their gold and brown bodies pressed against the glass, seemingly avoiding contact with the other reptiles. All of the serpents had one thing in common: dead eyes. Their cold, unseeing, yellow eyes seemed focused somewhere out in space as if seeking a command from an alien force or being—perhaps the Holy Ghost Himself.

Three elderly gentleman, their white shirts tucked neatly into their trousers, came forward out of the first row and lined up facing the preacher. Immediately two members with guitars stood up and began strumming on their instruments. They didn't exactly play a melody, but instead struck a series of chords that sounded almost like a disjointed instrumental version of an American Indian war chant. A third man joined in on a banjo, and pretty soon the entire congregation was on its feet, hopping and stomping, and twirling about with their arms waving in the air, while several women banged tambourines against the heels of their hands. The effect was almost hypnotic.

I looked over at Pete and got the shock of my life. My newest deputy was tapping his foot and swaying from side to side in time with the primitive music, his face nearly as red as his hair.

"Pete," I whispered. "What're you doing?"

He turned toward me and winked. "Just getting in the spirit," he whispered back. "Just trying to blend in."

Relieved, I decided to join in, too, and began doing my own version of the "green apple quickstep." Pete was right; we didn't want to be *too* conspicuous.

Suddenly, the music stopped and all attention was focused on the preacher and his assistant. She had removed the lid from the glass case containing the snakes, and was holding it out to Brother Ron. Without hesitation, he carefully reached in and extracted one of the writhing rattlesnakes, allowing it to drape itself comfortably along the expanse of his outstretched arm. One of the older men came forward, and Ron passed the snake to him. This procedure was repeated over and over, until each one of the snakes was being held by a church member. The music ramped up in earnest, and nearly everyone in the church got up and joined in the singing and dancing.

"Do you have The Faith?" asked Brother Ron.

"Praise Jesus!" shouted an old woman.

"Then He will not allow them to harm you!" shouted the preacher.

"Hallelujah! Amen!" shouted several church members.

The rhythmic banging of the tambourines and the repetitive strumming of guitars and banjos continued, while the dancing became more frenzied.

Eventually, the music ceased, and the snakes were returned, one by one, to the glass case. When it was full, Brother Ron's assistant replaced the cover and fastened it tight.

When the service ended, Pete and I waited until all the members of the congregation had left before approaching Brother Ron. He seemed genuinely pleased to see what he probably thought were new members, and greeted us warmly. "Welcome. Welcome. It is a joy to see you among us tonight."

What a line of bullshit, I thought. But, I played along.

"Nice to be here," I said.

Pete nodded his agreement.

"So, are you planning on joining our little church?"

"Well, that's a possibility," I said. "But, we were curious about something."

"Yes? What's that?"

"Well, we were wondering whether you folks drink...well...you know...do you drink—"

"Strychnine?"

"Well...yeah. Do you?"

"Why do you ask?"

"Well, I've been kind of reading up on your type of worship, and one of the things that surprised me was that usually along with handling the snakes, you often drink Strychnine...and...well...nothing happens to you. Is that true?"

The preacher's answer was a bit slow in coming, and I detected just the slightest bit of eye contact between him and his female assistant. Maybe I'd struck a chord.

"Well, it's true, but not quite exactly like you put it," replied Brother Ron. "We only drink it when the Holy Ghost moves us to. His power protects us. Otherwise there's no telling what might happen."

"Interesting," said Pete. He'd joined me at the front of the church, and most of his attention seemed to be focused on the case containing the snakes. "Mind if I take a look?" he asked Brother Ron.

"Not at all. Just don't tap on the glass or anything."

I figured this was as good a time as any to drop a little bombshell. "So, Brother Ron, how long have you and...I'm sorry, I don't know your lady friend's name—"

"I'm sorry," said the preacher. This is my wife, Winona. And I'm Ron, Ron Trentweiler."

After handshakes all around, I got back to business. "How long have you and Winona had your little church here?"

"Oh, I guess since around the middle of April. Why?"

Winona moved closer to the preacher.

"No particular reason. I was just curious. Where were you before?"

"Oh, we've kind of been here and there," replied the woman.

"Ever been in Centralia, Pennsylvania?" I asked. I knew what the answer *should* have been, but I was curious to hear the actual response. If they lied about it, there was a good chance they had something to hide.

As I expected, the question touched a nerve, because Brother Ron looked at his assistant, who narrowed her eyes in response.

"Why? Are you *from* Centralia?" she asked.

"Oh, no, no. It's just that I read a newspaper article not too long ago about a church similar to yours in that town, and I was just curious whether you knew about it."

Brother Ron laughed. "I must have read the same article, I think. Didn't somebody get bit by a snake or something?"

"Sure did," said Pete, who had joined me after getting his fill of snakes. "When I found your flyer under my windshield wiper, I showed it to Matt, and we were both curious as hell to see one of these churches for ourselves. Isn't that right, Matt?"

"Yeah. Yeah. It sure is something. I've never seen anything like it before. Is this kind of thing legal?"

"Absolutely," said Winona.

I'd checked, and with the exception of just a few states—Kentucky, Tennessee, and West Virginia, to name a few—snake handling was borderline legal in most of the United States. Where it wasn't, prosecutions were rare. But it was plain to me that these two would say— and perhaps do—whatever was necessary to maintain their practice. I decided to drop one more bomb.

"Do either of you know a gentleman named Billy Stillwater?"

After a brief hesitation, Brother Ron answered. "Can't say that I do. Should I?"

Winona remained silent.

"No, no," I replied. "Probably not. He was just a Meth dealer who got himself murdered a while back. That's all."

"Well, why on earth would *I* know about *him*?" asked Ron, indignantly.

His response was surprising. He either didn't know Billy at all, or else he was an excellent liar.

"Well, oddly enough," I continued, "he was poisoned with Strychnine."

The preacher seemed genuinely surprised by my answer.

I pulled out my badge and showed it to the couple. "I probably should have told you right up front who we were. Sorry about that. But, we've been investigating his murder ever since—"

"But—" The preacher's face was ashen.

"And since yours is the only church around that uses Strychnine in its service, I thought we ought to at least take a look at your little operation here."

"Well I wish you had told us that right away," said Ron, "instead of acting out this little charade. But, it doesn't really matter, because I really didn't know the man. I swear it. And besides, there are *other* uses for Strychnine—especially here in farm country. In fact, it's probably used for rat poison more than anything else. "

"That's true," I said. "And, believe me, we're just getting started checking that out. But, I must confess that after seeing your flyer, we both really wanted to see what one of your services was like."

The preacher smiled. "Not a problem. Come any time."

"Well," said Pete, "In the meantime, if either of you *hears* anything, give us a call, okay?" He handed his card to the young woman.

"Absolutely," replied Winona.

"Well," I said. "Thank you for your time,"

"Not at all," replied Brother Ron.

It had begun to rain, and its tempo increased on our way back to Roscoe, as Pete and I discussed what had just occurred. We both agreed that something about one of them wasn't quite right, but we differed in our opinion as to which one it was.

51

Treadwell, NY—three hours before Billy's murder

After Billy left, Winona decided it was time to come clean and make Ron aware of just how much was at stake if Billy were allowed to go unchecked.

"He knows everything," she said.

Ron listened in disbelief while she detailed all the events that had led up to her meeting him in the first place, including her relationship with her father and how they'd "arranged" for Miss Hattie to name his church as beneficiary of her insurance policy. He shook his head and cried, "No! No!" as she confessed to planting the snake in Miss Hattie's garden, as well as how she'd used other snakes to kill members in their own congregation at stops along the way to Treadwell. She even told him about the money from the insurance policies—but not the full amounts of their windfalls.

When she finished, she held her breath for Ron's reaction.

"What do you think he'll do?" he asked.

Winona thought she detected a note of desperation in his voice.

"I don't know. I haven't seen him since Dad and I left him and Mom—when I was just a kid. He says he still has the letter I sent him, and he wouldn't hesitate to use it."

"What letter?"

"I wrote him a letter not too long after Dad and I hit the road. I was young and stupid. I wanted to rub his nose in it; to let him know how much smarter we were than Mom and him. I told him about Miss Hattie."

"Then he probably knows about the others, too." It was a question rather than a statement.

"He might," said Winona. "He might not. But, even if he doesn't know, he might suspect. He's no dummy. It wouldn't take long for him to put two and two together."

"But what if we were married?" asked Ron. He let the implication of his words hang in the air.

"So what if we were?"

"Then they couldn't make us testify against one another."

Winona hesitated a second before replying.

"There you go with that marriage stuff again," she said. "Do you really want it that bad?"

"No," said Ron. "Well, *yes*. I mean, it *would* make sense, wouldn't it?—especially now."

Winona considered the idea. He was right after all. If Billy ever spilled the beans, it would be his word against theirs. Just imagine how ludicrous it would sound: A down and out drug dealer's word against the word of a preacher—and especially his wife.

"Let's sleep on it," she said. "I doubt he's going to tell anyone tonight, right?"

"Yeah," replied Ron. "I guess not."

"Good. Then I think I'll take a ride over to Oneonta and take in a movie," said Winona. "I need some time to think about this—*alone*. We need some kind of a plan."

"Don't you want some company?"

"No," said Winona. "I'd rather be alone. You just stay here and get some rest. Tomorrow we'll figure out what we need to do. Okay?"

"I guess," sighed Ron. "If that's what you think we ought to do."

"It is," replied Winona. "And don't wait up. I'll probably grab something to eat when the movie lets out." She grabbed a raincoat from the coat rack and gave Ron a hug. "I better get going."

As she started for the door, he grabbed her by the arm. "Wait a minute. I'll get my jacket and walk you to the truck."

It was raining heavily, and Winona quickly unlocked the door of the red Ford and got inside, cracking the window just wide enough to be able to see Ron's face through the opening.

"Don't worry," she said. "Everything's going to be okay."

"I sure hope so."

"It will be. Trust me."

Ron hurried back inside the church, and Winona headed out into the night—to God only knew where.

52

It had been two days since Pete and I had visited the church in Treadwell. I studied the contents of the white board set up in my office. The latest entries were "Brother Ron" and "Winona." Suddenly, I heard a commotion outside my office. I looked up just in time to see Rick hurry past my door, escorting someone toward the holding cell in the rear. Whoever he had in tow was making quite a racket.

"What've you got, Rick?" I called out.

"I'll be back in a minute," he replied. "I've got to get this guy to the tank."

A few minutes later Rick popped his head inside my door. "Guess who's back from rehab?"

The only person who came to mind was Wayne Sabolewski.

"Is it Wayne?" I asked.

Rick nodded in the affirmative.

You're kidding?"

"Wish I were," replied Rick. "He just got caught trying to break into a customer's car at Carl Peterson's used car lot over on Willow. Somebody left a laptop on the seat, and old Wayne was hoping to steal it, I'm sure. Must be back on the Meth."

"That's too bad," I replied. I was genuinely sorry to hear the news. "So why has he making such a racket?"

"He's afraid of going to county lockup. He claims he's got some information he wants to trade."

"What kind of information?"

"Don't know. He says he only wants to talk to you."

I tried to think of what kind of information a recidivist drug offender would have to offer, but all I could think of was perhaps the name of a dealer. Since Billy Stillwater had been killed, no one seemed to have picked up the slack. But, maybe things were about to change.

"Tell him to cool his heels for a while. I'll talk to him after lunch."

"Not a problem."

After wolfing down the contents of a deluxe cheeseburger platter, I was looking forward to talking to our latest "guest." Before I could make my way back to the holding cell, however, Nancy stopped me in the hall and handed me a folder containing several sheets of paper.

"Harold dropped this off while you were gone."

I took a quick look at the contents, and then did a double take. The mayor's signature was prominently displayed at the bottom of the final page.

"He actually okayed it?"

Nancy smiled one of "those" smiles. "I told you he would. Didn't I?"

She was referring to the paperwork I had submitted to His Honor, requesting authority to initiate an auxiliary police program. Apparently he had signed off on it, which was somewhat of a shock to me.

"I'll be a son of a—"

"Gun?" Nancy finished the sentence for me, using a different word than I had intended. "Well, I guess I'll see about putting an ad in the Shopper."

"You do that. Now, if you'll excuse me," I said with a chuckle, "I'm off to the holding cell to beat some information out of our prisoner."

Wayne looked terrible. He appeared even skinnier than he'd been the night I'd picked him up for breaking into the laundromat. According to Rick, Peterson had caught him red-handed trying to lift the laptop, and he had no qualms about pressing charges. Even if Wayne *was* only stealing to get money to feed himself, he'd still be spending some time behind bars—unless, as Rick indicated, he actually had some worthwhile information to trade for his freedom. And, even then, it was still up to Carl.

I unlocked the door to the holding cell and stepped inside, locking it behind me.

"Welcome back, Wayne. I didn't think I'd see you back here so soon."

The kid was sitting on the metal cot, his head on his chest. He was wearing a ragged pair of jeans and a sweatshirt—probably the same clothes he'd had on when I picked him up that night—and a filthy Mets cap that barely showed a trace of its original orange and blue colors through a thick coating of grime. It was hard to tell whether he was asleep or just avoiding my eyes, so I grabbed him by the shoulders and shook him hard.

"Sit up, buddy. You've got exactly five minutes to convince me that what you've got to say is worth hearing, or I'm going back to my office—and you're going to jail."

That seemed to do the trick, because he instantly started talking, barely able to keep his tongue out of the way of his words.

"I saw something the night Billy got killed," he said. "I *saw* something. I was *there* and I—"

"Okay. Okay. Relax. You say you *saw* something? What *was* it? What did you see?"

I had hoped at least for the name of the latest Meth dealer, but apparently Wayne had something even better in mind.

"That night. The night you picked me up. You asked me where I was when Billy got killed. And I told you I was at the diner until three."

"Yeah?"

"Well, I lied—sort of. I was there for a couple of hours, but the Greek threw me out. I had no place to go, so I thought I'd see if I could find Billy's stash."

"You mean you were there when Billy got killed?"

"I don't know."

"What do you *mean* you don't know? Either you were there when he was killed or you weren't. Which one is it?"

"Well, what I mean is I don't know if it happened *while* I was there, or *after* I left."

"Okay. Wait, wait. Let's start over again. The night Billy was murdered, you were in the parking area. Is that correct?"

"Yeah. I got there just after midnight. Nobody was around, so I went down by the river where I'd seen Billy go when he got me my stuff."

"And then what happened?"

"Well. It was raining, and it was all muddy, so I was having a tough time getting down to the river. All of a sudden I saw headlights and—"

"Was it Billy?"

"Yeah. And I got scared. He's a mean dude, ya know. I didn't want to fuck with him. So I hid behind some bushes."

"And then what?"

"Nothin'. At least not right away. Then, in a few minutes another truck pulled in alongside Billy's."

"Did you get a look at the driver?"

"Are you shittin' me? There's no way I was hangin' around that place. I waited until they turned off the headlights, and then I snuck past the two trucks as fast as I could and started headin' for the road. So you see what I mean, right?"

I shook my head. I had no clue what he meant.

"Well, it *probably* happened then," said Wayne. "But, I don't know for sure. Maybe somebody *else* came along, like *later*. I mean, I didn't actually see him get killed."

"So that's *it?* That's all you've got for me?"

"Well...yeah...but, I mean, doesn't that help?"

"Help what? That doesn't tell me a thing."

"Oh, I forgot. The truck, it was a Ford," said Wayne.

"What color?"

"Red. It was red."

"Well why didn't you say so? That's a little better. Do you know what year it was?"

"Shit. I don't know. Pretty new though, I'd say."

"How about the license plate. Did you get a look at the license plate?"

"Hell no. All I could think about was gettin' the hell out of there—before Billy saw me."

"Okay. Okay. You swear you're telling me the truth?"

"I swear on my mother's grave."

"Pick somebody else's grave," I said. "From what I've heard, your mother was a nice lady."

Wayne couldn't help but crack a smile. "Honest, Chief, I wouldn't make somethin' like that up. I swear."

"And that's it? That's all?"

"Well...by the time I got to the road, I heard the truck coming behind me."

"How much time had elapsed from the time you left the parking area and the time you reached the road?"

"Oh, ten minutes, maybe fifteen—tops. Whoever was driving shouted out the window as they drove by that I should forget all about what I'd seen or they'd find me and kill me."

"Was it a man or a woman?"

"I couldn't tell. Honest. I could hardly hear their voice, what with the rain and all. Besides, I was scared.

I just wanted them to leave so I could get the hell out of there—before Billy came out."

"But he never came out, did he?"

"Nope. I guess not. He got killed."

Wayne hung his head as if he actually had had feelings for his deceased drug supplier. The old Stockholm syndrome.

I took a moment to digest what Wayne had told me. Someone driving a red Ford pickup had met Billy Stillwater in the rest area that night. And that someone had left just fifteen minutes later—probably after killing him. Not too much to go on, other than the make and model of the vehicle—but it was something.

"Okay. Thanks, Wayne. I'll talk to Peterson. Maybe he'll agree to drop the charges. In the meantime, I'll see if Nancy can get you something to eat. Okay?"

"Sure," said Wayne, reassuming the position he'd held when I'd first entered the cell. "I'm sorry I fucked up," he whispered.

"So am I, buddy. So am I."

53

Treadwell, NY—1:30 AM, May 12, 2011

By the time Winona arrived back at the farmhouse, Ron was deep asleep. *Good,* she thought. *At least I won't have to do any explaining. He can think whatever he wants to.* She checked the newspaper for the Oneonta movie theater listings, read the review for *Thor 3D,* which had just opened, and memorized the plot. After making herself a cup of blueberry herbal tea, she slipped into bed alongside Ron, who was snoring heavily, oblivious to anything but his dreams. A minute or so later, Winona, too, was asleep.

In the morning, she found Ron already up, sitting on the sofa in the living room, underlining passages in his Bible in preparation for the next service. She plopped down beside him, and regaled him with the details of the film, and told him that she'd decided what to do about Billy—which was exactly *nothing.* She'd concluded that he really wasn't a threat after all.

"But what about that letter and him threatening to go to the police?" asked Ron.

"He's just bluffing. Even if he does have that letter, he can't *prove* I wrote it. Hell, that was almost twenty years ago. I don't even have the same handwriting anymore. He's always been that way—all bluff and bluster."

Ron sat quietly, almost as if he hadn't heard a word she'd said. He seemed to be lost in thought.

"I had a dream last night," he said softly, after a long pause.

"You *did?*"

"Uh huh."

"What did you dream about?"

"Us."

"Well that's nice. And what about us?"

Ron pursed his lips, apparently searching for the proper words. "I dreamed we were married."

"Well that's no big surprise. We just talked about it yesterday."

"I haven't stopped thinking about it," said Ron. "I really think we should do it. It'd be the best thing if—"

"Okay," said Winona. "You win. We'll do it."

"What?"

"I said, '*Okay.* You win.' When do you want to do it?"

Ron looked at Winona with a suspicious look on his face. "You mean it?"

"Yes, I mean it."

"So, what happened that caused you to change your mind?"

"Nothing," said Winona. "I swear it."

But Ron wasn't buying it for a moment.

"Something happened last night, didn't it?" he asked.

"*No!* I mean, no. What happened was that I went to the movies so I could think about *us*. You know how we women are; we just need time to work things out, that's all."

"And now you think we *should* get married. Are you for real?"

"Yep," said Winona with a smile. "So, what are you going to do now, chicken out?"

"No, no. Not at all. It's just that you took me by surprise, that's all."

Winona cuddled up next to Ron, running her index finger along the outside of his ear, causing him to squirm. "We *could* go over to Cooperstown," she said.

"We could go *today*," replied Ron. "There's a Justice of the Peace right there on Main Street, about six blocks from The Hall of Fame. And we could spend our honeymoon right there—in *The Hall*."

"Oh, you're *such* a romantic," teased Winona.

Ron smiled.

Winona stood up abruptly, and put her hands on her hips. "Wait a minute!" she shouted. "How did you know there's a Justice of the Peace in Cooperstown?"

"You're not the only one around here with a brain, Winona. Trust me. There's a Justice of the Peace right where I said. Now *do* you or *don't* you want to get married?"

"I do."

Ron smiled more broadly this time. "I was hoping you'd say that."

Winona, laughing hysterically. "You are such an asshole, Ron."

"Ah, yes," sighed Ron. "But I'm *your* asshole. And don't *ever* forget that."

Right after lunch, Winona and Ron drove to Cooperstown and obtained a license, and the following afternoon, after satisfying the required twenty-four hour waiting period, they were married in brief a civil ceremony that took place in a quiet, heavily carpeted room that more closely resembled a funeral home than a marriage venue. But Winona couldn't have cared less. They were now husband and wife. But, more importantly, they were immune from testifying against one another. They were safe.

54

Roscoe, NY

Peterson had consented to dropping the charges against Wayne, and I was about to release my "star witness" from the holding cell. But before I let him go, I wanted to make sure I'd know where to find him if I ever needed his testimony.

"Okay, here's the deal, Wayne. I can still bring charges against you for breaking into the car on Peterson's lot—even if *he* doesn't want to—but, I'd rather not. It all depends on you."

Wayne nodded.

"There's something I need you to do. I want you to spend your nights at the homeless shelter over in Livingston Manor, so I can find you if I need you to identify that truck you saw the night Billy was killed. Can you do that?"

Wayne nodded again, and looked at me with that look I'd seen a thousand times on the faces of the paid informants we'd relied upon back in the city. But, this was Roscoe, and people looked at things a little differently. I knew it was a crapshoot letting him loose, but the kid didn't have a record, and I certainly didn't want to give him one—especially for something as petty as trying to steal a laptop to feed himself.

"Well, what do you say? Is it a deal?"

Wayne shrugged his shoulders.

"Okay. Come on. I'll run you over to the shelter."

Wayne looked up at me, his face open and innocent. "Do you really think they meant it? About killing me if I talked?"

My silence spoke volumes.

* * * *

When I returned from Livingston Manor, the only sound I heard as I walked down the hallway at headquarters was that of Nancy typing away in her office. Although she was quite capable of using a computer, and actually did most of her record-keeping on one, she still preferred an old-fashioned Underwood electric typewriter for her letter writing. I'd actually grown quite fond of the sound, and found that it soothed my soul when I heard it.

I went into my office, sat down at my desk, and began studying the white board containing what little evidence we had collected on the Billy Stillwater murder case. After a few minutes, I got up, walked over to the board and added "red Ford pickup" to the slowly growing list of physical evidence. We also had a collection of names related to the case that included Wayne Sabolewski, Donna from Twin Islands, and now Ron and Winona Trentweiler, all under "Persons of Interest." Along with the red Ford pickup, there were: Strychnine, name change, and flashlight with DNA match—but that was pretty much it. Additionally, I had listed several motives, including: jealousy, alcohol or drugs, control of Meth market, revenge, and robbery.

As I stared at the board, something suddenly jumped out at me: the name Winona Trentweiler. If memory served me correctly, wasn't Winona the first name of Billy's sister? I pulled my notepad out of the top drawer of my desk and thumbed through it until I found an entry dating back to when I'd called Jefferson County, Alabama authorities when Billy's body had first been discovered. I was right! There it was. The name of Billy's sister was Winona—Winona Stepp. Some quick calculations told me that the woman I had met recently over at the Devoted Church of Jesus With Signs Following appeared to be just about the same age Billy's sister would be today.

I decided I needed to have another talk with the good reverend and his wife.

"Nancy," I called out. "Do me a favor, will you? Make me a copy of that photograph of Billy Stillwater's face that I took the day his body was found."

"Sure thing, Matt. It'll just take a minute."

There were too many coincidences that were starting to make sense, and I wanted to be absolutely certain I had all the facts before I started assembling the various pieces together into a completed puzzle that I could bring to the DA. Five minutes later, I was headed back to Treadwell, armed with the photograph of Billy and one of the flashlight that Bobcat had found.

The first thing I noticed as I pulled up to the farmhouse was the red Ford pickup parked in the driveway. It appeared to be less than five years old, and that would certainly qualify as a "late model," at least according to Wayne's limited powers of appraisal. Coincidence? I didn't think so, especially when I showed the couple the photograph of Billy. As I had hoped, I got the kind of reaction that gave new meaning to the expression "caught with their pants down." Winona's face lost all its color, and Ron's captured all that hers had given up.

"Okay, so I lied," said Winona. "So shoot me. He's my brother, okay? Or, more correctly, he *was* my brother. I happened to see the article in the paper about him after he was murdered, and I was totally shocked."

"Were you surprised that he was dead?"

"Not really. I always figured he'd come to no good. No, I was more surprised that he was—you know—*here*. I had no idea. I hadn't seen him since I was twelve-years old. Him and my old man left me and my mom high and dry, without so much as a dime or even a letter from either one of them. But, to tell you the truth when I found out he was dead I couldn't have cared less. As far as I was concerned it was good riddance to bad rubbish."

Ron was silent. But, I could tell by the expression on his face that he was probably hearing all of this for the first time. As if reading my mind, he spoke.

"Winona told me he was her ex-boyfriend," said Ron. "*He* said he was her brother, but Winona said 'no.' She said he was lying, and that he was just an old boyfriend who'd loaned her some money."

"So you saw him?"

"Yeah," replied Ron. "But just that once. Come to think of it, I guess it was the same day he was murdered."

"Did *you* kill him?" I asked, matter-of-factly, hoping to catch him off guard.

"No! Of course I didn't kill him." Ron's face had turned ashen.

"You said you'd like to," whispered Winona. "Don't you remember?"

Ron's face blanched. "Wh-a-a-t? What are you talking about?"

I wondered the same thing. What kind of game was she playing?

"Don't you remember?" continued Winona. "When I told you he was my first lover, you said you'd kill him if you ever got the chance."

"That's crazy! You're out of your mind, woman."

I pulled out the picture of the flashlight and showed it the couple. "Do either of you recognize this?"

"Why that looks like your flashlight, Ron," said Winona.

Ron studied the picture.

"Well, doesn't it?" Winona had a strange look on her face; disconnected, cold, and calculating.

Ron shrugged his shoulders.

Winona turned to face me. "It's been missing ever since...well...actually it's been missing ever since that night Billy came around. Isn't that right, Ron? We wondered where it'd gone."

"Where'd you find it?" asked Ron.

"Why don't *you* tell *me?*" I said. "After all, isn't *that* what you used to hit Billy over the head—before you poisoned him?"

"I already told you. I didn't poison anyone. That's just plain ridiculous."

"Can the two of you account for your whereabouts that night?" I asked.

"Of course," replied Ron. "We were right here—the whole evening. Isn't that right, Winona?"

Winona hesitated, then spoke. "Yeah, that's right. Well, *most* of the evening. I went to the movies alone after dinner, but when I left, Ronnie was here alright."

"Yeah. I was here the whole time."

"And he was here when I got home, too," said Winona. "I remember, because we talked about the movie I saw before we went to bed. It was *Thor* in 3D A real piece of crap, if you ask me—even if Natalie Portman *was* in it."

"That's right!" shouted Ron. "See, just like I told you. I was here the whole—"

"Of course," interrupted Winona, "he could have sneaked out *after* we went to sleep. But, I doubt it. I would have felt him leave. At least I think I would. But then again I'm a pretty deep sleeper and—"

"Okay. Okay. That's enough," said Ron. "I don't like the way this is going. Are you accusing me of murdering Winona's boyfriend—or brother—or whatever the hell he was? Are you? Because if you are, I want a lawyer. This has gone far enough."

"Actually," I replied. "*I'm* just doing my job. If you think you need a lawyer, that's up to you. Besides, I don't even have jurisdiction here. So, why don't we all just relax."

That seemed to calm Ron down a bit, because his face had returned to its normal color, and he appeared less tense. "Would anyone like a cup of coffee or something?"

"Actually," I replied. "I've got to be going. But there is one more question I'd like to ask you. Why did you lie to me about Centralia?"

Ron's face immediately turned scarlet. Winona studied her fingernails. Their reaction assured me that it definitely was them and their church that was involved in the insurance investigation I'd read about. But, for some reason they didn't want me to know about it. My guess was that the insurance company probably *did* have good reason to investigate them. But, unfortunately they just couldn't prove anything.

"Anyway," I continued, "If you don't mind, I'd appreciate it if you two didn't leave the area. In fact, I might ask you to come over to Roscoe—just to answer a couple more questions. Think you can you do that? We can even send a car."

"Well, I guess there wouldn't be any harm," said Winona. "Especially if we could help find who it was that killed my brother. Right, Ron?"

Ron hesitated; apparently he was considering his options, and had decided to play hardball. "I don't think so," he replied at last. "At least not without a lawyer present. I'm sorry, Chief, but that's just the way it's got to be."

"Well," I said, heading for the door, "that's your prerogative. But, I meant what I said about not going anywhere. If necessary, I can always get a restraining order. But naturally, I'd prefer that you cooperated. You two have a nice day. I'll be in touch."

The last thing in the world those two were going to have was a nice day—not if I had anything to do with it. On the way back to my Jeep, I copied down the tag number off the Ford. I couldn't wait to get back to headquarters so I could start doing some more digging. Nothing about Ron and Winona Trentweiler made much sense at all—and that spelled trouble.

55

Treadwell, NY—the same afternoon

The police chief had just left, and Ron was furious. "Winona," he shouted, "what in the *hell* was *that* all about?"

"You killed him, didn't you?" said Winona. "You got jealous, waited until I was asleep and you killed him."

"What are you talking about? That's crazy, Winona. *I* didn't kill anybody. Besides, how the hell would I have known where to find him? Answer me *that!*"

Winona was silent.

"Uh huh," said Ron. "*Gotcha!* You can't answer it, because it never happened—at least not the way *you* say it did. It was *you* who killed him. Wasn't it?"

"And what if I did?" spat Winona.

"So, you admit it."

"Someone had to shut him up. And *you* sure weren't going to do it."

Ron mumbled something under his breath.

"What'd you say?" asked Winona.

"Nothing."

"*What* did you say?" Winona's voice was measured and threatening.

"I said I should have known better than to ever believe you—about *anything*."

"Look, you loser. You're damned lucky you met me. If it wasn't for *me* you'd still be stuck back in that little storefront in Scottsboro, West Virginia, preaching for quarters. I'm the one who made you who you are. And you should worship the ground I walk on!"

"I'm sorry I ever met you," whispered Ron. He flopped down on the sofa, his head in his hands, and sobbed, "My life is over. I've come so far...and now it's all over. It's ruined."

"No it's not," said Winona, in a surprisingly calm voice. "Stop your whining. We can make this work. We're *good* together. Remember, they can't make us testify against each other. And without that, they've got nothing. It's all circumstantial."

"What about the flashlight?"

"What about it? We'll go buy another one just like it and tell him we were mistaken, that we found it."

"But what about fingerprints?"

"It's clean. Don't worry. I wore gloves," said Winona. "I'm not a complete idiot, you know."

Ron thought about what his wife had just said. She had admitted killing her own brother. He felt a shiver go through him as the implications of her words sank in. How could he *ever* trust her again?

"Look, Ron, I know what you're thinking. Relax. I did it for you—for *us*. It's always been about us. Besides, we've got a good thing going here. Let's not screw it up now. When this blows over—and trust me, it will—we can move again. But this time it'll be different. You'll see."

"But you tried to throw me under the bus, Winona. How can I forget that?"

"I was desperate. You'd have done the same thing if the shoe was on the other foot. Tell me you wouldn't have."

Ron wasn't comforted by her thought process. "I don't know, Winona. I've got to think this through. I need some time."

"Well don't take *too* long. We need to be on the same page here, or else—"

"Or else what? Are you threatening me?"

"No. But if I can't count on you, I'll have to make other plans. Maybe I'll have to leave—by myself."

"Don't pressure me."

"Then get with the program."

"I'm trying, Winona. I'm trying."

That night, Ron slept the restless sleep of a man whose whole world had been suddenly turned upside down. He even awoke several times during the night. And every time he woke up, he couldn't help noticing that Winona was sleeping like a baby.

How many other secrets was she hiding from him?

Only time would tell. And Ron felt his time was running out.

56

"I'm telling you, Pete, one of them did it. And my money's on that Winona. You should have seen her trying to put the screws to her old man. It was a regular Academy Award performance."

It was the morning after my visit to Treadwell, and Pete and I were sitting in my office, each staring at the contents of the white board, as I filled him in on the events of the previous day. Pete took a sip from his container of coffee, then inhaled sharply on his filter-tipped cigarette.

"I'm sure you're right, Matt. You've always had great instincts. But what can we prove? That's the big question. Do we have enough to be absolutely certain?"

"I think there's enough there to justify getting an arrest warrant. Just the fact that they lied about being in Centralia, for starters. They're definitely hiding something. If we can get the two of them in here, get them separated, and put some pressure on them, I'll bet one of them will crack."

"And what if they lawyer up? What then?"

"That's just a chance we'll have to take. I'm afraid if we wait, they're going to take off and we might not find them again."

Pete blew a series of perfectly round smoke rings into the air, each one smaller than the previous one so that they settled into a concentric grouping. "Okay," he said. "So what do we actually have?"

"Well," I said, "for starters there's motive. I'm guessing that Billy knew a lot more about his sister's past than she's told her husband, and he probably could have made it pretty uncomfortable for her with the preacher. I'll guarantee that very little of what she's told Ron about herself is true. Who knows, maybe Billy was trying to blackmail her."

"Could be," said Pete. "But we probably can't prove it."

"And as for opportunity, I don't buy that 'I went to the movies' crap that she was putting out there for a minute. It doesn't take a rocket scientist to check the newspapers for the movie schedule to see what was playing—or for that matter to buy a ticket. I doubt that either one of them can actually prove where they were that night. *And* we know Wayne saw the truck, so one of them was almost certainly there."

"Circumstantial evidence at best," said Pete between smoke rings.

"And," I continued. "Both of them have access to the Strychnine, so—"

"Objection! Circumstantial, counselor," said Pete with a smile.

"Damn Philadelphia lawyer! Screw you and your objections. *Most* of the convictions we get are based on circumstantial evidence, and you know it."

"Yeah. And so are the cases we lose."

"Well, I still think we should bring what we have to the DA and let him decide—and the sooner the better."

"It's your funeral," said Pete, grinding his cigarette butt into the ashtray. "When do you want to go?"

"No time like the present."

Forty five minutes later, we were sitting across from Sullivan County District Attorney Bill Bauer in his Monticello office, laying out the evidence as we saw it, and praying he'd issue an arrest warrant. It took some real effort on my part, but at last the DA agreed to issue the document.

"But, I'm warning you," shouted Bill, as we hurried from his office, "this better not turn out to be another Casey Anthony—or your ass is mine! I'm up for re-election this fall, and I don't want anything screwing that up. You understand?"

"Yeah, yeah," I muttered, as we shot out the door.

The DA's reference was to the not-guilty verdict rendered in a case in Florida where a mother had been accused of murdering her child. The woman, Casey Anthony, had been acquitted when the jury found the evidence presented by the state to be just a bit *too* circumstantial to warrant a conviction. The prosecution had been severely battered in the press, and I was certain Bill wanted no part of a similar fiasco—and neither did I. But the thought of a cold-blooded killer getting off Scott-free was more than I could bear.

I phoned ahead to the Delaware County's Sheriff's Department and explained what was going on. Technically, since the arrest was being made in their jurisdiction, I needed them to be there when I served the warrant.

"I know it's only a preacher and his wife," I explained to the deputy. "But, we're talking about a pretty nasty murder, and I would be surprised by anything these two might do--especially since I've already talked to them."

It was raining hard as I drove over Cat Hollow Road to Downsville, and then took the shortcut onto Knox Avenue to County Road 26. From there it was up and down the mountain, past the accumulation of junked cars that adorned a field at its base, and over the West Branch of the Delaware River into Hamden.

I turned east onto Route 10, speeding through Hamden, Delancey, and Frazer in that order, before slowing the Jeep as I rounded the bend by the SUNY campus just before coming into Delhi. Then, it was about a seven-mile run along Route County Road 14 until I reached Treadwell—and the road to the Devoted Church of Jesus With Signs Following.

A white Delaware County Sheriff's Department cruiser sat waiting for me at the entrance to the dead-end, and I coasted to a stop behind it at the intersection. I pulled on a rain jacket and exited my Jeep, hurrying through the downpour to the shelter of the other police vehicle. As I climbed in through the passenger door, my olfactory senses were immediately assaulted by the aroma of a thick layer of cigarette smoke that hung like a blue cloud in the car's interior.

After a brief conversation with Deputy Koestner, I handed him the signed warrant and returned to my Jeep to await his departure for the church. A minute or so later, the cruiser pulled out and headed up the dirt road with me following close behind in my Jeep. By now, the heavy rain had turned the road's surface into a mixture of gravel and mud, so I reached down and threw the lever on the Jeep's transfer case, putting the vehicle into four-wheel drive.

Evil waited patiently at the end of the road, spinning its wheels.

57

Treadwell, NY

"I picked up a couple more rattlers this morning," said Ron, matter-of-factly. "Got them from Frankie Farrell over there on Davis Mountain Road."

Farrell was an active member of the church who had made it known that he could supply all the snakes Ron and Winona could use. He hadn't disappointed.

"Did you put them in the barn?" asked Winona.

"Not yet. They're still in the rear compartment of the truck. I didn't want to try bringing them into the barn while it was raining so hard. But, as soon as it stops, we'll go out and get them. Okay?"

Winona nodded.

"Got some mice, too," Ron added.

"Uh huh. That's good, Ronnie."

Winona turned her attention back to the book she'd been reading. Ron marveled at her composure.

Suddenly, the slamming of several car doors caught the couple's attention.

"Now who the hell can that be?" asked Ron to no one in particular.

Winona got up off the couch, strolled over to the living room window, and peered through a pair of white, lace curtains to see who the unexpected visitors might be.

"Shit!" she exclaimed. "It's that damned police chief and he's got somebody from the sheriff's department with him. I've got a lousy feeling about this, Ron."

"Go in the bedroom and let me handle it."

The sound of a sharp knock on the front door, followed by two more, rattled through the living room. Ron straightened his shirt collar and brushed a stray strand of hair from his forehead before opening the door.

I pulled my vehicle to a stop right behind the deputy's, which was blocking the driveway in front of the innocent looking farmhouse. As I exited the Jeep and approached the front porch, I could see Winona peeking out from behind the window curtains. Then, she disappeared.

The sheriff's deputy preceded me onto the porch and knocked several times on the heavy wooden door. After a brief delay, the door opened and the preacher appeared in the opening.

"Ron Trentweiler?" said Deputy Koestner, standing erect in his black tunic, gray slacks, and western-style hat.

"Yes? Can I help you?"

"I've got an arrest warrant for you and your wife, Winona Trentweiler, for the murder of William Stillwater. You have the right to remain silent. Anything you say or do can and will be held against you in a court of law. You have right to speak to an attorney. If you cannot afford an attorney, one will be appointed for you. Do you understand these rights as they have been read to you?"

"But—"

"Do you understand these rights as they have been read to you?" repeated the deputy in a flat monotone, as if Trentweiler had never opened his mouth.

Ron nodded his head.

"Put your hands behind your back, please," I said, removing a pair of handcuffs from my belt.

Ron did as he was told, and I placed the cuffs on his wrists, ratcheting the steel bracelets tightly enough to elicit a slight yelp from the good pastor.

"Where's Mrs. Trentweiler?" asked the deputy.

Just then, the sound of a slamming door split the air, catching us all by surprise.

"The back door!" I shouted. "She's fleeing the scene!"

"Stay here with him," ordered Koestner. "I'll go get the woman."

The deputy pulled his Glock 37, semi-automatic pistol from its holster and headed across the living room floor into the kitchen toward the back door, his weapon held in front of him. At the same time, I heard a truck door slam, followed by the distinctive whirring sound of a starter motor turning over a big V-8 engine. Turning my head, I caught a glimpse of the red Ford careening down the driveway. The two patrol cars parked there only slowed Winona down for a second. When she realized the driveway was blocked, she shifted into reverse, and then shot around the two vehicles, over the lawn and out onto the muddy dirt road, traveling as fast as conditions would allow.

Deputy Koestner came running around the side of the house, headed for his cruiser.

"I'll call for backup!" he shouted, as he vaulted into the car and started the engine. He pulled forward, spun around hard, and gunned the engine, propelling the vehicle over the lawn, past my Jeep and down the road. Its rear end fishtailed wildly as the back wheels fought to gain purchase in the mud, which was growing thicker by the minute thanks to the torrential rain. I looked at Trentweiler. His face was as white as a ghost.

"Please," he pleaded. "You're making a big mistake."

"Never mind that," I said. "You're coming with me!"

I pushed him out the door and onto the front porch, guiding him down the steps and over to my Jeep. I opened the rear, passenger-side door and carefully pushed him onto the back seat, his hands handcuffed behind him.

"Don't move," I said, as I locked the door.

I silently thanked the mayor for the heavy wire cage that separated prisoners in the back from the front compartment, along with tamper-proof locks that could only be opened by the driver.

For a brief instant I thought of leaving the chase to Deputy Koestner and returning to Roscoe with the preacher. But, I decided that that could wait, and opted to join in the pursuit instead. I flipped on the roof-mounted light bar, hit the siren, and started off down the road, wiper blades slashing against the pouring rain and all four wheels pulling me over the muddy surface.

This was going to be fun.

58

Winona's mind spun wildly as she flew down the road in her pickup at breakneck speed. The combination of the pouring rain and the muddy surface made it difficult to control the direction of the vehicle, but if the going was tough for the four-wheel-drive truck, she could only imagine how difficult it must be for the police cruiser. If she could just make it onto the paved highway, she thought, she had a good chance of putting some real distance between herself and the pursuing police car. When she and Ron had purchased the used pickup, one of the things she'd insisted upon was the largest engine available, a 5.4 liter, 300-horsepower beast. Now, as she increased the distance between the Ford and the pursuing cruiser, she knew she'd made a wise choice.

Images of her dead father, her murdered brother, and Ron all flashed through her mind's eye. She could picture Ronnie desperately trying to make sense of what was happening and callously laughed aloud at his naïveté. However, a quick glance in the rearview mirror revealed another image—one that disturbed her even more—that of a Plexiglas case with two rattlesnakes in it, sliding around behind her on the floor of the extended cab. *Oh shit, I forgot about them.* She could just make out the buzzing sound the two serpents made, as the case bounced crazily around in the confines of the rear compartment of the truck.

Winona slowed the pickup just enough to make a wide, swinging right turn out of Crowter Lane and onto County Road 14. As she entered the intersection, she looked quickly to her left for any signs of oncoming traffic, but the driving rain made it all but impossible to see if anyone was headed in her direction. She sucked in her breath and took a chance. The solid asphalt surface of the highway welcoming the Ford's tires with a resounding screech signaled that it was safe to increase the pressure on the accelerator, which she did immediately. The pickup shot down the highway like a greased pig pursued by a mob of teenagers at a county fair. Winona twisted the wiper control mounted on the stalk of the steering column to its maximum setting, but the increased wiper speed barely made a dent in the flow of water across the windshield.

"Fuck!" she shouted, as she pressed even harder on the gas pedal.

A glimpse in the rearview mirror revealed that the police car had receded in the distance, but she knew it was capable of making up ground quickly now that they were on a solid roadway. She needed to lose it, and lose it fast. Her best chance was to make her way onto the back roads of Franklin, which were mostly dirt, and hope to outmaneuver her pursuer until she could find a spot to hide.

In the rear of the cab the sound of the agitated rattlesnakes was reaching a crescendo; the buzzing sounded like miniature castanets keeping pace with an impossibly fast flamenco dancer. Up ahead was the junction with Route 357. Winona careened left at the Y, and headed west onto the two-lane highway toward Franklin. The rain had let up a bit, enough to see that the police cruiser was closing fast. *Just a few more miles*, thought Winona. Then, she could lose him.

59

I'd never been involved in a high-speed pursuit before, and unlike what I'd seen in those old Burt Reynolds *Cannonball Run* movies where everyone drives at a hundred-miles an hour while listening to music and enjoying the scenery, the real experience was nothing like the cake walk they portrayed in the films. Added to the tension of just trying to maintain control of the Jeep was the fact that I had a prisoner bouncing around in the rear compartment of my vehicle, who most likely would sue me, the Roscoe city government, and anyone else he could if anything happened to him. But, I couldn't worry about that now.

Not being a native of the area, I could only guess where the suspect was headed, but common sense told me that it probably wasn't the interstate highway. That would be a suicide move if ever there was one. Up ahead, Deputy Koestner appeared to be gaining on Winona, as his cruiser's pursuit engine reached its maximum torque, propelling the white and gold vehicle over the blacktop at a dizzying rate of speed.

In less than thirty seconds, he had caught up with the suspect, and it looked as if he were going to pull alongside, perhaps to attempt a pitting maneuver. Suddenly, just as the deputy's vehicle drew even with the Ford, the truck swerved hard to its left, catching the right front fender of the police cruiser and sending it careening wildly into the oncoming lane. I pumped hard on the Jeep's brakes and managed to slow down enough to miss the spinning cruiser, which had come almost to a stop in the road. I continued on after the Ford.

Ahead of us was the little town of Franklin, its main street only a few blocks long, lined with ancient houses and the occasional retail shop. I thanked God that it was raining and that most likely no one would be out and about on the sidewalks. At the rate of speed that Winona's truck was traveling, it was doubtful that she'd be able to stop if an unsuspecting pedestrian dared step into the roadway. I faced the same dilemma.

The bright reflection of the Jeep's flashing, multicolored lights bouncing off the many windows lining the little town's main thoroughfare, made it seem as if a squadron of police vehicles were in pursuit of the Ford. The sound of the digital siren reverberating off the buildings only served to reinforce the illusion.

A glance in my rearview mirror revealed that there were now at least two police cruisers behind me, spaced so closely together that they gave the impression of being one long vehicle—and they were closing fast. Suddenly, the truck ahead slowed down abruptly. In fact, its speed decreased so quickly that at first I thought its engine had quit. But I soon discovered otherwise. It was making a sharp right turn.

I braked hard with my left foot and stepped on the accelerator with my right, sending the Jeep into a controlled slide around the corner, while maintaining the same distance between it and the fleeing suspect's vehicle.

In the distance, through the driving rain, I could see the faint outline of what appeared to be a large, concrete structure—perhaps a dam, or some sort of spillway—off to the right. Was that the end of the road? I wasn't sure. If it was, Winona was done for. I pumped the Jeep's brakes gently, slowing the car enough to where I felt I had a bit more control. The rain-soaked windshield made it nearly impossible to see. Everything was a blur.

Just when I thought it couldn't rain any harder, however, a torrent of water cascaded onto the glass and completely obliterated my vision. I slammed on the brakes and screamed aloud involuntarily, as the Jeep went into a spin. In the back seat, the preacher's voice matched mine with its intensity.

After what seemed like an eternity, the spin ended and the Jeep came to a sideways stop in the middle of the road. I opened the door and stepped onto the roadway.

The pickup had disappeared.

60

When Winona saw the sign for the Sidney Dam, she made the right turn onto the road that eventually crossed over Ouleout Creek, where it flowed from beneath the dam before heading downstream. She breathed a sigh of relief because she knew that she was only minutes away from escaping. However, what she hadn't counted on was the newly-erected, black and yellow striped wooden barricade that announced "Road Closed: Flooding Ahead" that blocked her escape route.

By the time she saw the barrier through the rain it was too late, and despite slamming on the brakes, the Ford crashed through the barricade and slid off the road into the roiling water of the creek, where it landed upside down, moving downstream with the flow of the heavy current.

Winona screamed as the pickup bounced along on its roof, half underwater, as metal scraped against rock, slowing but not stopping the vehicle's movement downstream. Totally panicked, she tugged on the door handle, desperately trying to open the door. But the water had shorted out the electrical system and the power door locks held tight, trapping her inside the truck. In the darkness, screaming wildly, Winona kicked hard against the padded surface of the door panel, but it wouldn't budge.

"Ronnie!" she called. "Help me!"

But there was no reply, no sound at all—except one.

At first, the noise didn't make any sense. It was a kind of buzzing, almost like the sound a personal vibrator makes. Oddly, it was a noise with which she should have been familiar, but in her nervous state, she failed to recognize it. Then, she remembered. The snakes.

"Oh God, please help me," she cried. "I don't want to die."

Winona felt a warm dampness spreading across her crotch, as she lost control of her bladder and urinated in her pants. She was crying uncontrollably now, like a small child afraid of the dark. Cold water was beginning to seep through the microscopic spaces between the windows and their frames. Eventually, she knew, the cab would fill with water and she would drown.

But before that could ever happen there would be the snakes.

Winona felt something touch her shoulder.

61

I watched helplessly as the red Ford truck disappeared from sight, the heavy current propelling it downstream like a bottle cap caught in the flow of a storm drain headed toward a distant catch basin. I closed my eyes and said a silent prayer, but deep down I knew it was in vain. There was no way she would ever survive.

A minute later, the rain began to subside, and a hint of sunlight peeked through the dark gray clouds. By the time the two police cruisers had come to a stop behind the Jeep, the rain had stopped completely. Deputy Koestner and a fellow officer joined me at the water's edge, and I explained what had happened. The second officer walked back to his vehicle and called for emergency services. There was barely a hint of urgency in his voice.

Suddenly, from behind me I heard a scream.

"Winona! Winona!"

It was Trentweiler. He was kicking at the inside of the back door of the Jeep, desperately trying to get out. I walked over and unlocked the nearside passenger door, reaching inside to grab the distraught preacher's left arm, handcuffed to its counterpart behind his back.

"I'm sorry," I said. "I'm really sorry. There was nothing I could do."

Trentweiler sobbed, crying, "Winona. Winona."

"I'm afraid she's gone," I said, verbalizing the obvious.

"I know," whispered Ron. "She's been gone for a long time, but I just didn't want to see it."

62

What Winona had felt brush against her shoulder was just a mouse. When the truck had turned over, the container holding the mice that Ron had bought that morning had opened, and now its inhabitants were skittering around the inside of the truck, which was rapidly filling with water. Their high-pitched squeaks reverberated against the cab walls, as the rodents desperately treaded water and fought to evade the snakes. Winona alternately cried and laughed hysterically, tears streaming down her face.

Then, the first rattler struck.

It was a stabbing blow to Winona's neck, the force of the strike surprising her with its intensity. She'd never imagined a serpent could bite that hard. The fangs ripped into her neck like a hot dagger. Instantly, deadly venom erupted from the pits at the base of the hypodermic-like fangs and coursed through her veins toward her heart, which pumped furiously in response to the adrenalin rush that had begun with the onset of the chase.

The second snake scraped against her leg, and Winona twitched involuntarily at its touch. It was all the incentive the serpent needed to strike. A searing pain followed, as the rattler plunged its fangs through the material of her jeans and into the soft flesh beneath. Fresh venom entered Winona's bloodstream, mixing with the scarlet fluid making its way through her body's supply line. But, instead of bringing life-giving oxygen to her heart, her veins now carried a liquid cargo of death.

The squeaking of the mice and the buzzing of the snakes joined the drumming inside Winona's skull, as all three sounds combined in a discordant melody that could only result in a morbid finale.

Water was pouring unchecked into the cab now, as the truck's doors were battered and deformed by the vehicle's deadly roller coaster ride over the rock strewn creek bed. A window shattered, then another, and the cab filled completely. But Winona hardly noticed. The venom was working on her nervous system and her senses were failing rapidly. Her heart was shutting down.

One final image filled Winona's mind's eye before she died. It was that of Walt Witkowsky's face, and the surprised look it had contained that day—the day she had ended his life.

Then, mercifully, it was over.

Epilogue

It's been four months since Winona Trentweiler met her maker. Ron Trentweiler was eventually cleared of any wrongdoing, and even gave back what money was left from Winona's insurance scam to the churches of those families involved. But the little church he started in Treadwell has been abandoned; and the former preacher is back to living in a rented trailer. Last I heard, he'd taken a job at the Wal-Mart over in Oneonta, selling plumbing fixtures.

Billy Stillwater's Meth lab, long rumored to have existed in the hills overlooking Roscoe, was finally found by some hunters, and as a result—or maybe just due to dumb luck—Harold was re-elected as mayor in September. Nancy found two college freshmen for our police auxiliary program, and I'm looking forward to seeing Rick and Bobcat each take one of them under his wing.

Poor Wayne Sabolewski never could overcome his Meth addiction, and the last I heard he was seen hitchhiking in the direction of New York City, probably to be swallowed up by its streets and lost in its inhospitable jungle.

Oh, and Don Brann finally got himself a real security camera and a solid metal back door installed at his laundromat. Guess he intends to stay for a while.

Can't say that I blame him. I feel the same way about Roscoe.

Val and I just celebrated four months of her being cancer free, and we have high hopes that the worst is behind us. Doctor Radford assures us that the odds are in her favor and somehow I believe he's right. Maybe it's because I discovered that he's a fly fisherman. Or maybe it's just because he's such a damn good doctor. Either way, there's hope. And, to quote Martha Stewart: "That's a good thing."

ACKNOWLEDGMENTS

As is always the case with writing a novel, there are countless individuals without whose help the book might never have been written.

My thanks for technical assistance to: Bill Bauer, attorney; Chris Freitag, retired police captain; and Tom Koestner, retired FBI agent.

For their graphics design assistance, my appreciation to: Gary Kabasakalian, graphics designer and Linda Hawley, fellow author and "techno freak."

For general support and inspiration, I thank all the members of the various internet writing groups to which I belong, including (but not limited to): Author Central on Facebook, Book Blogs, The Read On WNC, Mystery & Thriller Writers Group on Facebook, Good Reads, and Book Town.

For permitting me to use and "abuse" their good names as characters, I am eternally grateful to the "real" Bill Bauer, Nancy Cooper, Rick Dawley, Chris Freitag, Pete Richards, and my good friend and "error detector," Don Brann.

Last, but by no means least, my eternal gratitude and love to my wife, Becky, for her unending support, and her countless hours spent scanning, reading, critiquing, and editing. She is my muse.

OTHER BOOKS BY JOE PERRONE JR.

As The Twig Is Bent: A Matt Davis Mystery—
Someone is raping and strangling women in the
Chelsea district of Manhattan—but who? The
only clues: a signature heart carved into each
victim's breast (inside, the initials "J.C" and
those of the deceased); copies of the New
Testament with underlined passages referring to
infidelity; and fingerprints of a juvenile arrested
in the '60s. *As The Twig Is Bent* is an explosive
thriller that rips the lid off the sordid underbelly
of Internet sex chat rooms, and propels the
reader on a no-holds-barred journey toward its bone-chilling
conclusion. CAUTION: Contains graphic sexual material that may be
inappropriate for some readers.

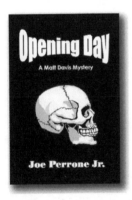

*Opening Day: A Matt Davis Mystery—*Young
girls are coming through a pastoral Upstate
New York fishing village—but, they aren't all
coming out—alive! The remains of a female
corpse are found in the waters of Matt's secret
fishing hole, with no identification whatsoever.
Complicating matters is the fact that several
other young females have gone missing during
the same time period. Are they alive, or have
they, too, been murdered? *Opening Day* is a
spellbinding tale of murder in the Catskills that
picks up where *As The Twig Is Bent* left off.

Escaping Innocence: A Story of Awakening—
David Justin is an Italian-Catholic, height-
challenged youth, who is desperate to escape
the bonds of sexual repression and adolescent
innocence that hold him captive in the Age of
Aquarius. Determined to cross that invisible
line that separates childhood from manhood, he
and his friends approach every encounter with a
member of the opposite sex as a potential "first

time." Their efforts are heroic yet laughable at the same time. But, this is "The Sixties," the era of "Sex, Drugs, and Rock 'N' Roll," and David will not be deterred—or will he? *Escaping Innocence: A Story of Awakening* is a classic coming-of-age novel for all ages.

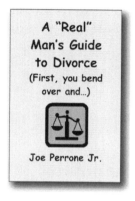

A "Real" Man's Guide to Divorce (First, you bend over and...) is just what it seems: a hilarious look at the serious subject of divorce—from a pointedly, one-sided, male perspective. This is the perfect book to keep in that "special" reading room. Filled with lots of sage advice, and highlighted by a glossary with actual definitions of legal divorce terminology, along with some less-than-actual, humorous definitions. If you thought divorce wasn't a laughing matter, think again!

NOTE: All of Joe's books are available in paperback and Kindle editions through Amazon.com. Autographed copies of Joe's books can be purchased on his website at: www.joeperronejr.com.

A NOTE FROM THE AUTHOR

Dear Reader:

I hope you enjoyed *Twice Bitten*, and if you did, I invite you to post an objective review on Amazon.com or any other literary website of your choosing. We independent authors rely upon our readers to get the word out about our books. And one of the most helpful things a reader can do is to tell others about our work. Without you, the reader, all our creative efforts would go unappreciated and unrecognized. Thanks to all of you who have chosen to purchase and read my books.

Please note: If you select one of my books for your book club, it would be my pleasure to entertain discussion questions during a group Skype session, hosted at your convenience. I welcome your questions and comments, and will make every effort to respond to each reader who contacts me. You may reach me via email at: **joetheauthor@joeperronejr.com**. To follow my writing career and to learn of new books, or to just follow my blog, please visit my website at: **www.joeperronejr.com**.

Best fishes,

Joe Perrone Jr.

Made in the USA
Charleston, SC
19 January 2012